PRAISE FOR AGATHA AWARD FINALIST
BETH GROUNDWATER

Deadly Currents

"A heart-racing debut with as many twists and turns and unexpected upsets as a ride through the rapids itself."—Margaret Coel, author of *The Silent Spirit*

"A thrilling journey . . . filled with river lore, vivid descriptions of the duties of the river rangers, and loving depictions of the varied characters."—*Alfred Hitchcock Mystery Magazine*

"An entertaining read . . . A classic and well-written murder mystery; you won't be able to put it down."—*Colorado Country Life*

"Groundwater kicks off a new series that combines outdoor action with more than a modicum of old-fashioned detection."—*Kirkus Reviews*

"With a fresh locale . . . this is a promising new series."—*Library Journal*

"The amiable cast, along with Groundwater's fascinating firsthand knowledge of rafting, makes this a series worth watching."—*Mystery Scene*

"*Deadly Currents* comes rushing at you from the first page like roiling whitewater and culminates in a riveting climax that lives up to this book's name. If you like outdoor adventure and gripping characters, this one's a must-read."—Sandi Ault, Mary Higgins Clark and WILLA Award Winning Author of the Wild Mystery Series

"An exciting ride from the very first chapter, with a courageous heroine in a fascinating line of work."—Nancy Pickard, author of *The Scent of Rain and Lightning*

A Real Basket Case

An Agatha Award Finalist for Best First Novel

"*A Real Basket Case* and its author are a welcome addition to the mystery genre."—*Crimespree Magazine*

"An enjoyable mystery...*A Real Basket Case* should not be missed."
—Romance Reviews Today, RomRevToday.com

"A clever, charming debut novel. Quick-paced and well written with clear and comfortable prose, *A Real Basket Case* is a perfect afternoon read for cozy fans."—SpinetinglerMag.com

"A crackling good novel with the kind of twists and turns that make roller coaster rides so scary and so much fun!"—Margaret Coel, author of *The Drowning Man*

"Groundwater brings new meaning to the term menopausal in this flawlessly crafted mystery. Her gutsy, power surging heroine keeps the pressure on until the final chapter."—Kathy Brandt, author of *Swimming with the Dead*

"Beth Groundwater has put together the perfect mixture of humor, thrills, and mystery. A terrific debut!"—Christine Goff, author of the Birdwatcher's Mystery series

FATAL
DESCENT

BETH GROUNDWATER

FATAL
DESCENT

MIDNIGHT INK
WOODBURY, MINNESOTA

First Edition
First Printing, 2013

Book design by Donna Burch
Cover design by Lisa Novak
Cover image: Woman: Aurora Open/The Agency Collection/PunchStock
         The Rio Santo Domingo: Michael & Jennifer Lewis/
         National Geographic/PunchStock
Editing by Connie Hill

Midnight Ink, an imprint of Llewellyn Worldwide Ltd.

Library of Congress Cataloging-in-Publication Data

Groundwater, Beth.
  Fatal Descent : an RM Outdoor Adventures mystery / by Beth Groundwater. — First edition.
      pages cm. — (RM Outdoor Adventure Mysteries ; 3)
   ISBN 978-0-7387-3482-8
   1. White-water canoeing—Fiction. 2. Colorado—Fiction. 3. Mystery fiction. I. Title
   PS3607.R677F38   2013
   813'.6—dc23   2012050857

Midnight Ink
Llewellyn Worldwide Ltd.
2143 Wooddale Drive
Woodbury, MN 55125-2989
www.midnightinkbooks.com

Printed in the United States of America

To river guides everywhere, a hardy breed
who labor long hours with little pay
to provide river runners with a safe
and fun experience.

ONE

We are now ready to start on our way down the Great Unknown. . . . The men talk as cheerfully as ever; but to me the cheer is somber and the jests are ghastly.

—JOHN WESLEY POWELL

"I COULD KILL HIM."

With hands on her hips, Mandy Tanner surveyed the pile of gear heaped in the back room of the outfitter's building. The rafts, oars and paddles, sleeping bags, mats, and tents were all there, as were the kitchen supplies, water jugs, coolers, portable toilet, first-aid kit, handheld radio transceiver, and myriad other supplies needed for a multi-day rafting trip. But Gonzo, one of the guides and their provisioner, had forgotten to bring some vital equipment—camping lanterns to light their campsites in the evenings.

Mandy swallowed to tamp down the frustration threatening to clog her throat. That meant the only light they would have at night would be thin beams cast by flashlights or headlamps. Could they make do? No, dammit. They had to have at least two lanterns, and preferably a third for backup.

Mandy's fiancé and business partner, Rob Juarez, gave a shrug. "Gonzo will find some."

How could Rob be so nonchalant? She gazed at his infuriatingly calm and handsome face. "The clients will start arriving any minute, and I was counting on Gonzo's jokes to put everyone in a good mood. He's supposed to be here to meet and greet them instead of running around Moab trying to beg lanterns off another outfitter. With so many outfitters closed for the season, it'll be tough finding them."

Contrary to her better judgment, Mandy and Rob had assigned Gonzo Gordon, their best rafting guide, to provision this expedition, their first outside of Colorado. She would have preferred to let Gonzo learn the ropes on a local trip that was less complicated. But Rob had suggested it to show their support of and trust in Gonzo, who was making good progress in his alcohol rehabilitation program. And Gonzo had assured her—multiple times—that he could handle being the "Quartermaster," as he had dubbed himself.

"'No problemo', he kept telling me," Mandy said as she stared at the equipment pile, "and now look where we are."

Rob put a firm hand on each of her shoulders and turned her to face him. His puppy-dog brown eyes crinkled with worry as his gaze searched her face. "Yes. Look where we are. We are in Moab, Utah, ready to embark on our first combo rafting and climbing trip. We have twelve paying clients and all the gear we need except for two lousy lanterns." He cocked his head. "You don't usually get this stressed out by trip snafus. What's got *mi querida* wound up so tight?"

While he waited for an explanation, he massaged her tight shoulders, easing the tension out of them. "Take a deep breath."

Mandy did, inhaling Rob's familiar aroma of leather, soap, and the grassy outdoors, and blew the breath out slowly. This was no way to start out. She needed to be relaxed and cheerful for the clients to make sure they felt excited and confident about taking the five-day, hundred-mile trip down the Colorado River. They would travel along the placid waters of Meander Canyon, the whitewater rapids of Cataract Canyon, and a finger of Lake Powell that had flooded lower Cataract Canyon before they took out at Hite Marina. She couldn't let her own worries cloud the clients' perceptions of the upcoming adventure.

"You're right. I'm sorry. It's not Gonzo's fault. It's mine for not going over the manifest with him. I've been too distracted to manage the setup for this trip as well as I should have."

"This is the way it's going to be as our business grows, Mandy," Rob responded with frustrating reasonableness. "You'll have to trust our employees to do their jobs. You can't do everything. And what's been distracting you?" He grinned lasciviously. "The handsome hunk you're going to marry in a few months?"

Mandy finally smiled. She playfully slapped the standing waves tattoo on one of his muscular biceps. "Sure, I can't keep my hands off your bodacious bod."

Rob turned his face to show her his profile. "More like bashed-up bod."

She traced a gentle finger down his crooked nose, accidentally broken by one of his best friends when Rob tried to break up a fist fight between fishermen. "The bashes just make you look more hot, my macho mountain man. No, the problem is the handsome hunk's mother, who has to talk to me every single bleeding day about the wedding plans."

"Ah-ha." He gave a knowing nod of his square bronzed chin. "The truth comes out."

Mandy's parents had been killed in a car accident the summer before her senior year of high school. So after Rob's mother finished gushing over the news of their engagement, she offered to help Mandy plan the wedding.

"At first I was really glad to have her help, because I know a lot more about planning a rafting trip," Mandy swept an arm toward the pile of supplies, "than a wedding. But, sheesh, all the details are driving me crazy. The colors, the cake, the bridesmaid dresses and gifts, the meanings of the damn flowers—"

Rob stopped her with a kiss, which deepened into a long, savoring smooch that warmed her to her toes. She couldn't help but respond in kind. Finally he pulled back but kept his arms around her, his hands caressing her back. "Mama is so excited. She hasn't planned a wedding before."

"But your sister was married." Before divorcing her abusive husband.

"I must've never told you that they eloped," Rob said with a frown. "They robbed Mama of what she views as a mother's God-given right. She sees our wedding as a way to make up for that."

"I guess that explains some of her mania…"

"And Catholic Hispanic mamas live for weddings," Rob added with a laugh. "Mama's the star of her neighborhood in Pueblo. The other ladies gather around her every Sunday after church to hear about the plans. She's in the spotlight and loving every minute."

Mandy tilted her head and grinned playfully. "Maybe *we* should elope!"

"No way, José. And don't ever joke about that to Mama. She'd have a heart attack." His brow furrowed. "You know she's going to be a big part of our lives after we're married. Are you going to be able to get along with her?"

"I'm sure it's just the wedding that's making us both crazy now. I think your mom's great, Rob, and she's been wonderful, really, about welcoming me into the family. We won't have any issues after we're married." At least, Mandy hoped so.

She had a thought, and with a laugh, changed the subject. "I wonder how she's getting along with Lucky right now." Rob's mom had volunteered to let Mandy's golden retriever stay with her during the trip. "He's a good dog, but he can be rambunctious."

Rob smiled. "She loves dogs. You may have a problem making her give up Lucky when we get back."

Kendra Lee, their second-best rafting guide, walked into the room. She stopped and put a hand on a jutted-out hip. Her eyes twinkled and a broad grin split her beautiful ebony face. "The first clients have arrived. Can you keep your hands off each other long enough to check them in?"

Rob released Mandy and yanked her blond ponytail. "Got your happy face on?"

Mandy flashed him a bright, perky smile. "Yes, now that I've realized your mom won't be able to reach me for five whole days. In a way I'm glad there's no cell phone service on the river and we can only radio out from a few locations. I'm sure your mom doesn't like it, but I'm really looking forward to a break in wedding planning."

Rob glanced at the radio transceivers. "Since the radio is really just for emergencies, hopefully we won't have to make *any* calls on it."

———

Mandy stepped into the front room of the building with Rob, leaving Kendra in the back room to deal with packing the food. They were borrowing the building of a Moab-based outfitter that had closed up shop in the middle of September. Mandy and Rob's own business, RM Outdoor Adventures, was based in Salida, Colorado. The RM stood for both Rocky Mountains and Rob and Mandy. Along with renting the other outfitter's building to check in clients and gear, they were able to run their trip under the other company's Utah rafting license because they had hired their expert climbing guide to come along.

Like most of those who worked in the adventure travel field, Mandy and Rob juggled multiple jobs. Besides their joint business, Mandy worked as a seasonal river ranger on the Arkansas River in the summer and as a ski patroller at Monarch Mountain in the winter. Rob stitched together a patchwork of construction and carpentry jobs during the off-seasons. And, he was extending their outfitting business into the shoulder spring and fall seasons by adding fly-fishing, horseback riding, and other trips that were not dependent on Colorado's summer snow melt that kept its whitewater rivers gushing.

This climbing and rafting trip was one of those experiments. It was taking place during early October when most of the outfitters had already shuttered their doors. Mandy flashed Rob a crossed-fingers-for-good-luck sign behind her back as the two of them stepped up to the counter. Hopefully the experiment would work.

Two women stood at the other side of the counter. They both had tightly curled hair, though the younger one's was a lighter brown and longer than the older one's. Their similar heart-shaped faces and features showed they were related. Probably mother and daughter, Mandy surmised. The mother's leathery skin and smattering of wrinkles and sun spots indicated she was a middle-aged outdoorswoman. In marked contrast with her daughter's loose T-shirt, the mother wore a V-necked stretch top that clung to her curves and showed some cleavage.

"Hello, ladies." Rob held out a hand. "I presume you're here for our Cataract Canyon rafting and climbing trip."

The older woman shook his hand and eyed him up and down. "I must say I'm looking forward to the scenery." She shot an amused grin at her daughter, who rolled her eyes.

Rob just smiled and said, "I'm Rob Juarez and this is my partner and fiancée, Mandy Tanner. We'll be your lead guides on the trip."

While Mandy shook the women's hands, she thought, thank goodness he likes using that word fiancée so much. She bet Rob couldn't wait until they were married and he started calling her his wife. Her independent streak had not quite reconciled itself to that term, but she had to admit that she liked the idea of staking her own claim on Rob by calling him her husband.

The women introduced themselves as Elsa Norton, the mother, and Tina Norton, the daughter. Mandy remembered that Tina, a college junior majoring in elementary education at the University of Wyoming, had booked the trip. She had been a little worried about missing classes for it.

"I remember taking your call," Mandy said to Tina. "Were your professors okay with you taking this trip?"

Tina nodded. "It worked out great. I'm only missing three classes and a lab, and I can make up the lab after I get back on Friday."

"As a professor at the university myself," Elsa added, "I was ready to jump in and make some calls for Tina if I had to. Missing one or two classes is nothing compared to the experiences this trip will allow her to share with her future students."

Rob cocked his head as he slid release forms into two clip-boards. "What do you teach?"

"Geology," Elsa replied.

"You'll find gobs of cool formations in the Canyonlands." Mandy checked the trip roster. "We have three of you signed up. Where's—?"

"Three?" Elsa raised an eyebrow at Tina.

Tina fidgeted, glanced at the wall clock, then back at her mother. "I told you I wanted this to be a family trip, since I'll be busy student-teaching soon and I don't know when we'll have the time later on."

"Family? Who else did you invite? Your cousin Kathy?"

"No." Tina rubbed her hands on her jeans, took a deep breath, and faced her mother. "Dad."

Elsa's eyes bugged out. "Your father? You invited Paul on this trip? When were you going to tell me?"

Mandy turned to Rob, and a meaningful glance flashed between them. *Trouble.*

Tina's chin quivered. "I kept trying to bring it up, but I could never find the right time. I figured it would all work out once he appeared." She burrowed her head into her shoulders like a frightened turtle.

Elsa finally seemed to realize that Rob and Mandy were watching the argument. She turned to them. "Tina's father and I have been divorced for a year. For good reason." She glared at Tina. "How could you do this to me? To him? Do you know how miserable the two of us will be?"

Mandy nudged Rob and pointed at the trip roster, which also listed tent assignments. They had allocated two 4-man tents and five 2-man tents to the trip, thinking the two families would occupy the larger tents. The Nortons were one of those families.

A man walked into the room. He was of medium height and medium build, with graying, mousy-brown hair and bifocal glasses. He blinked as his eyes adjusted to the lack of sunshine. Mandy was struck with the thought that mousy was an appropriate description for the whole man—his nondescript clothing, pallid skin, withdrawn demeanor, and thin-fingered hands all fit. All he lacked were twitching long whiskers on his clean-shaven cheeks.

Then a smile lit up his face. "Tina!" He held out his arms.

"Dad!" Tina ran into his embrace.

Elsa Norton crossed her arms, murder in her gaze.

Paul Norton glanced at his ex-wife, then at Tina. "When did you tell her I was coming?"

Tina cringed. "Just now."

"Cripes." Paul looked up at the ceiling, then squared his shoulders and walked toward the counter, Tina tucked under one arm. He stopped in front of Elsa. "I'm sorry. I thought you knew and were okay with this."

"No, I'm not okay with this," Elsa said between clenched teeth. "But I can't back out now. I've already taken the leave and arranged for a sub. And I'm sure these good people aren't going to give me a refund at this late date." She swept a hand in Mandy's and Rob's direction.

Paul touched her shoulder, but when she flinched, he quickly removed his hand. "For Tina's sake, we can make this work. We've already done enough arguing for a lifetime. Let's just try to have a fun vacation."

Elsa glanced at Tina, who looked hopefully from her father to her mother. Elsa exhaled, unclenched her arms, and held up her hands. "For Tina's sake, I'll try to be civil, but I'm not sharing a raft with you—or a tent either." She raised an eyebrow at Mandy.

Mandy took her cue. "It's no problem. We'll put you and your daughter in a 2-man tent and Mister Norton in another 2-man tent." How she was going to reshuffle the other tent assignments, she had no idea.

Elsa nodded. "Good."

"It's probably best for me to be in my own tent, anyway," Paul said, "because I snore like the dickens."

"Does he!" Elsa covered her ears with her hands. "I had to wear earplugs to bed when we were married."

Paul's assumption he could have a tent to himself was a leap. The trip instructions had explicitly said that all tents would be shared because of the tight space on the rafts. But Mandy decided to wait until she had juggled tent assignments before she said anything to him. Maybe she really could put him by himself and spare some other guy a bunch of sleepless nights.

Paul sniffed. "The snoring's probably related to my allergies. So I should pitch my tent away from the others each night."

"We'll keep that in mind when we arrange the campsites," Rob said glibly.

While Rob went over the release forms and packing lists with the Nortons, Mandy scanned the roster and tried to think. Besides the Nortons, there was the six-person Anderson family—two parents and three grown children, one of whom was married—and three women from different parts of California. She had allocated a 4-man and a 2-man tent to the Anderson family and had assigned 2-man tents to herself and Rob and Gonzo and the climbing guide. She would now have to put Kendra and the three women clients in what would have been the Norton family's 4-man tent. Could the four strangers all get along?

Mandy and Rob said their goodbyes to the Nortons after inviting them to join the group for a pre-trip meet-and-greet dinner at Milt's Stop & Eat. The local burger and shakes joint had been recommended to them by the owner of the building they were using. He had told Rob that it set a tone of informality for clients and helped them to start shedding their business-suit personalities prior to getting on the river.

Just as Mandy was going to fill Rob in on the tent shuffle, three women walked in, giggling and chatting with each other. They all looked to be in their thirties and were a variety of races—white, Hispanic, and black. They stepped up to the counter, and after a few more snippets of chattering, turned as a group and looked expectantly at Rob and Mandy.

"Hi, gals," Rob said. "Here to check in for the Cataract Canyon rafting and climbing trip?"

"You bet your sweet *cojones* we are!" the Hispanic woman said, tossing her long black hair over one shoulder and eyeing Rob's athletic build.

Mandy stiffened.

Rob, however, took it in stride and went into his spiel. "I'm Rob Juarez, and this is my partner and fiancée, Mandy Tanner." He put an arm around Mandy's shoulder. "We'll be your lead guides on the trip."

"Damn, ladies, he's taken." While her companions laughed, the Hispanic woman winked at Mandy. "Don't worry, honey, we're just having some fun. We're all happily married, but this is our annual gal-pal escape from the hubbies and munchkins. I'm Vivian Davis, but you can call me Viv." She held out a hand to Mandy.

Mandy smiled and shook it, then looked at the other two. "And you are ... ?"

"Maureen Heedles," said the petite blond-haired white woman, shaking Rob's and her hands, "but call me Mo."

"Betsy Saunders," said the black woman, also shaking their hands.

"I hadn't realized you three knew each other," Mandy said, "since you live in different California cities."

"We all attended high school and community college together in LA," Mo replied. "We go way back. And, as you can tell, we're a real mixed bag."

Betsy grinned. "Our husbands are, too. Viv's is black, Mo's is Asian, and mine is white, so our kids are all hybrids."

"Too bad they don't run on electricity. Our grocery bills would be a lot lower," Viv quipped, causing all three to laugh. They started comparing notes on what their hapless hubbies were planning to cook, or take-out, while they were gone, which set them to laughing again.

Once they had quieted, Rob slid release forms on clipboards to them across the counter and asked them to read and sign them.

Mo looked up from hers at Mandy. "Is it possible for the three of us to share a tent? We plan to do a lot of catching up with each other while we're on this trip."

Relieved, Mandy said, "Sure, we can arrange that."

But she needed to break the news that they would have to share with Kendra. She took a deep breath and plunged in. "We're tight on space in the rafts, though, and can only bring so many tents. We can't afford to have any bed space in a tent go empty. You'll be in a 4-man tent. Do you mind sharing with our other female rafting guide? Her name is Kendra Lee."

The three women looked at each other and nodded. "No problem," Betsy said. "Is she here? Can we meet her?"

"She's in back organizing gear. I'll bring her out." Mandy went into the back room.

When Mandy entered, Kendra looked up expectantly from her checklist of food items. She was sitting cross-legged on the floor surrounded by boxes, bags, and cans of food. "What's up?"

"I had to shuffle tent assignments when I found out the Nortons really aren't a family," Mandy said. "The father and mother are divorced. So, I need to put you in a 4-man tent with the three solo female clients. Turns out they really aren't solo and they all know each other—call each other gal-pals."

Kendra grimaced. "So I'll be the odd gal out."

"They seem really nice and said they didn't mind having you. They want to meet you."

"I was going to talk to you about tent assignments." Kendra rose to her feet and flashed a sheepish smile at Mandy. "See, Gonzo and I have started seeing each other."

"Get out!" Mandy slapped Kendra on the back. "That's great. How'd you keep it from all of us?"

"We wanted to make sure it was going to work out before we spilled the beans. I didn't say anything when you told me a couple weeks ago that you were planning to have me share a tent with a female client, because Gonzo and I weren't, you know, doing the sleeping bag samba yet." Kendra grinned happily.

Mandy returned Kendra's smile. "Glad to know you've found a compatible dance partner." She studied the roster in her hand. "I don't think I can swing putting you two together, though. I've got Gonzo in a tent with Tom O'Day, the climbing guide, and if I put you in that tent instead, there's nowhere for Tom to sleep. Paul Norton's in a tent by himself now, because he said he snores like the dickens. I'd hate to subject Tom to that. And I certainly can't put him in with the women."

"Maybe Tom snores, too." Kendra looked hopeful.

"I'll ask him when he shows up," Mandy said, "but I still want to introduce you to these women. Sorry to say it, but you'll most likely end up bunking with them."

Kendra sighed. "Okay. It's only for a few nights anyway."

Mandy gave her an elbow nudge. "As they say, absence makes the heart grow fonder. Maybe Rob and I can swap places with you and Gonzo one night."

Mandy led Kendra out of the room and made the introductions. Before long the three pals were chatting with Kendra, asking her questions about the upcoming trip.

"Will we see many birds?" Viv asked. "I'm a bird watcher, and I want to add some Utah species to my list."

"What about animals?" Betsy pulled a book for identifying animal tracks out of her backpack. "My hobby is identifying wildlife prints."

"And I'm hoping to see some fall-blooming wildflowers," Mo said. "That's my thing." She held up a camera. "I've got a whole wall of my kitchen plastered with wildflower photos, and I want to add to my gallery."

By the time Kendra had fielded all of their questions, she was smiling. "This trip is perfect for you three."

"We always pick an outdoor-oriented trip for our getaway," Mo replied. "The last one was a four-day horseback ride in Oregon."

Betsy rubbed her rump. "It took weeks for my butt to recover from that one."

All four women laughed.

Viv waved her arm toward the door. "Time to pack our dry bags, gals."

Mandy walked them to the door. "Remember our meet-and-greet dinner at six."

The last one out, Betsy, turned and whispered to Mandy, "Thanks for putting Kendra in our tent. We're going to love having an expert's brain to pick."

Mandy smiled. Another problem solved. After the women left, she faced Kendra. "You okay with this?"

Kendra nodded. "Yeah, they all seem pretty nice. Not sure how much sleep I'm going to get, though."

"More than you would get with Gonzo," Mandy shot back with a wink.

Laughing, Kendra retreated to the back room.

Returning to her position behind the counter next to Rob, Mandy said, "We may need to rescue Kendra from those chatterboxes. We can't have a sleepy rafting guide, especially in Cataract Canyon."

Rob shrugged. "We'll cross that bridge when we come to it. If need be, she can sleep with you one night, and I'll bed down outside."

Mandy leaned on her elbows and looked at the roster. "You know, when we were planning this trip, I imagined all sorts of things going wrong. I never dreamed that tent assignments were going to be such a challenge." She wondered if this tent shuffle was a sign of more client issues to come.

With a laugh, Rob said, "Hopefully the Anderson family will be okay with theirs."

"We can't do anything about it if they aren't!"

TWO

*In the duel of sex, woman fights from a
dreadnought and man from an open raft.*

— H. L. MENCKEN

WHILE MANDY AND ROB were checking the signed release forms
for errors, the front door to the outfitter's building swung open. A
breeze came through the doorway, stirring up the papers. Mandy
slapped her hand on them to keep them from flying, then looked
up. A very tall, thin young man stepped through the door and
swept his shoulder-length straight brown hair out of his face. He
wore a tattered T-shirt and torn jeans, and his angular chin and
cheeks were covered with two-day-old stubble. The breeze brought
the strong scent of body odor to Mandy's nostrils. She wrinkled her
nose and wondered if the guy was homeless.

"O'Day!" Rob shouted and came out from behind the counter
to clap the man on the back.

Mystery solved. Mandy moved to join the men. Tom O'Day was the climbing guide they had hired for the trip. Rob had interviewed him when he, Gonzo, and Kendra had come out a month ago to take an orientation rafting trip down Cataract Canyon. Still recovering from a cracked rib, Mandy hadn't gone on that trip.

Rob put an arm around Mandy's shoulder and pulled her toward him. "Meet Tom O'Day, Mandy. Tom, this is my partner and soon to be ball-and-chain, Mandy Tanner."

Mandy glanced at Rob and caught his playful wink.

O'Day grinned and held out a hand, but his blue, almost gray, eyes were assessing her. "Glad to meet you, Mandy. Call me Cool. Everyone does."

"Nice to meet you, too, Cool." Mandy didn't say anything about his pungent state, but she prayed that it wasn't normal for him. Yes, by the end of a multi-day rafting trip everyone got a little ripe, but they usually didn't start out that way.

After they shook hands, Cool looked down at his filthy clothes. "Sorry I'm such a mess. I just got back from a two-day climb that took longer than I expected. I figured I should come over here first before I head home and shower. I promise I'll have all my shit together by tomorrow morning."

Mandy held back a frown. O'Day didn't seem to be taking their trip very seriously. What was he doing out climbing when he should have been preparing for it?

"We were hoping you could join us for a meet-and-greet dinner with the clients at Milt's Stop & Eat in…" She glanced at the clock. "A little over an hour. Can you make it?"

"I can try."

"We'll expect you," Rob said firmly. "First you should meet Kendra, though. She and Gonzo Gordon—you remember him, right?— will be in charge of packing the gear onto the vehicles after dinner. You'll need to make sure all the climbing equipment gets to them."

Cool frowned as he followed Rob and Mandy toward the back room. "Sounds like a late night."

"Doesn't have to be, if your gear is all ready," Rob said smoothly. "But tomorrow morning will be early. Mandy and I want all the guides here at six a.m., so we can get our act together before the clients show up at seven."

Cool groaned. The sound made Kendra raise her head. And Kendra's looks made Cool let out a wolf whistle.

Kendra rose with a forced smile. "Dream on, honey. Too bad for you I'm not available."

"Damn, the first two babes I meet on this gig are taken," Cool said. "Who's the lucky guy?"

Kendra blushed and glanced at Rob. "Gonzo."

Rob's eyes widened. "Really? Since when?" He looked at Mandy. "Did you know?"

She shook her head and grinned. "Not until about an hour ago."

"Cool," Rob said. "And speaking of cool, this is Tom O'Day, the climbing guide—he goes by the nickname Cool. You weren't around when Gonzo and I talked to him on our orientation trip."

Cool and Kendra shook hands, then Cool scanned the equipment pile. "Is one of those 2-man tents for me?"

"Yep," Rob said. "You'll be sharing with Gonzo. That'll give you two a chance to do a lot of talking, so he can learn as much as possible from you."

A shadow crossed over Cool's face. "Makes it kind of hard to bed a babe. But I guess Gonzo and I can work something out, take turns sleeping outside." He leered at Kendra. "I bet he won't want to be without you for four long, lonely nights."

Kendra shot Mandy a look that said, "What a sleazeball!"

"One more question," Mandy said to Cool. "Do you snore?"

"Nope." Cool's eyebrows lowered. "I hope Gonzo doesn't. I can't sleep in a tent with someone who saws logs all night." He looked at Kendra.

She shook her head, then shrugged at Mandy. So much for putting O'Day in with Paul Norton.

Cool made plans with Kendra to meet back with Gonzo and her at the building about an hour after dinner to load equipment. Then he rushed off to shower.

While Mandy and Rob returned to the front room, she played back the conversation with the climbing guide in her head. Something bothered her about it.

Rob peered at her. "What's wrong?"

"I don't like what Cool said about bedding babes and taking turns sleeping outside with Gonzo. Since we two 'babes'"—she wrinkled her nose in distaste—"are taken, is he planning on picking up one of the female clients and sleeping with her?"

"Maybe he was just trying to do Gonzo a favor," Rob said, looking thoughtful.

Mandy put her hands on her hips. "He better not have plans to hit on the clients. That's totally lame."

Rob frowned. "Some casual flirting with the guides is kind of expected on these trips."

"I know, I know. Like what went on between you and Viv Davis. That's okay. But Cool strikes me as being a little sleazy, like he's planning on taking it a lot further." She stared at the door through which O'Day had exited. "We'll have to keep an eye on him."

———

An hour later, Mandy strode at a fast clip with Kendra to Milt's Stop & Eat. The aspens and cottonwoods back in Salida, Colorado, had already shed their yellowed leaves. However, here in Moab, three thousand feet lower in altitude, the trees still retained their brilliant gold colors. The lowering sun flashed dancing yellow lights off the cottonwood leaves twirling in the slight breeze. The darkening sky held just a few puffy white clouds, and no rain was predicted for the first couple days of their trip. The weather, at least, was cooperating.

Mandy felt a little nervous about making a good impression on the clients. She had been too busy making an ice run and helping Kendra pack the coolers to wash up. Kendra, however, even though she had been working hard all afternoon, looked beautiful and serene as usual. Mandy had missed greeting the Anderson clan, too, and regretted that. She hoped that at the dinner she could make them feel welcome and confident that they would be well taken care of.

As she and Kendra neared the restaurant's parking lot, the mouth-watering aroma of grilled meat wafted toward them. Mandy spotted Gonzo Gordon standing beside their fifteen-passenger van. He had taken the van on his quest for camping lanterns. He waved two of them triumphantly in the air. A wide grin split his pale, freckled face and the breeze teased his dreadlocked blond braids.

Kendra clapped her hands. "Success!"

"Success, indeed!" He held out his arms for her then, hesitated.

"It's okay." Kendra slipped into his embrace. "Mandy and Rob know."

Gonzo gave her a quick kiss, then glanced at Mandy, almost begging for approval.

Of the relationship or of his successful mission, Mandy couldn't tell. But she knew the recovering alcoholic still needed all the positive feedback he could get. Relieved that he hadn't come up short, she gave it to him.

"Good job on finding the lanterns, Gonzo, and I'm really stoked for you and Kendra, too."

His tense shoulders visibly relaxed. "And I've got a surprise for you." He untangled himself from Kendra and opened the van door to reveal a third lantern. "Since they weren't our stock, I thought it would be safer to bring three. I tested all of them, and they work."

"Great thinking, quartermaster."

Gonzo puffed out his chest and tossed back his locks, then struck a pose. "Master and commander of the expedition stores, that's me."

Kendra snickered and Mandy laughed.

"Time to meet the clients, Gonzo," Mandy said. "We'll need you to turn on your usual charm tonight."

After Gonzo stowed the lanterns and locked the van, Mandy led them from the parking lot to the outdoor patio on the other side of the fifties-style diner. Rob had said he would get there early and secure tables. When he saw them, he waved them over to two long plastic-on-metal picnic tables he had pulled together. There was space for sixteen on the benches, and he had positioned a lawn chair at one end to make room for seventeen, the headcount for the trip.

The three gal-pals were already sitting at one end. Kendra took Gonzo over to meet them. He greeted them boisterously, and they all seemed to instantly fall in love with him, as Mandy knew they would. Along with being an expert boatsman, Gonzo was exceptional at entertaining clients and putting them at ease. The gal-pals were in good hands.

She scooted up next to Rob. "How were the Andersons?"

"A little uptight," he replied. "I think this trip will do them all some good. They could use a strong dose of enforced relaxation. But you can see for yourself. There they are now." He nodded his head toward the front of the building.

A group of six people had stopped by the diner's sign so one of them could take a picture of it. All were dressed in what looked to be brand-new, brushed nylon zip-off pants, sun-protection button-down shirts, safari hats, and expensive multi-sport sandals. Many of their shirts still showed the creases from the packaging. Someone had taken the suggested packing list to heart.

The older couple had happy smiles on their face, and one of the two young men swung his arms in anticipation. But one of the two young women was looking around at the take-out window and out-door seating with her nose turned up in disdain. When the young man with the camera asked the rest of the group to pose in front of the sign, she rolled her eyes, but grudgingly cozied up to the others.

Oh, brother. Mandy squared her shoulders and plastered a bright smile on her face.

Rob waved the group over and introduced them to Mandy. The parents, both in their fifties and carrying some extra pounds, were Diana and Hal Anderson. A comb-over was ineffective in hiding Hal's bald patch, and gray roots peeked out along the precise part in Diana's hair. As Mandy remembered, the clan was from Omaha, Nebraska. The older Andersons looked like typical well-to-do, middle-aged mid-Westerners, who probably got most of their exercise from playing golf.

Her assessment was verified when Rob asked Hal where he got his tan—that extended to his collar line—and Hal answered with, "Golf! Diana and I play every Saturday we can, her with her lady friends and me with the guys."

While Diana shook Mandy's hand, the older woman said, "I'm both excited and nervous about this trip. It's been a long time since we took the kids camping, and we've only gone rafting a few times as a family. Living in Omaha, we have to travel pretty far to find whitewater."

"Where have you gone rafting before?" Mandy asked.

Diana ticked the trips off on her fingertips. "The Big Sandy River in Kentucky—the easy part, Big Horn Sheep Canyon on the Arkansas, and some river in the Texas hill country."

"The Guadalupe?"

"That's it!"

Mandy nodded. All of those river sections contained Class I to III rapids, which were easier than the Class III and IV rapids they would encounter in Cataract Canyon. These folks would likely need some coaching, but she could tell that Diana was looking for reassurance.

"It's great that you've been on some rafting trips before," Mandy said. "We've taken beginners with no experience at all on Class III to IV runs and they've worked out fine. With your experience, I'm sure you'll have no problems."

"Phew, that's a relief."

The blond and blue-eyed young man with the camera reached over his mother's shoulder to shake Mandy's hand. He was a younger and more athletic version of his father.

"I'm Alex Anderson," he said. "I made the reservation. And I'm the family rafting expert. I go to the University of Wyoming, so I've rafted western rivers like the Yellowstone in Montana, the Snake in Wyoming, and the Arkansas in Colorado."

Rob broke off his conversation with Hal Anderson to ask, "What sections of the Arkansas?"

"Brown's Canyon and the Royal Gorge."

"You'll handle Cataract Canyon just fine, then. You may even be able to give the rest of your family some pointers. What's your major?"

"Geology."

"What a coincidence," Mandy said. "A geology professor from the University of Wyoming is also coming on the trip."

Alex's face went blank for a moment, then he said, "Yeah, I know her. Elsa Norton. She suggested this trip when I told her I wanted to plan a whitewater and climbing adventure for my family." He glanced around. "Is she here?"

"Not yet," Rob said, "but I'm sure she and her daughter and husband will be along soon."

"Husband?" Alex's eyes widened in surprise.

"Ex-husband," Mandy amended. "Now, who's this next to you?" She made a special effort to smile, since it was the woman who had turned up her nose at the diner and was now watching the flies buzzing the outdoor tables with dismay.

"Oh, this is my oldest sister, Alice," Alex said. "I'm the baby of the family."

"And the favored son," his sister quipped.

"Nice to meet you, Alice." Mandy noted the woman's firm handshake and wiry, athletic build. "Do you live in Omaha, too?"

"Yeah."

Not much of a conversationalist. Mandy cocked her head. "What do you do there?"

"I'm a PE and health teacher at Marian High School."

"Ah, that makes sense. You look really fit."

Finally a smile appeared on Alice's face, a little smug one. "Thanks."

Diana leaned in and touched Mandy's arm. "Both of my girls went to Marian. It's the only Class A girl's high school in Nebraska. Very exclusive, and they provide an excellent education. I'm so pleased Alice is working at her alma mater."

"What do you do to stay in such good shape?" Mandy asked Alice, to draw her out some more.

"I coach the girl's swimming and lacrosse teams, and I mix it up with them a lot." Seemingly tired of the conversation, she looked around. "Does this place have a restroom?"

Rob pointed. "In the back."

Alice walked off, leaving the last two members of the Anderson family in front of Mandy and Rob, along with Alex. Kendra had come over to introduce herself to Diana and Hal Anderson and had taken them to meet the others.

"This is my sister Amy." Alex swept a hand toward the young couple next to him. "And her husband, Les Williams."

Also blond and blue-eyed, Amy was attractive, but in a softer, more rounded and feminine way than her athletically fit sister and brother. When she shook hands, Mandy noticed that, like her mother and sister, Amy's fingernails were professionally manicured and painted with a light pink polish. She wondered if the three women had had a salon day together recently and thought, *why bother?* By the end of the trip most of their nails would be broken and mud-caked. At least, that's how Mandy's always came out, so she never bothered with manicures.

While she shook hands with Mandy, Amy said, "I'm the middle child. Les and I live in Omaha, too."

"What do you do there?" Mandy asked.

"I'm just an old-fashioned housewife," Amy said timidly and glanced at her husband. "I cook and clean and garden. Les is the breadwinner."

Amy's husband looked to be in his mid-thirties, about ten years older than his wife. He had the large, bulky build of a bar bouncer or former football player, but of one who had gone a little soft around the edges. He had a tight grip around his wife's waist, and his hand-shake was almost bruising. He eyed Mandy up and down until she shifted uncomfortably under his scrutiny.

"I'm a corporate security officer." Les said it with almost a swagger, as if the title should mean something to Mandy and Rob.

"Sounds important," Rob said.

Good, Mandy thought. Rob had caught on that this guy expected some buttering up.

"It is. Mostly hush-hush, too." Les released his wife and rubbed his hands together. "I'm starving. I hope this place makes a good burger."

"That's what they're known for," Rob replied. "And their shakes. They have all kinds of flavors and they're really thick."

"Oooo, I'd better stay away from those," Amy said. "Got to keep my figure for Les."

Rob swept a hand toward the line in front of the order window. "Go ahead and get whatever you want. Tell them to put it on RM Outdoor Adventures's tab."

The Nortons had arrived while Ron and Mandy had been talking to the Andersons, and they were in the food queue along with the others. Mandy looked around. No sign of Tom O'Day yet. Cool was playing it just a little *too* cool.

After they had all gotten food and taken their seats, Rob suggested they go around the table while they were eating and share their names and occupations. "And tell us something else about yourself, like your favorite food."

This was a common ploy on pre-trip get-togethers for multi-day trips. Mandy would make a mental note of the favorite foods. Then she would make a last-minute run to the local City Market grocery store to buy whichever items she could that would pack well.

Gonzo set a light tone for the sharing by clapping a hand on his chest. "I'm Gonzo Gordon, the best river guide you'll see this side of the Mississippi, and I'm being modest here. I'm also your quartermaster, in charge of supplies, so if we run out of TP, come beat up on me. And, I'm one of your two climbing guides..."

He raised a questioning eyebrow at Mandy, but she shook her head. *Don't mention Cool.*

"...and my favorite food is—what else?—pizza!" he finished with a bow.

"Where the heck is O'Day?" Mandy whispered to Rob.

"Don't worry, I'm sure he'll be here."

When it was Alex Anderson's turn to talk, he said, "I've got two new favorite foods now. It's a hard choice between this awesome chocolate shake," he held up his tall Styrofoam cup, "and the best tater tots I've eaten in my life." In his other hand, he held up a greasy paper tray of Milt's specialty tater tots that came with every order. He nodded his head toward Rob. "Great choice for dinner tonight."

Mandy was sure his oldest sister wouldn't agree, as her tater tots remained untouched. While the introductions continued, Mandy noticed Alice frowning at the plastic utensils. After sawing away at something in her turkey Cobb salad with her plastic knife, she leaned over to make a disparaging remark to her brother-in-law. Les laughed and nudged his wife to join in.

Just as the last introductions were made, Tom O'Day sauntered up. He wore tight jeans and a pearl-button shirt, opened wide enough to show off some of his chest hair. His damp long hair was tied back with a strip of rawhide. When he brushed past Mandy, she caught the whiff of a strong musky aftershave.

Rob introduced O'Day to the others and asked him to share. While he spoke, Mandy noticed his gaze locking onto each of the female clients at the table. All except for Diana Anderson, who had her hand on her husband, Hal's, knee, and Amy Williams, who was under the protective arm of her husband, Les.

Rob stood, told Cool to grab some food, then launched in to his pre-trip speech. He reviewed what they had mostly covered both in pre-trip emails and again when the clients had checked in for the trip, but it never hurt to give out directions multiple times.

After taking a few questions, he clapped his hands together. "Okay, who knows how many rafting guides it takes to screw in a lightbulb?"

Mandy knew this joke. She assumed Kendra, Gonzo, and Cool all did, too, and were wisely keeping their mouths shut.

Rob looked around as a few clients shrugged. "The answer is eleven. One to screw it in and ten to talk about how big the hole was." He paused for the chuckles to die down. "We'll be seeing some whopper holes on this trip. Now, I don't want to run you off if you want to socialize some more, but be sure to get a good night's sleep. We expect you to be at the outfitter building at seven o'clock sharp!"

Prompted by Gonzo, a collective groan went up, mostly in good fun, except for Alice Anderson and Les Williams, who seemed to really mean it.

"Why so damn early?" Les asked.

"We've got a full day planned for you," Rob replied. "We'll stop for lunch where you can see some petrified wood logs, some of which are still sticking out of the solidified mud sandstone that preserved them, and—"

"I care a lot more about getting a good night's sleep than seeing a few old logs," Les said.

"Well I, for one, am looking forward to seeing them." Alex's hard stare at Les was a challenge.

"Me, too," Paul chimed in.

Rob held up a hand. "The petrified forest isn't the only reason we're leaving early. We plan to reach the Little Bridge campsite by mid-afternoon, so anyone who wants to can climb to some caves in the cliffs before dinner. It's seventeen miles downstream. Since we'll be floating on flatwater the whole way, it'll take some time to get there."

Les made a face but remained silent.

Most of the group stood and started to leave, throwing their trash in the diner's oil barrel trash can on the way out. The Anderson family all left theirs on the table, however, as if expecting a bus boy to clean up after them. There was no such thing. Kendra jumped up to clear their trash.

Cool O'Day had taken a seat near the gal-pals and was chatting them up while he ate his Cowboy Burger with cheddar and jala-peños. "You know what would make this burger better? If it was drowned in marinara sauce and mushrooms." He patted Mo's knee. "Like Mo here, I have a hankering for Italian food. Goes good with cool nights like this."

Viv leaned in. "Is October a good time to be taking this trip?"

"Hell yes," Cool replied. "You get bigger water in May, but fall's for taking it slow, savoring the experience. Know what I mean?" He waggled his eyebrows suggestively then put a hand on his heart. He sang a few lines in a deep baritone from a song Mandy didn't recognize, something about autumn weather turning leaves to flame and spending precious days with you. He ended with a flourish and a bow, obviously begging for applause.

The women all accommodated him, laughing while they clapped. They seemed to enjoy Cool's attention and weren't in a hurry to leave.

After saying goodbye to Paul Norton, Rob put an arm over Mandy's shoulder and drew her close. "What do you think? We got a good group?"

On most multi-day trips, personality problems cropped up and had to be smoothed over, and Mandy could see the potential here. But no more than usual, really. No one seemed ready to kill anyone else yet.

"So far, so good," she said to Rob.

THREE

MANDY STOOD OUTSIDE THE outfitter building the next morning, sipping her second travel mug of coffee. She hadn't gotten much sleep the night before, because added to the excitement she felt before embarking on any whitewater rafting trip was the anticipation of a first descent down a river that was new to her. While butterflies battered her stomach, she chaffed her arms and stomped her feet to generate some warmth.

The eastern sky's rosy hue portended the sun's rise in about twenty minutes, and Mandy was anxious to feel its warming rays on her face. The morning air was still a chilly fifty degrees. Once the sun rose, though, the temperature would rapidly climb with it to about seventy-five. Mandy and the other guides had finished prepping and loading the vehicles while wearing fleece jackets and zip-off pants, but they would shed their jackets and lower pant legs soon. As usual, Gonzo wore shorts regardless of the temperature, as he did until winter snows hit the Rockies.

The three gal-pals, Betsy, Viv, and Mo, were the first clients to arrive a few minutes prior to seven. After Mandy greeted them, they sheepishly admitted that they had been up late chatting over a couple of bottles of wine.

With a smile, she replied, "No problem. That's what vacations are for. You can nap on the river today. Help yourself to some breakfast." She swept an arm toward the door of the outfitter building, where she had put out coffee, donuts, and fruit on the counter inside.

The women stumbled into the building to soak up some energizing caffeine and sugar, and Mandy returned her attention to the trip's small caravan. The vehicles sat with full gas tanks and engines running, so heaters could warm the interiors. The exhaust steam rising around the dark hunks of steel made her think of hunkered-down dinosaurs, with the prehistoric-looking backdrop of Moab's looming sandstone formations in the background. This area of the American West was prime dinosaur fossil territory, after all.

First in line was the large pickup truck piled high with gear and towing the raft trailer. The two large oar rafts that would carry most of the gear and few or no passengers were strapped on the bottom, with the two smaller eight-man paddle rafts on top. Most of the clients would ride in those. Besides the climbing aspect, the paddle rafts were another unique feature of their trip. Most outfitters just offered oared rafts or even larger motorized rafts called J-rigs in

Cataract Canyon. Mandy and Rob were giving their clients the opportunity to power a small 8-man raft through the rapids rather than just holding on while the guide did all of the work.

The fifteen-passenger van idled behind the pickup truck. All of their clients would ride to the river in that, along with Kendra, Gonzo, and Mandy. Kendra would drive and Gonzo would entertain. As for Mandy, she wanted the opportunity to size up their clientele some more on the half-hour drive along the Potash-Lower Colorado River Scenic Byway to the put-in at the Potash Boat Ramp.

Rob would drive the pickup truck, with Cool O'Day riding, so they could talk about the climbing side trips planned. Last in the lineup was a beat-up old Subaru with three deeply tanned young men inside chowing down on donuts. Rob had hired the out-of-work river guides to drive their vehicles to the Hite Marina on Lake Powell, their takeout point, and leave the keys in the marina office.

By seven fifteen, all but one of their clients had arrived, loaded up on breakfast, and found seats in the van. The missing man was Paul Norton. Mandy looked up where he was staying on the roster and called his motel. Reception buzzed his room, but there was no answer. She had just about decided to send the guys in the Subaru to the motel to roust Paul out of his room when he arrived in his car.

He parked and jogged over to Rob and Mandy. "I'm sorry. I had so much trouble getting to sleep, worrying about Elsa's reaction to me showing up unannounced, that I slept through the alarm. Thank God I asked for a wake-up call, too, but that came twenty minutes late."

"No problem." Rob clamped a hand on Paul's shoulder. "Remember you're on vacation now. While you're stowing your stuff in the back of the truck, I'll get you some breakfast. How do you take your coffee?"

Looking relieved, Paul answered, "Black will do." He ran back to his car.

Rob winked at Mandy. "There's always one."

She rolled her eyes. While he went inside the building, she helped Paul secure his dry bag in the back of the truck. Paul climbed into the van's only empty seat, next to his daughter, Tina, in the third row. Elsa Norton, sitting on the other side of Tina, didn't acknowledge his presence and stared out her window. The Anderson clan filled the last two rows in the back, and the three girlfriends were in the second row.

Once Rob had returned with Paul's coffee, donut, and banana, Mandy climbed in the front seat next to Gonzo. Then they were off, heading west, with the rising sun blazing through the rear window. As soon as they were on the way, Gonzo got on his knees, facing the back of the van. He had been reading up on Native American rock art. Since there was a good example along the ride, he was going to brief the clients on it before they stopped to get out and look at the panel.

"On the way to the put-in," he shouted, "we're going to see some awesome petroglyphs right on the side of the road, so get your cameras out. Anyone know the difference between petroglyphs and pictographs?"

He waited.

Mandy turned around and saw that Paul Norton's face had a smug expression, but he wasn't volunteering what he knew.

When no one piped up, Gonzo explained, "Pictographs were painted on cliff walls with natural paints made from crushed minerals or plants of different colors mixed with a binder made from fats or blood."

He paused. After Tina Norton wrinkled her nose and issued the "Eew" he was waiting for, he added, "Now that's one way to suffer for your art! But we're not going to see pictographs today. We're going to see petroglyphs. They were chipped into the dark desert patina or rock varnish you find on a lot of the sandstone cliffs, exposing the lighter sandstone underneath. The way to remember the difference is that the root words 'petro' and 'glyph' mean 'rock' and 'carve' and 'picto' and 'graph' mean 'paint' and 'write.'"

Mandy turned around again to make sure everyone was comfortable and could hear. In the back row, the two older Andersons were straining forward, heads cocked. Adding to their difficulty in hearing was the fact that Alice was talking softly, but laughing loudly, to her sister's husband, Les, sitting next to her in the row in front of her parents.

Mandy put a hand on Gonzo's arm to stop him. She shouted over the seat back, "Excuse me. Is anyone having trouble hearing Gonzo?"

Diana and Hal nodded and raised their hands.

"Gonzo's already talking as loudly as he can. Could everyone keep it down so the folks in the back can hear him?"

She waited, and Les stopped laughing and straightened. The van was silent except for Alice, until the woman sensed everyone's gaze and stopped. She pursed her lips and crossed her arms.

"Thank you," Mandy said.

Gonzo resumed his spiel, explaining that no one knows the true meanings of the various rock art symbols. Anthropological experts and modern tribes descended from the ancestral Puebloans who created the rock art all have different interpretations.

Before facing forward, Mandy glanced back to see if Diana and Hal were okay. Hal caught her eye and gave her a thumbs-up. Alice's glowering stare back was unnerving, however, but she remained silent. Mandy returned her gaze to the meandering road in front of her. Sometimes on guided trips she felt like she was a kindergarten teacher or a cat herder.

"There's always one," Kendra said in a low whisper.

Mandy nodded. "I'm afraid that's going to become our mantra for this trip."

———

By mid-morning, after the hustle and bustle of loading the rafts, everyone picking which raft they were going to ride in and launching, Mother Nature had worked her magic on Mandy again. The sun's warmth, the peaceful open surroundings, and the calmly flowing water of the mud-brown Colorado River eased the tension out of her shoulders and put a smile on her face. The towering red sandstone cliffs of Meander Canyon on either side of the river drew her gaze, and her spirits, skyward.

She rested her oars and drank deeply from her water bottle while she watched a peregrine falcon circle overhead in the clear blue expanse. She pointed it out to Elsa and Tina Norton, who had opted to sit in the front of her heavily laden supply raft. That way, they were separated from Paul, who was in one of the nearby paddle rafts being guided by Kendra and Gonzo. The three women watched the hawk spot its prey, swoop down, and disappear behind a willow bush on the shore. Then it rose again with some small creature wriggling in its talons.

"Poor thing." Tina shielded her eyes from the blazing, late-morning sun as she watched the hawk leave.

"I'm sure there are many more mice or moles where that one came from," Elsa replied. "And that beautiful bird may have a nest full of hungry babies to feed. It's survival of the fittest. The strong flourish, and the weak don't, rightfully so."

Mandy thought maybe Elsa was no longer referring to the falcon or the mouse, but to someone closer to home. That was confirmed when Tina frowned and glanced at her father in Kendra's raft just in front of them.

Kendra had positioned him in the rear next to her after watching his feeble paddling strokes. She was talking to him, giving him some pointers. All of the guides would be doing that with the less-experienced paddlers in the next few days, getting them prepared for the big water near the end of the trip.

Looking hopefully at her mother, Tina said, "Those who are weak in some areas may be strong in others. Everyone should get a chance to prove themselves."

"I know you're not talking about that damn mouse anymore," Elsa said curtly. "I gave your father plenty of chances." Her freezing glare at him in Kendra's raft made Mandy shiver involuntarily. "Our marriage is over," Elsa continued. "I've moved on." She buried her nose in her paperback mystery novel, ending the conversation.

Tina sighed and gave a Mandy a weak smile. She held a romance novel in her hand but didn't seem anxious to read it, so Mandy asked her what she did when she wasn't studying or taking classes.

Tina was soon chatting happily about her experiences volunteering at a preschool for underprivileged children.

Listening with one ear, Mandy scanned the other rafts. Rob was oaring the other supply raft, with Cool O'Day snoozing in the front. Besides Paul Norton, Kendra had the three female friends in her paddle raft. They seemed to be getting along well with her, asking for pointers and listening to her advice. Being a birdwatcher, Viv had watched the falcon, too, with the binoculars strung around her neck.

Gonzo, in the lead paddle raft, had gotten stuck with all six of the Anderson clan. The parents, Diana and Hal, sat in the back with him. They happily swatted ineffectively at the water with their paddles while Gonzo and their son, Alex, took turns giving them advice and demonstrating. Les Williams had started out with powerful strokes in the front of the raft. But when he realized they were never going to go much faster than the relentlessly slow river current in Meander Canyon, he gave up and rested his paddle in his lap.

His wife, Amy, and sister-in-law, Alice, had yet to show much interest in paddling. Amy was painting her toenails to match her manicure. Mandy had to laugh that someone would think of bringing nail polish on a whitewater river camping trip.

Alice sat with arms crossed while she quietly scanned the river banks, looking bored. She had only asked Gonzo one question so far, what the piles of foam floating in the river were. Her repulsed expression revealed that she thought they were some kind of pollution or waste.

The guides had used the opportunity to explain that the foam piles were natural phosphates washed off the native yucca plants during rainstorms. Kendra scooped up some on a paddle and let

Paul and the three women feel its slimy smoothness between their fingers. Gonzo did the same for the passengers in his raft, but Alice refused to touch it.

"Hey, Paul," Gonzo shouted to Kendra's raft. "I noticed you brought a fishing rod. Catfish love to slurp the bugs that get stuck in those foam piles. So a good place to throw your line is into a big batch of foam, like the one stuck behind that sandbar." He pointed and Paul replied with a thumbs-up signal.

"You catch 'em, we'll fry 'em." Gonzo shouted and returned the thumbs-up.

Hal asked Gonzo, "You get any trout in the Colorado?"

"At the headwaters, shoot yeah, but not here," he replied. "Water's too muddy and doesn't hold enough oxygen for them. 'Bout all you'll find in this part of the river is bottom feeders like catfish, chub and carp."

Hal crossed his arms. "Not very good eating."

"That's what cornmeal, onions, and secret spices are for," Gonzo replied.

Amy cocked her head. "What secret spices?"

"My special recipe. Can't tell you what's in it, because ... it's a secret!"

While Gonzo laughed and the others smiled, Alice gave only a dismissive sniff. After a conversation about campfire recipes started up between Gonzo, Amy, and Diana, Alice yawned and licked her lips. She turned around and interrupted the conversation to ask Gonzo for a bottle of water. He passed one to her through Alex, and she took it without thanking either of them.

Mandy remembered that the whole Anderson family, except for Alex, had treated the guides like porters at the put-in. The five of them had stood off to the side, talking about the ugly structures of the Potash mine just upstream and taking photos. The others had done all of the work, lugging gear and rafts between the vehicles and the river bank. The Andersons hadn't even carried their own personal dry bags to the river. She hoped they weren't going to expect the guides to wait on them hand and foot for the whole trip.

As she watched Amy and Alice, Mandy wondered whether the two women might be happier sitting in her raft, where they weren't expected to paddle. And if they spent some time with her, maybe Mandy could drop the hint that they would enjoy the trip more if they actually pitched in and *did* something.

When Tina took a break in her story-telling, Mandy asked her, "Do you and your mother want to take some turns in the paddling rafts?"

"Oh yes, I do," Tina said, "especially in the whitewater section."

When Mandy looked at Elsa, she nodded and said, "Me, too."

"I'll make sure that happens," Mandy said. "We'll keep mixing it up so you have plenty of time in a paddle raft—but we won't put Elsa in the same one as Paul."

Elsa cracked a smile. "Smart gal. You wouldn't want to have a murder on your hands."

Mandy gave the expected response of rolling her eyes in jest, but inwardly she shuddered. She had just come off a summer of river rangering where she had experienced much more than her fair share of murders—and the disastrous effects on those she loved. The absolute last thing she wanted to deal with, even more than Rob's mother's wedding mania, was another dead body.

The flotilla reached the petrified forest site below Thelma and Louise Point around twelve thirty, perfect timing for lunch. While they beached the rafts, Cool told the story of how the point had stood in for the Grand Canyon in the movie. The National Park Service wouldn't give the movie makers permission to crash a car in the Grand Canyon, but the Utah state park authorities were happy to oblige.

Mandy and Kendra set up the portable toilet upstream behind a screening stand of tamarisks and willows.

Then Gonzo gave the toilet speech. "Listen up, folks. Here's the scoop on pee and poop. Whenever we stop on the river bank, any of you guys who need to 'water the river' should head downstream. Women should head upstream and find a private place in the trees to squat. The chemical toilet is for number two only, or any woman who doesn't want to squat."

Gonzo held up a roll of toilet paper in a plastic bag. "This here is the key to the john. If it's in camp, the toilet is available. If it's gone, the toilet's occupied. Everyone got the idea?" He waved the bag in the air.

Alice gave a snort and marched upstream. Diana gratefully took the key from Gonzo, and Amy followed her mother.

After everyone had relieved themselves, Rob led the clients through a grove of river cane to the petrified logs with Mandy bringing up the rear. The other staff stayed on the river bank to make lunch and set up a handwashing station.

Each of the river guides had picked an area of study to bone up on before the trip. Rob took geology, Gonzo had chosen the ancient tribes and their rock art, Kendra studied the wildlife, birds, and tracks, and Mandy had chosen the plant life. She had gone on a short hike with a Moab herbalist and plant expert the day before the rafting trip. She was glad she could put that education to use when Mo Heedles stopped and pointed at a small bush with grayish-green spiky leaves and small yellow flowers.

"What plant is this?"

Mandy bent down and fingered the prickly flowers. "That's snake broom." She waved the group over to look. "Native Americans would make a poultice out of this plant to put on snake bites. One of the Moab guides told me that when a friend got stung by a wasp on a camping trip, he mixed some of the crushed flowers with a little beer and put it on the bite. His friend said it helped—took away the pain and swelling."

"Hell, just drinking the beer would do that!" Les gave a hearty laugh and turned away, obviously disinterested.

Mo frowned at him, then turned to Mandy. "That was fascinating. Thanks." She took a photograph of the plant and scribbled a note in a small journal she carried with her.

When they reached the petrified logs, Rob admonished the group not to touch them or pick up any pieces. Then he explained how they were created by a sudden flood that washed them down to the mouth of the ancient river where they were covered by a mud flow. Over time the mud solidified into sandstone and minerals leached into the wood, dissolving it and leaving mineralized impressions. The geology hounds, Alex, Elsa, and Paul, seemed most interested in the site, taking photos and asking questions. After a few perfunctory photos posing in front of the logs, the others grew restless.

Mandy suggested it was time for lunch.

When they returned to the beach, Gonzo explained how to use the handwashing station, a hygiene requirement of the Park Service. All of the food preparers had used it before making lunch, and they were supposed to urge the clients to use it before every meal.

Les skipped the handwashing and looked around with hands on his hips. "Man, it's time to get this party started! I need some beer. Where's the coolers?"

No one said a word.

Mandy shot a glance at Rob. While neither they, nor any of the other outfitters, provided alcohol on the trip, they had told the clients there would be room in the coolers for canned or boxed beer and wine if they wanted to bring some. Les had brought a whole case of Budweiser. Hal and Diana's box of white wine seemed small in comparison.

Rob walked over to Les and put a hand on his shoulder. "We need our wits about us when we're on the water. So, we're going to hold off on the alcohol each day until we reach our final campsite. You can have all you want then, but in the meantime, Kendra's made some lemonade and iced tea for us."

Les made a face, but when he looked around and saw that no one wanted to join him, he shrugged. "I'll go with the flow if nobody wants to have some fun. Hell, this trip's been downright boring so far."

Mandy bristled at that, but Rob just forced out a laugh and said, "That's what relaxation is all about. Glad to know we delivered!" He clapped a bewildered-looking Les on the back and went to wash his hands.

Diana approached Mandy while holding her "Americone." It was half of a large flour tortilla rolled into a cone and filled with fresh taco salad. The cooks had mixed crushed tortillas in with the salad to soak up the juices.

"This is genius," Diana said. "You don't need plates or napkins or anything. I'll have to remember it for our next barbecue. And it's delicious, too." She took a large bite.

Mandy smiled. Minimizing trash and the need for utensils was the whole point of the meal. "Thanks. There's plenty, so if you want more, feel free."

After everyone had had their fill, Mandy and the other guides cleaned and packed the kitchen gear and toilet and stowed it all back on Rob's raft. Then Mandy got everyone's attention.

"We want to mix up the raft positions a little," she said. "Elsa and Tina were in my raft this morning, and they'd like a chance to paddle this afternoon. Anyone else interested in moving?"

The silence was deafening.

Finally, Alex raised his hand. "I'll give up my spot. I don't need the practice."

"You can take my place in Rob's oar raft," Cool said to Alex. "I'll hang out with the ladies this afternoon in Kendra's raft."

Mandy looked around for other volunteers.

Her cheeks reddening, Amy nudged her husband. "They can have our spots, don't you think?"

"Sure," Les said lazily. "Maybe I can stretch out and take a nap on one of the oar rafts, since there's not much else to do."

"I'll set up a comfy spot for you on my raft." Mandy flashed a grateful smile to Amy.

With that issue resolved, they quickly loaded the rafts and pushed off into the current. Once underway, Cool pointed out Dead Horse Point above them and told the legend of where the name came from. Cowboys had rounded up wild mustangs on the point and corralled them there with a brush fence across the narrow neck of land onto the point. They picked out the horses they wanted and left the rejects trapped behind the fence to die of thirst within sight of the Colorado River 2,000 feet below.

"How awful!" wide-eyed Amy said, while her husband just shook his head at her reaction.

"Here's a better story about the point, then," Cool replied. "Remember the scene in *Mission Impossible II* where Tom Cruise is rock climbing?"

Peering at the point, Les said, "Sure do. I couldn't believe that prissy little movie actor would do something so dangerous."

"That scene was filmed on the edge of Dead Horse Point. He was on cables, but they erased them in the movie," Cool answered, "and his stunt double did the riskiest parts."

Les snorted. "Figures." He smugly folded his arms across his chest, as if he could show Tom Cruise a thing or two.

Mandy said to Les, "I noticed how strong your paddle strokes were this morning. You know, when we unload the rafts at the campsite, we could really use someone athletic like you."

The comment had multiple purposes—to butter up Les, to make sure he wasn't miffed about putting off his beer drinking, and to get him in a helping frame of mind. They really did need help unloading the rafts. Hopefully, if she could get Les to realize pitching in was expected of the clients, the rest of the Anderson family would follow his lead.

"I guess I could lend a hand," Les replied. "As long as it doesn't put off cocktail hour too long."

"No problem," Mandy said. "The more hands we can get in a bucket brigade to unload the gear, the quicker it goes. Shouldn't take more than a few minutes if everyone helps. Then we guides will fix dinner and set up camp while you folks pitch your tents and relax."

"I could help," Amy said timidly.

Les snorted. "You? Lugging these big sacks?" He patted one of the tent dry bags he had been lounging against. "No, don't worry your pretty little head over that."

"Pitching a tent isn't very hard," Mandy offered. "And if you haven't done it before, one of us could show you how."

"Sounds like fun," Amy said, while Les looked doubtful.

To continue softening Les, Mandy said to him, "I guess from the looks of you, a corporate security officer has to stay in good shape. What do you do for work, exactly?"

Les waxed eloquently about the importance of his position, the hush-hush nature, the element of danger. But when Mandy probed further, with appropriate ego-stroking comments about how important it all sounded, it seemed like the job mostly involved paperwork, such as processing and checking on employee clearances. It all sounded like a huge bore to her, but it was easy to feign interest with a remark here and there.

After a while Mandy tried a couple of times to steer the topic toward Amy and her activities, but Les kept dismissing his wife's life as trivial and returning the discussion to himself. Finally he yawned mightily, leaned back on the dry bags and pushed his hat over his face to take a nap. Then Mandy and Amy could talk quietly about Amy's home life.

Soon, Mandy had trouble stifling her own yawns. There was no way she could tolerate Amy's sedate, mostly indoors existence, catering to Les's whims. Mandy mused to herself that if she were in Amy's shoes, she would go out back and shoot herself—or Les.

FOUR

Should you shield the canyons from the windstorms
you would never see the true beauty of their carvings.
—ELISABETH KÜBLER-ROSS

LATER THAT AFTERNOON, THE group reached the Little Bridge camp-site and tied the rafts to some sturdy tamarisk trunks. Gonzo made hasty work of widening steps that had been cut by a previous party into the tall sand bank rising about five feet above the water. Again, one of the first items unloaded from the raft was the steel box toilet that was set up a discrete distance from camp. Rob then organized a bucket brigade line to pass gear from the rafts up to a wide, sandy area about twenty yards from the river bank. Mandy was glad to see the Andersons pitching in.

Once the unloading was complete, folks picked tent locations and the guides helped the clients figure out how to pitch their tents. Mandy told everyone to just toss their sleeping bags and gear bags inside the tents, that there would be time to organize their gear later. After folks had grabbed a piece of fruit or a granola bar for a snack—or a beer in Les's case—she got everyone's attention.

"We're going to divide into two groups, so you have a choice of activities. Cool and Gonzo will take one group over to the cliff wall above us to try some climbing and rappelling." She swept an arm toward the red sandstone cliff rising above the downstream side of the camp. It was riddled with caves about halfway up, a three-story climb. "You'll get an awesome view of the river from those caves, so be sure to take your cameras.

"For those who aren't feeling so daring, Kendra will lead a short hike back into the canyon. You can take photos there of the wildflowers, the beautiful amphitheater formed by the cliff walls, and any wildlife you see. And, of course, you have the option of doing nothing and hanging out here. Rob and I will stay here to cook dinner. Now, who wants to go with Kendra?"

Kendra stepped away from the group and held up her hand. As Mandy expected, Diana and Hal Anderson walked toward her. Their daughter Amy did, too, as did Tina Norton. That surprised Mandy, since both of Tina's parents seemed to be opting for the more adventurous climb.

"Don't you want to hike with your daughter?" Elsa asked Paul Norton.

He shook his head. "I've always wanted to try climbing. It's one of the reasons I came on this trip." When she frowned, he said quietly, "Let's just try to get along."

That left eight clients with Cool and Gonzo. "Can you handle so many?" Mandy asked Cool.

Cool began tossing helmets to the people in his group. "Sure, we'll rig up two belay lines, with Gonzo in charge of one and me in charge of the other."

Elsa sidled over next to Cool, and with a sigh, Paul stepped toward Gonzo.

After explaining how to fit their helmets to their heads, Cool addressed the climbing group. "This will be a short, easy ascent to those caves, to give your climbing muscles a first stretch. After some time for photo ops, we'll rappel down. This will prepare you for more challenging climbs later."

"Just be sure you're back before dark, so folks can organize their tents before dinner," Mandy reminded him.

He gave a quick nod. Then he looped a gear harness across his chest and over a shoulder that clanged with carabiners, removable anchors and other hardware. Next, he shouldered a large backpack stuffed with ropes, gloves, and belay harnesses. Gonzo did the same. After making sure everyone had a full water bottle, they headed for the boulder hill at the base of the cliff.

In the meantime, Kendra had waited patiently until everyone in her group had dug out a camera and filled water bottles. Though she didn't need to wear much sunscreen to protect her own black skin, she reminded the others to be sure to put some on. Once everyone was ready, with a nod to Rob and Mandy she led her group into the canyon.

"Ah, alone at last." Rob snaked an arm around Mandy's waist. "Come here, *mi querida.*"

After a quick glance around to make sure they were alone, Mandy joined Rob in a kiss that deepened and lasted until she was reeling and wanting more.

Rob pulled back and gazed into her eyes. "I needed that."

"Me, too, and I wish we could finish this in the tent." Mandy gave his butt a squeeze before releasing her hug. "But we've got a lot of work to do."

With a finger to her lips, Rob said, "Save my place. We'll pick this up again later."

He winked and headed for the gear pile. They both knew this was the way it would be for the rest of the trip. Quick snatches of alone time when they could find it. But as Mandy watched the muscles bunch in Rob's sexy thighs while he hefted the camp stove, she smiled. She could always watch him—and anticipate the nights when those thighs would be next to hers.

They worked companionably together, comparing observations on the clients while they set up the kitchen, handwashing station, three-stage dishwashing station and folding camp tables and chairs. Rob agreed with Mandy that Les Williams was proving to be an ass, but Rob thought he could handle him.

"You've done a good job with him so far," Mandy said. "I just wish the whole Anderson family would pitch in more."

"Hey, they're on vacation," Rob said with a shrug. "If they don't want to pitch in, that's their privilege. They paid for it."

"You're right," Mandy said, blowing hair out of her face, "but it's always the clients who roll up their sleeves who get the most out of these trips. The Andersons don't know what they're missing out on."

"It's their loss, not ours. I'm more worried about the Nortons. Keeping Elsa and Paul from arguing and putting a damper on the whole group is going to be tough."

"At least the three women have been no problem so far. They're a lot of fun and enthusiastic."

They went to work on the meal. Mandy chopped vegetables and started a pot of rice boiling on the gas stove for stir-fried rice. Rob fried spring rolls on the griddle side of the large gas stove, then set them aside in a covered pot to stay warm while he fried chicken breasts that had been marinated in teriyaki sauce. They stirred up pitchers of lemonade and iced tea and put out s'more makings for dessert later.

By the time Kendra returned with her group, Mandy and Rob had laid out a buffet line, and all of the food was being kept warm in pots on the stove.

"See anything interesting?" Mandy asked.

Amy shrugged. "Some pretty wildflowers. I think I'll organize our tent and lie down for a bit before Les and the others come back." She headed for it.

"That cryptobiotic soil is fascinating," Hal said. "Some of the crusty mounds were five or six inches high."

"I thought they were strange-looking anthills," Diana said, "until Kendra explained the crust was a mix of lichens, mosses, fungi, algae, and—" She snapped her fingers. "What's the term for that bacteria again?"

"Cyanobacteria," Kendra answered. "The mucus they secrete is what holds the soil clumps together."

"And it's amazing how those teeny tiny organisms can do that huge job of retaining water and controlling erosion."

"But only if you don't step on them," Kendra said. "You all were great about staying on the trail."

"I thought that bridge formation in the back of the canyon was pretty spectacular," Tina chimed in. "I snapped some good photos of it before we had to head back."

"Great," Mandy said. "You can show them to your folks when they get back."

"What can I do to help?" Kendra asked, and before Mandy could answer, Tina said, "Me, too."

What a nice change from the Andersons, Mandy thought. "You can collect driftwood for a fire later, Kendra. And Tina, after you wash your hands, you can set out the spring rolls and dipping sauce for an appetizer."

Kendra and Tina quickly went to work. In the meantime, Hal Anderson dug their wine box out of the cooler. After asking for cups, he poured white wine for Diana and himself. They sat and drank at one of the camp tables and watched deepening shadows crawl across the river while munching on the spring rolls Tina brought them.

About a half hour later, as the sun dipped below the pink cliffs behind the campsite, gilding the upper rim golden red, Cool and Gonzo arrived with their group, all chattering enthusiastically about the climb.

Mandy came out of the tent she was sharing with Rob, where she had been laying out their sleeping bags. She flashed a greeting smile at the group. "How'd everyone do?"

Les pumped a fist in the air. "I was first to the top."

"After the guides, that is," Alice added.

"Well, of course," Les said with a scowl. "They had to set up the route. But I beat your bro fair and square."

"Were you racing?" Mandy asked.

"Not really," Alex replied as he dug a beer out of one of the coolers and tossed it to Les. He popped the top on another one, drank some, and let out a satisfied "Ah," then smacked his lips. "Les and I were the first two to go up, so of course, he turned it into a race."

Hand on his hip, Les said, "Why not? Adds an element of excitement." He looked around. "Where's Amy?"

"Napping in your tent, I think." Mandy pointed.

Before walking away, Les said, "You shouldn't feel bad, Alex. At least you didn't get beat by a girl, like Paulie boy here."

Paul bared his teeth in a nervous smile, looked at his daughter and explained, "Elsa and I went next, and she reached the top before me."

Mandy glanced at Elsa, who quickly wiped a triumphant smirk off her face. In a nonchalant tone, she said to Tina, "Your father and I weren't really racing. It just turned out that we got on the two ropes at the same time."

I bet, Mandy thought. Elsa, like Les, seemed to have that type A personality that grabbed at competition whenever it could. These were the type of clients that Meander Canyon was best for, cutting them off from their electronic devices and forcing them to slow down and savor life.

Cool came up behind Alice Anderson and Betsy Saunders and draped an arm over each, pulling them close to him. "The lovely ladies did great, too," he said with a salacious grin.

Alice slid out of his grasp. "I'm going to clean up before dinner." She walked away.

Still holding on to Betsy, Cool tried to throw an arm around Mo Heedle's shoulders, but both women twirled out of his grasp.

"We're going to clean up, too," Mo stated firmly, and the three women headed for their large tent.

Mandy frowned. The last thing she wanted was Cool carrying the flirtation thing too far and pissing off the female clients. RM Outdoor Adventures couldn't afford to deal with a sexual harassment lawsuit.

Left with empty arms, Cool gave a shrug and went to work stowing the climbing gear back in one of the rafts. Gonzo snatched a spring roll and gave a toodle-oo wave with his fingers to Kendra before going to help Cool.

Mandy raised an eyebrow at Rob, but she couldn't really say anything to him about Cool in front of the others. They would have to talk about him later in the privacy of their tent.

––––

Everyone had worked up an appetite. They descended on the Chinese meal like a swarm of locusts on a cornfield and stripped the pots bare. Dusk had descended, so the camping lanterns had been brought out and lit, and most of the group had applied bug repellant or donned long-sleeved shirts and pants.

Exhausted now after her mostly sleepless night and work-filled day, Mandy struggled to maintain a perky smile and posture. She silently calculated how long it would take to clean up and put the campsite right before she could crawl into her sleeping bag.

Too long.

The clients had all settled back into camp chairs with s'mores and mugs of decaf or regular coffee. The three girlfriends passed around photos of their families to show the others. Kendra roasted marshmallows over the small driftwood fire burning in the metal fire pan for those who wanted seconds on dessert. She slapped Gonzo's hand playfully when he grabbed a chocolate bar to eat by itself.

Rob started a discussion on the differences between Meander Canyon, with its slow-moving flatwater, and Cataract Canyon, with its whitewater rapids. Cataract also had twice the water volume, from the confluence of the Colorado and Green rivers. Both canyons had their pluses. Meander Canyon offered more chances to interact with nature and examine the geology and history of the Utah Canyonlands while taking hiking, swimming, and climbing breaks. Cataract Canyon offered the thrill of surfing an almost continuous string of roaring rapids—an hours-long roller coaster ride.

Rob leaned forward in his chair. "Here's a challenge. I'd like each of you to choose which canyon you think you're going to enjoy the most. At the end of the trip, we'll talk about this again to see if anyone changes their mind. Surprisingly, I've been told that a lot of people do."

By then, Mandy felt sure she could predict which canyon each of their clients would say they preferred, but she listened carefully to see if her people-reading skills were right.

Of course, the older Andersons, Diana and Hal, chose Meander Canyon, especially Diana. With a shudder, she said, "I'm still worried about those huge crashing waves in Cataract Canyon that I keep imagining."

Alex laughed and patted his mother's hand. "You'll end up whooping and hollering like the rest of us. I guarantee it! And, of course I choose Cataract Canyon. If there was a way to get there without going through this slow stuff, I'd probably do it."

As Mandy expected, the type-A personalities of Elsa Norton and Les Williams chose Cataract Canyon. Alice Anderson, too, who had looked so bored during that day's float downriver, chose Cataract Canyon.

Betsy, Viv, and Mo spent a lot of time discussing the choice. They noted their interests in animal tracking, bird-watching, and wildflower identification, respectively, and said they had enjoyed the quiet float and challenging climb that day. However, they all had a sense of adventure, too. They wound up refusing to choose, no matter how much Rob needled them, saying they had chosen the trip for both and thought they would like both equally.

When her turn came, Amy shyly looked in her lap. "I think Meander Canyon is beautiful, but I can't wait to see the rapids in Cataract Canyon."

That was Mandy's first surprise. She wondered if Amy was just trying to please her husband and choose the same as him.

When it was Paul Norton's turn, he shifted in his seat. "Well, you all know Elsa has a doctorate in geology and teaches it at U of W. But, I also have a Master's Degree in geology. Elsa and I met while we were graduate assistants together."

He put a hand on his daughter's shoulder. "When Tina here came along, I decided I needed a steady job with health insurance to support my family, so I became a letter carrier with the postal service. I still collect mineralogy specimens for a hobby, though, and I'm finding the rock layers we're passing through to be fascinating."

Paul held up the page on Rock Sequences of the Canyonlands in the copy of the waterproof *Canyonlands River Guide* he had brought along. "If anyone still thinks the Earth is only six thousand years old after traveling through these hundreds of millions of old layers of rock, they've got their heads in the sand. So, I think I'll choose Meander Canyon, because the slow pace makes for easier rock study."

Mandy cringed at his slap at those who took the Bible literally and looked around the group to see if anyone had taken offense. Thankfully, no one was frowning. She tended to feel out river clients about their beliefs on the age of the Earth before going into much detail about the rock layers they were seeing. There didn't seem to be any creationists in this group. In fact there hadn't been any mention of religion at all. Mandy hoped they could avoid the troublesome topics of religion and politics for the rest of the trip.

Coming last, Tina Norton glanced back and forth between her two parents, who had made different choices, as if conflicted about which one she should align herself with.

"C'mon, Tina," Elsa urged. "You always liked water slides when you were a kid."

Paul set his jaw. "This isn't a competition, Elsa."

"No?" Elsa spat back. "Haven't you always competed against me for Tina's affection? Isn't that why you secretly arranged to come along on this trip?"

"That's not true," Paul said. "I didn't know about the trip before Tina asked me to come."

When Elsa glanced at her, Tina nodded. "I just wanted to be a family again, even if just for a few days," she said mournfully.

Most of the others seemed uncomfortable and avoided looking at the Nortons, except for Alex Anderson, whose serious gaze went back and forth between his professor, Elsa, and her ex-husband. Realizing the argument was putting a damper on the evening, Mandy nudged Gonzo, who was sitting beside her.

He took the hint and leapt to his feet. "Well, now that we know everyone's opinion on that and the light from the fire has died down, it's time to move on to some stargazing." He pointed to the sky. "Has anyone ever seen the Milky Way as clearly as you can tonight?"

All of the clients' heads tilted back so they could gaze at the star-studded sky.

"Man, it's hard to pick out any constellations with all those stars!" Viv said.

"The only one I know is the Big Dipper, and that's not too hard," Mo added.

Cool O'Day turned out to be quite a stargazer, plus he pulled out a well-worn book on the Navajo interpretations of the constellations. He and Gonzo started a little competition between them and got everyone involved in identifying Greek constellations as well as some of the Navajo ones.

Finally, Hal let out a big yawn and stretched his arms wide. "Well, I'm ready to hit the sack."

Looking grateful, Diana said, "Me, too." She got out of her seat and held out a hand for Hal. While the two of them walked to their tent, the three gal pals said they, too, were going to call it a night, and left.

When Kendra rose to go with them, Mandy put a hand on her arm. "Kendra, could you come with me to check on the rafts?"

Kendra gave her a quizzical look, but she said, "Okay."

Mandy strapped on her LED headlamp and turned it on, and Kendra did the same. The two of them walked to where the rafts were beached on the sand.

Once they were out of earshot of the others, Mandy turned to Kendra. "I don't like the moves I've seen Cool putting on the female clients. Could you feel out Betsy, Viv, and Mo? See if he's bugging them, if they're okay with it or not?"

"Sure. But what'll you do if they're not?"

Mandy pursed her lips. "Rob or I will have to tell him to cut it out. The last thing we want is some client complaining about sexual harassment."

"Oh, I don't think it's as serious as that." Kendra raised an eyebrow. "He's just flirting, making the trip a little more exciting for them."

"Maybe so, but he's laying it on a little too thick. Let me know tomorrow what they say. Sometime when we're away from the others."

Kendra nodded and headed for the 4-man tent she would share with the gal-pals. Mandy made sure all of the rafts were still secure before she returned to the tables. By then, everyone but the guides had left. Gonzo and Cool were washing pots and pans by the light of a camping lantern and dropping them into the dishnet hanging off one side of the kitchen prep table to dry. Rob, wearing his headlamp, was scouring the campsite for food droppings and trash. They had already tied down the locked food coolers on the rafts, and the trash bags would be joining them.

Mandy asked Rob, "Did the ranger briefing have any black bear sightings?"

"No, but better safe than sorry," he said as he knotted the trash bag. "The rangers said the bears don't usually come down to the main river channel, but they'll often follow stream corridors in the fall looking for prickly pear cactus and hackberry tree fruits to fatten up for hibernation. We don't want to entice them into camp with any easy pickings here."

Raised voices from the 4-man tent being shared by Hal, Diana, Alex, and Alice made both of them turn. Mandy couldn't make out what the argument was about, because they all seemed to be talking at once and the tent was far enough away that the words were indistinct.

Finally, the tent flap was thrown back, and Alex stormed out. He wore his headlamp and was lugging his sleeping bag.

"Fine! I'll sleep outside," he shouted and stomped away from the campsite.

Mandy hurried to catch up. "Anything I can help with?"

"Crap, no," he said. "Alice is just being difficult, and I'm not in the mood to put up with it. It's a nice night, so I don't mind sleeping outside. No rain's predicted, right?"

"Not for a couple of days, at least. You want to bed down near the guide tents?"

"I'd rather be alone, if that's okay." He shifted the sleeping bag. "Commune with nature and watch the stars, you know? Pretend I'm roughing it on my own, if you get my drift."

"Sure." She wondered if he had deliberately picked the fight to get out of the family tent.

"I'll bed down somewhere back in the canyon."

"Did Cool or Gonzo brief your group on cryptobiotic soils?"

Looking puzzled, Alex shook his head. "What's that got to do with anything?"

Mandy explained about the fragile soil layer, then said, "We guides have been asked by the Park Service to keep clients off soils that haven't already been damaged." She pointed to a ten-foot-tall jumble of huge boulders behind the campsite. "The ground around that rock formation has been trampled already, and the trail goes past them. I suggest you lay your bag just on the other side of the rocks. I remember a cleared area there, and you'll be close enough to hear the coffee call for breakfast."

"Sure thing." He grinned, his white teeth glowing in the light from their headlamps. "I don't miss many meals. I'll be as hungry as a bear come morning."

Mandy laughed with him then watched as he disappeared around the rock formation into the black night. *He should be all right. Right?*

Shaking her head, she said out loud, "Of course he will."

While she helped Gonzo pack the cooking utensils, pots, and pans, Mandy wondered if the spat between Alex and his sister was real, and if so, if it would linger into the next days—or even the rest of the trip. She hoped not. It could cast a pall over the whole group, spoiling the experience. She was beginning to think that dealing with all of the personalities on this trip might be worse than dealing with Rob's mom.

Nah.

When everything was shipshape, Mandy and Rob said good-night to Gonzo. Cool had already retired. Mandy brushed her teeth then headed for Rob's and her tent. While he went to stow the trash on the rafts and brush his teeth by the river, she changed into a sleep T-shirt and flannel pants and sat there wondering about Alex. She finally crawled out of the tent, slipped on her Tevas, and turned on her headlamp.

She found Rob relieving himself in the river, the arching stream glittering in his headlamp. He was obviously seeing how far out over the water he could reach. She giggled and surprised him.

He turned only his head, and when he saw it was her, he leered. "Like what you see?"

Putting a hand on her hip, Mandy cocked her head and flapped her shirt front as if she were overheated. "Always."

Rob tucked himself in and rinsed his hands in the river. "Went at least thirty feet. Think I'll invite the rest of the guys to a pissing contest tomorrow night."

"Don't you dare!"

He picked up his toothbrush and water bottle from a rock and squirted some toothpaste onto the brush. "Miss me already? I'll just be a few more minutes."

"I came to tell you I want to check on Alex."

"He's a big boy. I'm sure he'll be okay."

"Probably, but I also want to make sure he's not destroying any cryptobiotic soil. I explained it to him, but I didn't show him exactly what it looked like."

"Worrywart!" He stuck his toothbrush in his mouth and waved her away.

Smiling to herself, Mandy walked quickly through the campsite, rubbing her arms. Once the sun went down, the temperature dropped at least twenty degrees, and the T-shirt wasn't enough to keep her warm. She let out a big yawn. She would just take a peek around the boulder pile to check on Alex, then hurry back to her warm tent, snuggle up to Rob and go straight to sleep.

As she rounded the formation, she heard the sound of a zipper unzipping, then someone whispering "Sssh." Why would Alex be shushing himself?

She was about to clear her throat and announce her presence when she saw Alex's bare back gleaming in the moonlight—and his bare butt. He was on his knees facing away from her and was rhythmically thrusting his hips forward.

Mandy gulped, thinking she had witnessed him in a very private sex act, but then she heard a moan—a female moan. A naked female form was on her hands and knees in front of Alex, back turned to him, with his hands cupping her breasts. Her head was down, bobbing with Alex's thrusts as her soft moans quickened in pace.

Who's with him? Mandy couldn't see the woman's face. She stood frozen, worried that the amorous couple would hear her if she moved, but she couldn't stay. Their rapid panting signaled they wouldn't be preoccupied much longer.

Mandy decided that they were so engrossed with each other, she didn't need to worry about making noise. Her face burning now, she slipped around to the other side of the rock formation. Now she knew the reason Alex had picked a fight with his sister— so he could have a rendezvous with some woman on the trip.

She stood in the shadows, her mind racing through the female clients. Mandy had seen no signs of an attraction developing between Alex and Tina that day. Could it be one of the girlfriends, looking for a little extra excitement on this trip away from the hubbies? Could the relationship explode in their faces, ruining the trip?

Mandy was about to sneak quietly back to her tent when soft footsteps came trotting around the side of the rock formation. She stood stock still in the shadows and held her breath. The woman passed about eight feet in front of her but didn't notice Mandy because her attention was focused on buttoning her shirt. The moonlight gleamed on the woman's short dark curls.

Elsa!

FIVE

Mother Nature may be forgiving this year,
or next year, but eventually she's going to come
around and whack you. You've got to be prepared.
—GERALDO RIVERA

MORNING CAME EARLY AFTER a disturbed night, and Mandy groaned when Rob lifted the tent flap, letting in the cool morning air and exposing a lightening sky. The sun wouldn't be over the canyon rim for another hour or so, but it was time to get the coffee brewing and breakfast started for the clients.

After she had told Rob about discovering Alex and Elsa *in flagrante delicto,* he had reached for her with his own ideas for lovemaking. Then the two of them had stayed awake for another half hour discussing the possible complications. Rob finally convinced her they could do nothing about Alex's and Elsa's affair, and the best thing was to ignore it and hope the two continued to keep their relationship secret.

She pulled on some warm clothes, stumbled into the willow and tamarisk thicket upstream to relieve herself, then washed her hands and face at the handwashing station after refilling the water can with cold river water. Fully awake after that, she scooped coffee grounds into a metal campfire coffeepot and poured in water from the purified water jug. She turned on the gas stove and put the pot on a burner. While Rob woke Gonzo and Cool in their tent, she went to the rafts to unload breakfast fixings from the coolers.

When she reached the rafts, she pulled up short. Muddy streaks covered the tops of the coolers, and they were twisted in their lashings as if someone—or something—had been tugging on them. The dry food metal boxes had also been disturbed and moved, but their locks had held. Muddy streaks smeared the sides of the rafts, too. The streaks looked like they had come from the paws of a hungry animal, a large one.

What happened here? A bear?

Mandy had never heard of bears getting into anchored rafts, which were the recommended place to store food away from animals and were frankly the safest place to store anything vital to a float trip. She scanned the nearby river bank, but saw no prints or damaged vegetation—or a bear hulking in the underbrush.

Next, she did a quick mental check to see if anything was missing. They had brought ashore all of the clothing dry bags, tents, and sleeping bags the night before, and the PFDs were still tied together to the front of each raft. The water jugs were all accounted for, as were the oars, first aid kit, and other gear—except for a waterproof metal ammo box containing their permits and the radio. It was gone.

Shit!

Remembering that the ammo box had been sitting loose next to one of the dry food boxes versus clipped to one of the raft fittings with a carabiner, Mandy's heart sank. She scanned the river bank, hoping the ammo box hadn't been knocked into deep water. She spied a metal corner sticking out of the water next to the first step that had been carved in the sand bank.

Yes!

She clambered over the rafts until she reached the one next to the box, which was stuck bottom-up. She tugged and tugged at it until the mud released it with a wet sucking sound. But the damn thing was open. The plastic bag with the permits inside came loose and floated out into the water. Mandy snatched it up with a surge of relief. When she looked inside the ammo box, though, she blew out a breath. The radio transceiver was coated with mud, and the external antenna was broken.

No way in hell is that going to work.

Rob appeared on the bank. "What happened here?"

Mandy held up the muddied ammo box. "I don't know. Bear maybe. Everything else seems to be okay, but our radio is toast."

"What?" Rob stepped into one of the rafts and took the radio from Mandy. He rinsed the mud off of it in the river then tried keying it on, but nothing happened. "Crap. These things are supposed to be water-resistant."

Then he looked around at the raft. He pointed to the lid of one of the coolers that showed four closely spaced long mud streaks, as if left by four claws. "It does look like a bear left that, but it's sure big for a black bear."

"I wonder why we didn't hear anything," Mandy said. "Our tent was closest to the water."

Rob shrugged. "The bear was sneaky, I guess, or we were dead to the world after getting to sleep so late. I hope it wasn't in camp."

"I don't see any prints on the river bank here. Go check for paw prints in camp while I clean this mess up," Mandy said.

After Rob left, she splashed river water on the mud stains to rinse them off. Then she gathered eggs, bread, strawberries, and other breakfast ingredients.

Rob returned and took some of the supplies. "No bear prints in camp, and nothing's been messed with there. I'm still amazed a bear attacked the rafts. There's never been a sighting of one along the river. But we're running behind. C'mon, let's get some food cooking."

As she left the rafts, Mandy scanned the river bank again. "It's odd that there aren't any prints in the sand here, either. Maybe it swam over to the rafts from upstream."

"I'm just glad it didn't do more damage." Rob hefted the radio. "I'll crack this open and let the parts dry in the sun for a day. Maybe I can get it working after it dries."

Mandy worried her lip. "In the meantime, we have no way to call for help if we need it."

Of course, there were very few spots along the river where they could call anyway. Radio repeaters had been installed only where outfitters would most likely need to call in, like at the confluence or at the end of Cataract Canyon to request a pick up or to rendezvous with others. But the lack of a radio still made her nervous.

Back at the camp kitchen, she saw Kendra had quietly exited the women's tent and was ready to help. The five staff quickly divvied up the work of preparing breakfast while Rob and Mandy filled in the others on the bear's thwarted attack on the rafts.

"Good thing its claws didn't puncture any of the raft tubes," Gonzo said while toasting bread on the griddle.

Kendra paused in chopping onions, mushrooms, and tomatoes for omelets. "That would have set us back at least an hour while we patched and reinflated the tubes."

"Usually bears don't come down to the main river," Cool said while setting up a buffet line with plates and utensils. He placed a bowl of strawberries and jam and butter at the end for toast. "I'm surprised none of us heard anything."

As soon as the coffee was hot, Rob bellowed "Coffee!"

Some folks had already started stirring in their tents and making forays to the screened portable toilet. While the omelets bubbled on the griddle, the clients queued up for coffee, which Cool poured into mugs through a strainer to catch the grounds. Within minutes, most of the group had settled into camp chairs around the folding tables to eat. The only one missing was Alex.

"I guess Alex didn't hear your call," Mandy said to Rob with a raised eyebrow. *Probably worn out after last night's gymnastics.*

Being one of the last out of the tents, his sister Amy hadn't filled her plate yet. "I'll get him," she said. "Where'd he bed down?"

"Behind those rocks." Mandy pointed toward the rock formation at the back of camp, and Amy trotted in that direction.

Mandy had filled her plate and taken one delicious bite of hot, cheesy omelet when a piercing scream rent the air.

Mandy leapt to her feet. "The bear?"

"Crap!" Rob dropped his plate on the prep table, grabbed the camp shovel and ran for the rocks.

Mandy snatched a couple of pots to clang together that she hoped would scare away the bear and followed Rob.

Gonzo came running with a metal marshmallow fork and the largest of their camp knives. "Stay here!" he yelled to the clients, some of whom had stood and were moving toward the formation.

After the three of them rounded the rock formation with makeshift weapons raised, they stopped dead in their tracks.

Amy was on her knees by Alex's sleeping bag, sobbing hysterically.

No bear was in sight.

"Amy? What is it?" Mandy asked.

Amy said nothing, only shook her head, her eyes wide and distressed.

Mandy stepped closer and looked over Amy's shoulder. She gasped.

Alex's face was raked with claw marks. Where his head lay, a dark maroon stain spread out in the sand. One of the claws had ripped into his neck, opening the jugular vein. His body had been pulled partway out of the sleeping bag, but as far as Mandy could see, the head wound seemed to be the only damage. As the coppery scent of dried blood filled her nostrils, gorge rose in her throat.

Murmuring "*madre de dios*," Rob dropped to his knees by Alex's head and felt his neck for a pulse. He looked at Gonzo and Mandy and shook his head. "His body is cold. This happened hours ago."

That brought another agonized wail from Amy.

Mandy knelt beside Amy and put her arms around her, offering what comfort she could. She tried to pull Amy away from Alex's body, but the woman wouldn't budge. She looked at Gonzo. "Bring something to cover him with. And keep the others away from here."

Too late.

Diana stepped around the rock formation, pushing her husband's hand off her shoulder. "—and something could have happened to Alex," she was saying to him over her shoulder.

She turned to the scene in front of her and stopped. Her eyes grew wide and her mouth fell open. A keening wail escaped her lips as she stumbled forward and sank to the ground next to Amy. Mandy released Amy and let mother and daughter grasp each other. Tears streamed down their faces.

Hal came up behind them and put a hand on each. His wrenchingly sorrowful gaze at Mandy was pleading, *please don't let this be true.* "Is he—" He couldn't finish the question.

All Mandy could do was nod in horror. She could barely believe it herself and felt frozen and powerless, unable to think of what to do.

Amy's husband, Les, and her sister Alice appeared next and took in the scene with shocked expressions and "Ohmigods." Alice grabbed her father's arm, and he turned and took her in his arms. Les rested his hand on his wife's shuddering shoulder.

Before long, everyone in the group had piled up behind the grieving Anderson clan. They stood quietly, clutching each other. Silent tears dripped down Elsa Norton's cheeks, as she held a hand over her mouth. But she wasn't the only person outside of the Anderson family who was crying. Mandy realized with a shock that she, too, had wet cheeks.

Finally Hal asked, "What happened here?"

Rob got to his feet and looked around on the ground. He pointed to a bear print in the soft sand near Alex's head. "We think it was a bear. But I don't understand why one was here and why it attacked him."

"You didn't tell us there were bears around here," Les said.

"They usually stay way up in the remote stream canyons," Rob replied, "and don't come down to the river. There's never been a bear attack reported anywhere near the river."

"Why'd you let him sleep by himself?" Alice asked angrily.

Mandy was already wishing she hadn't.

"It was his decision. And we had no reason to think he'd be in danger," Rob said.

As the guide with the most experience in the area, Cool jumped in to defend the decision. "I've done it many times myself," he said. "Yeah, we follow the park guidelines about storing food on the rafts, but no guide has ever seen a black bear anywhere near the river. We've only seen them while hiking in the high country."

"Did the bear go anywhere else in camp?" Les asked, his jaw set. "Were the rest of us in danger?" He looked around. "Are we in danger now?"

Mandy's chest constricted. Les didn't seem to be worried just about his own or his family's safety. She could see lawsuit written all over his face as his eyes narrowed in a calculating way. Sure, the liability waivers that all of the participants signed protected RM Outdoor Adventures legally, but that didn't mean Les couldn't get nasty about it.

"We saw signs this morning that a bear tried to get at the food on the rafts," she said quietly, trying to set a calm tone and keep others from raising their voices. "But it didn't succeed. And we checked everywhere in camp. We didn't find any prints."

Betsy Saunders inched her way toward the bear print. She examined it and a couple more on the surrounding ground with a frown on her face.

"How are you going to protect us?" Les asked, his face turning red. "You don't have any guns, do you?"

Rob raised his hands, palms out. "I'm sure the bear's long gone by now. It didn't eat—"

Mandy cleared her throat loudly.

Rob looked at her, then back at Les. "It didn't do anything else to Alex. Something made it run off. And we'll be leaving here, too."

"But what about Alex?" Diana wailed.

Silence.

Time to act. Mandy turned to Gonzo. "Gonzo, could you take everyone except the Andersons back to camp and pack up?" Then she faced Cool. "Cool, please get the first-aid kit and a jug of river water."

Cool, Gonzo, the Nortons, and the three female friends turned and silently walked away.

Alice gave Mandy a quizzical look, "First aid?"

Mandy wasn't going to drop the bombshell that the large first-aid kit also contained a body bag. "We'll clean him up as best as we can. You all can stay or leave while we do it, or take care of him yourselves, if you want."

She took a deep breath and faced the Anderson family. Her arms hung at her sides. She had never felt so helpless. She had no freaking idea what to say next, but from some reserve of strength the words came.

"We're deeply, deeply sorry that this happened to Alex. We'll do whatever we can to help you, to respect your grief, to—" Here the words failed her.

She glanced at Rob, who gave her a nod of support and added, "This has never happened to us on a trip, so we're feeling our way here."

"But please," Mandy said, "know that we care—about Alex, about you and your feelings. So if you need or want anything, anything at all, please ask."

Diana reached out to stroke Alex's cold face. Hal bent down to wrap his arms around her.

"I want my son back," Diana sobbed.

———

A half hour later, Rob, Mandy, Hal, and Les each picked up a corner of the black PVC body bag with Alex's rinsed body inside. They carried it through the campsite, with the three Anderson women forming an impromptu funeral procession behind them, and laid it gently on the ground by the rafts.

Before cleaning Alex's body, Mandy had taken photographs of the scene, in case any questions arose later. She and Rob also had a short discussion away from the Andersons about what to do next. Their options were very limited.

While they had been preparing Alex's body, the others had packed the tents and sleeping bags and were washing dishes. Half-eaten omelets and toast went sliding into the trash bag. Obviously, after the shock, no one felt like finishing breakfast. Gonzo had made another pot of coffee, though. He refilled cups and handed them around.

The sun was up over the canyon rim now, warming the air, so many of the campers were shedding their fleece jackets. People hugged the coffee cups, though, as if hoping the warmth could make the horror go away.

Mandy took a grateful sip, then said, "Everyone gather 'round, please. First of all, we want to warn all of you to stick together in camp. We think that bear is long gone, but just in case, no one should go off by themselves. Now, I need to ask, did anyone wake up during the night, maybe because they heard something?"

Elsa raised a tentative hand. "I woke up, but it was from a hot flash, I'm sure. I didn't hear anything."

"Anyone else wake up or leave their tent for any reason? Maybe you scared off the bear without realizing it." Mandy looked around and was met with head shakes.

Rob glanced at her to see if she had any more questions, then addressed the group next. "Mandy and I need to tell you what we plan to do next."

"Can't we just go back to the put-in and call the whole trip off?" Hal asked.

Rob shook his head. "We don't have a motor, only oars and paddles. A powerful motor is the only way to make your way upstream on the Colorado River. The current's too strong."

Paul stepped forward. "Can you call for an emergency helicopter pickup?"

Again, Rob shook his head. "Cell phones don't work in the Canyonlands. And the bear destroyed our radio. Besides, there's no repeater here, so we wouldn't have been able to call from here anyway."

Hal tried another tack. "Can we hike out?"

"There's no trail out of this side canyon," Mandy said, stepping up next to Rob. "The cliffs are too steep. There is a trail out of Lathrop Canyon, about six and a half miles downriver. It used to be an ATV trail, but a flash flood washed out a section last spring and only hikers can use it now. Our best hope of finding someone who can get word to emergency services is meeting another group on the river. But there's a chance someone might be on that trail, too."

Rob took a sip of coffee. "Mandy and I have put together a plan. We propose that I take Alex's body in my oar raft, along with two strong paddlers. We'll head to Lathrop Canyon as fast as we can. We may find some hikers at the campsite there. If not, I'll hike up the trail for at least a half hour, looking for someone before turning back. The rest of you can follow at our regular pace and meet us there. If we don't find anyone there, we have no choice other than to continue down the river."

Mo looked concerned. "Why can't you hike all the way out of Lathrop Canyon?"

"It's a four-mile steep uphill trek to the White Rim Road from the beach," Mandy said. "And there's no guarantee Rob will see any four-wheel drive vehicles on the road when he reaches it. Hardly anyone's on it at any time of the year, and it's even more unlikely now. And from there, it's another long seven-mile hike to the park road. Our chances of seeing someone on the river are much better—and quicker, we think, especially at the confluence. But we're going to try scouting the Lathrop Canyon trail, just in case."

Diana covered one of Hal's hands with hers, then looked at Mandy and Rob. "I know you're trying your best. I just hope we can take care of Alex soon."

"It seems likely that we'll have to keep on going," Alice said to her mother, "maybe even all the way through Cataract Canyon."

Mandy saw a look of relief pass over Paul's features before he masked it with a respectfully somber frown. Yes, the Andersons were half of their party, and they had experienced an awful tragedy. But the other half of the clientele had paid good money for the trip, too, and shouldn't be expected to give it up. She and Rob had discussed splitting the group, with everyone but the Andersons and one of them continuing on, if they could get word out and arrange for a motor launch to retrieve them and Alex's body. First, however, they would have to find some way of contacting the outside world.

Les stepped toward Rob. "I'm strong. I'll volunteer to paddle with you."

Rob clamped a hand on his shoulder. "Thanks."

"I'll take the other paddle," Cool said. "I'm not as experienced at river guiding as Gonzo, Kendra, and Mandy, so they should stay with the others."

With that decided, they quickly loaded the body bag into Rob's oar raft. The three men tied the bag down, then Rob stepped onto the bank to give Mandy a quick hug. "Keep an eye out for that bear."

"I will. You be careful, too, on that trail by yourself. We can't have you turning an ankle up there or anything." Mandy took strength from his hug, then stepped back. A strong sense of foreboding crawled up her back.

Rob pulled out the sand anchor and got into the raft with it. Mandy gave them a push off from the river bank and waved goodbye. With Rob oaring in the middle and the other two paddling in the front, the raft was soon out of sight.

The others turned to washing and packing up the rest of the gear. When Mandy went to dump dishwater in the river, Betsy Saunders approached her. "Can I talk to you privately?"

"Sure," Mandy said, curious to hear what was obviously bothering the woman. "I need someone to get the toilet and carry it back with me. I shouldn't do it alone, just in case that bear is still around. Do you mind?"

"I don't mind. I'm not worried about the bear."

That comment made Mandy give Betsy a sharp look, but the woman obviously wasn't ready to talk yet. She kept her lips clamped tight until they were out of earshot of the others. Then she put a hand on Mandy's arm.

"Something's not right about this bear attack."

Mandy turned to her, but kept on walking. "What's not right?"

"I've done a lot of research on bears and bear attacks, as well as their prints," Betsy said. "And no bear will stop after killing an animal. They kill to eat, especially in the fall, to fatten up for winter hibernation."

"Maybe it was scared away before it could start … eating … Alex."

Betsy shook her head. "By what? You asked if anyone left their tent and no one did. None of us scared it away. And another thing. There were no defensive wounds on Alex. That one swipe on his neck was fatal, but he didn't die instantly from it. Why didn't he try to defend himself?"

"I don't know." Mandy pictured Alex's body again in her mind. "You're right that there weren't any scratches on his arms." *Strange.*

They had reached the portable chemical toilet. Mandy looked around but saw no signs of wildlife, bear included, so she indicated Betsy should stand a few feet away. Holding her breath against the smell, Mandy removed the seat so she could screw on the watertight cap that kept the odorous contents secure while the large metal box was roped into a raft. While working, she thought about what Betsy had said.

"Maybe Alex was sound asleep when the bear attacked," she said to Betsy. "Then after it happened, even if he woke up, he could have fainted from the pain or the blood loss."

Mandy picked up the toilet seat and grabbed one of the handholds on the side of the box. She waved Betsy over to take the handhold on the other side. They both grunted when they lifted the box.

"Maybe." But Betsy's skeptical expression showed she seemed to think otherwise. She teetered a bit as they started back toward camp with the box between them. Before she could say anything else, a rustling in the nearby willow grove made both of them drop the box and stare into the shadows under the willows. "What's that?"

Is the bear back? Mandy stepped toward the willows, looking for a dark bulk while tensed to run. A rock squirrel skittered out, chattering at them as they ran. Relieved, she said, "Just a squirrel."

They both picked up the box and started walking again.

"Something else was strange about the scene," Betsy said. "I only saw a few paw prints on the ground near Alex. There should have been more. And they were all from the front left paw. No front right paw and no back paw prints."

Mandy stopped and stared at Betsy. "That's odd."

"And that's not the oddest thing about it," Betsy said. "I would bet my life that those weren't black bear paw prints. They were too big. And the claws were wrong."

"What are you saying?"

"Those tracks were from a grizzly."

SIX

*The wind whips through the canyons of the American
Southwest, and there is no one to hear it but us—a reminder
of the 40,000 generations of thinking men and women
who preceded us, about whom we know almost nothing,
upon whom our civilization is based.*

—CARL SAGAN

AN HOUR LATER, MANDY plied her oars through the silty waters
of the Colorado River and tried to figure out what Betsy's observations meant. After checking with the remaining Andersons, who had
agreed, Mandy had decided to take the rest of the group to their originally planned next stop, the native American ruins across the river
from Lathrop Canyon. That would give Rob time to look for hikers
on the Lathrop Canyon trail before they rejoined him, Cool, and Les
around lunchtime. The group could eat lunch at the picnic tables
there while the guides decided what their next move would be.

When they pushed the rafts off the river bank, Mandy had wound up solo in hers, because her raft was overloaded with extra gear that normally would have been stowed on Rob's. Though the rafts stayed close together, that left Mandy time alone to think. After they had gotten back to camp, Betsy had opened her wildlife tracking guidebook to show Mandy grizzly and back bear prints and claw marks. While very similar, there were marked differences. Mandy had told Betsy that she needed to talk to Rob, and in the meantime, she asked Betsy to keep the information to herself.

No grizzlies had ever been spotted in the whole state of Utah, so there was no way Alex could have been attacked by a real grizzly bear. But Betsy had been so sure the prints were grizzly, even when Mandy pointed that out to her. Mandy had to agree—the tracks looked more like grizzly than black bear. And then there was the strange fact that they had all come from the same foot. Could the other odd details Betsy had observed about the death scene mean that someone had staged the death to look like a bear attack, using a preserved bear claw to cover the real cause of death?

If so, how was Alex really killed—and by whom? If he had been murdered, that meant the killer was still among them. A chill ran down Mandy's spine. Could the killer be plotting more deaths? The convenient destruction of the radio pointed to that strong possibility. And if so, like the aquatic life hidden under the murky surface of the Colorado River, secrets must be lurking under the surface of Alex's supposedly accidental demise.

Deadly secrets.

Mandy's mind returned full-circle. Maybe she was overreacting. Maybe Betsy really wasn't as knowledgeable about bear prints as she seemed to be. Unfortunately, in the process of moving Alex's body, all of the prints had been obliterated. So Betsy's observations couldn't be confirmed—unless the photos Mandy took included some of the prints. Maybe they could be blown up to show the prints were all from the same paw, and maybe a bear expert could determine that they were grizzly.

But first they had to get off the river.

While Mandy's mind—and gut—were in turmoil, the float to the Lathrop ruins was quiet. Kendra had the four remaining Andersons in her paddle raft, and she politely gave her passengers space to grieve and talk quietly among themselves. Gonzo tried to impart some river knowledge to the six clients in his raft to keep them distracted. He got Viv talking about the many species of swallows inhabiting the cliffsides, and she was able to spot mud, barn, and cliff swallows darting in and out of shadowed crevices with her binoculars. When Mo asked about the dying tamarisk trees she had seen along the river banks, Gonzo got Mandy's attention. He passed the question along to her, since it was her area of expertise.

Mandy put aside her mental quandary to explain the park's strategy to control this destructive invasive species. Imported from Europe and Asia for use as landscape ornamentals, the tamarisks quickly spread throughout the Western United States. They displaced native trees and thirstily drank much more water than native plants. Being a variety of salt cedar, their leaf residue increased the soil salinity, killing even more native vegetation. The US Agricultural Service imported tamarisk leaf beetles from China to feed on the trees, releasing them in 2001. Since then, long patches of tamarisks along the Colorado and Green rivers had been defoliated and native willows were returning.

By the time the discussion moved on to identifying some of the fifteen native varieties of willows, Mandy saw that Kendra had maneuvered her raft close enough so the Anderson family could hear, too. Realizing the distraction might be good for them, Mandy pointed to a large stand of green willows on the river bank.

"Those tall willows that grow in groves like bamboo are coyote willows. The beavers that live along the river love to feed on them."

"But we haven't seen any beaver dams," Paul said.

"There's no way they could dam the Colorado," Mandy said with a smile. "It's too big. And the canyon streams are seasonal. They're dry most of the year. So, the beavers that live here don't build dams."

At that moment, a great blue heron swooped past the rafts. With a reverent "Aah," Viv tracked its flight with her binoculars.

"See where it landed," Kendra said while pointing. "If you look in that hackberry tree, you'll see at least three heron nests. Usually herons are loners and nest on the ground. But here in the canyons, coyotes are a big threat to them. So, like the beavers, the herons have adapted to this unique environment. They live in communities in the treetops so they can protect each other from the hungry coyotes."

Diana leaned her head against Hal's shoulder. "Alex told me that this was one thing he wanted us to see, how the river canyons have forced wildlife to adapt." She looked at her daughter Alice. "Maybe you're right about finishing the trip. Then we'd be honoring his wishes."

"But what do we do about his body?" Hal asked Mandy.

Mandy knew what he meant. After a few days on the river in that black PVC bag, Alex's body would start to decompose. "If we can't find a powerboat on the river to take Alex and you all back to Moab," Mandy said, "we'll dunk his body bag in the river each night to keep it cool. It's watertight, so no water will get in." She didn't know what else they could do.

Hal bit his lip and nodded. He looked away, and Mandy realized he was fighting tears.

They rounded a bend, and Gonzo pointed out a wide beach on river left. "There's where we pull in to look at the ruins."

They beached and anchored the rafts. Then Mandy gently asked the Andersons if they wanted space and time to themselves or if they wanted to join the group in hiking to the ruins.

"Seeing everything is what Alex would want us to do," Alice said, and Amy agreed.

Hal stepped out of the raft. "I'd rather hike than sit here."

Diana sniffed and swiped a tear off her cheek, then with a determined set to her chin, she gave a nod, too.

Gonzo led the clients onto a well-worn trail that slanted up the cliffside to a ledge overlooking the river. Mandy realized that while she couldn't do much to alleviate the Andersons' grief, she could at least address another nagging issue of the trip. She signaled Kendra to hang back in the rear with her.

Once the others were out of earshot, Mandy asked, "I haven't had a chance to bring this up with everything else that's been going on, but what did Betsy, Mo, and Viv say about Cool's flirting when you asked them last night?"

Kendra's brow furrowed. "They tried to say it was no big deal, that they viewed it as a compliment. But..."

"But what?"

"Their body language said something else. I think they're a little uncomfortable with it."

"Damn." Mandy kicked a stone off the trail. "I'm definitely going to have to tell him to back off."

"That wasn't the only problem, though," Kendra said.

"What else is Cool doing?" Mandy asked angrily.

"He's not the other problem. Les Williams is. Seems he made a sleazy remark to Viv. She said she was embarrassed to tell me about it since I'm black, but it also made her mad. Les made some comment about what a fox she was and asked what she was doing sleeping with a black man when there were handsome white guys like him around who are available."

Shocked, Mandy stared at Kendra. "The nerve!"

"And available?" Kendra snorted. "The flaming bigot is married, and his wife is on the trip!"

"What did Viv do?"

"She brushed him off by saying pretty much the same thing. She said she stomped off before she could say anything really foul to him—or slap him like she really wanted to."

What a low-life. "Given how much Les controls Amy, I guess I'm not surprised. Trying to pick up other women is another way to prove no woman controls him, that he can do whatever he pleases."

"It's assholes like him who make me glad I've got Gonzo." Kendra gazed at her boyfriend, marching in front of the group and gesturing toward the river, his Rastafarian braids bouncing with his boisterous movements.

"Sounds like it's getting serious," Mandy said with a grin.

"Not yet, but he treats me right. Really respects me, you know?"

Mandy nodded. "I know. And when you find a guy like that, you hang on to him."

Though Rob had a frustrating tendency to want to take care of her, he did respect her. And he had backed off and let her be her own woman when she needed to. Yeah, she was glad she had Rob, too.

They caught up with Hal and Diana, who had lagged behind the others. While talking with Kendra, Mandy had noticed that Hal seemed to be having trouble with the uphill climb, stopping a few times to catch his breath. He was breathing heavily now, sucking in huge gasps of air while Diana stood beside him looking worried.

Mandy was worried, too. This was a very short uphill hike compared to some of the others they had planned. Hal hadn't listed any health issues on the client medical form, other than mild hypertension. But Mandy knew clients often lied, afraid that their medical problems would mean they wouldn't be accepted for trips. Or maybe he was just particularly susceptible to altitude sickness, though Moab was only about 3,000 feet higher in altitude than his home in Omaha.

When Mandy asked Hal if he was okay, he waved her off and started walking again. Watching his bowed shoulders, she thought maybe his grief was weighing on him. She hoped that was it. But she feared otherwise.

Once they all reached a large ancient granary built under an overhang, they took turns peering into it. Gonzo explained it was constructed out of stones cemented together with a mud made of sand and clay mixed with urine, blood, feces, or other organic matter.

Tina wrinkled her nose and said, "Yuck."

Turning from the nearby handprint and bighorn sheep pictographs that she was photographing, Elsa asked, "Why'd they store their food in such a remote place?"

"Actually, they didn't store food in the granaries." Gonzo swept an arm toward the wide sandy flatland between them and the river. "Down there is what we call 'Big Bottom.' These bottoms are where the ancestral Puebloans, or what used to be called the Anasazi, grew their squash, beans, and corn in the summers. After the harvest, they'd hide their seed stocks and tools from other tribes in these granaries before heading to the highlands in the cool months to hunt for deer and other meat."

"Ah, so these are hiding places," Elsa said with dawning understanding. "That's why they're so remote and high up."

Gonzo pointed out a design on the rock wall that archaeologists thought was a solstice calendar and took them to another smaller granary and some more rock art. By then, it was approaching noon, so Mandy signaled for them all to head back to the rafts and paddle across the river to the Lathrop Canyon campsite. The whole time they had been on the cliffside, she and Kendra had scanned the river for other boats but neither of them had seen any.

They were totally alone.

———

After they beached at Lathrop Canyon, tying off their rafts next to Rob's containing Alex's body, Mandy led the group to the campsite. She saw Cool and Les sitting at one of the picnic tables in the shade. "Where's Rob?"

"Not back yet," Cool said.

Worry started to nibble on Mandy's psyche. "How long has he been gone?"

Cool checked his watch. "Over an hour."

Mandy looked toward the back of the campsite, where the trail took off, with hands on her hips. "Maybe I should send someone after him." She hoped he wasn't injured. They had agreed he wouldn't take more than an hour to look for hikers on the trail.

Just then Rob appeared around the bend, his steps plodding and dejected.

"Any luck?" Mandy yelled.

Rob shook his head. Once he was near, he said, "The trail was deserted, and there's no evidence that anyone's been at the campsite here in days. The latrine doesn't even smell. This isn't a very popular hiking trail even in season."

"Kendra and I didn't see anyone on the river from the ruins either." Mandy chewed on her lip. "I guess our only choice is to keep moving."

She scanned the campsite. The women clients had already spied the latrine, the last they would find on the river before the Hite Marina, and they were making good use of it. Kendra was setting up the handwashing station for them to use afterward. Cool and Gonzo were carrying lunch supplies to the picnic tables.

The next thing she saw made her heart lurch. She grabbed Rob's arm. "Look." Diana and Hal had walked to the river bank. They stood there silently hugging each other in front of the body bag in Rob's raft.

When Amy made a move to join them, Alice stopped her and said, "Let them be." She put her arms around her sister and held her stoically while Amy cried into her shoulder. Les joined them and put his arms around both of them.

"I wish we could do something for them," Mandy said.

Rob gave Mandy's hand a squeeze. "So do I, but I think all we can do now is feed everyone and get back on the river." He walked toward the picnic tables and Mandy followed.

The rest of the clients took seats at one of the picnic tables where Gonzo had put out tortilla chips and salsa. They picked at the food while waiting for the guides to finish preparing the rest of the meal. As she laid luncheon meats and sliced cheeses on a plate, Mandy looked around at the quiet knots of people in the campground.

Could one of them really have killed Alex? And why set up an elaborate bear attack scene, when conking him on the head with a rock that presumably could have fallen from the nearby formation was enough? Did the killer want him to suffer?

She knew from past experience that murderers often didn't look or act any differently from normal people in a casual setting. But she still couldn't help scanning their faces. She hoped to spot some clue, some window opening onto a soul that was twisted enough to not only kill a fellow human being, but to plan out that killing so it looked like a bear attack.

Who could do that?

She really wished she could pull Rob aside to talk about Betsy's observations, but there wasn't a private enough place here, out of earshot and sight of everyone else. She stepped back from the finished buffet and announced lunch was served. The group dined on make-your-own submarine sandwiches and pickles while chipmunks scampered through the tree branches and scanned the ground for dropped crumbs. Hal, Diana, and Amy just picked at their food, barely eating anything. During the meal, the rest of the group dithered over whether they should stay at Lathrop Canyon and camp there, waiting for someone to appear.

"The problem is that the rafting season is officially over now," Rob said. "As far as I know, we're the only commercial trip on the river this week. So, we'd be counting on private boaters coming by. On this section of the Colorado, that probably means they're not under power and probably don't have any way of calling out either. They may not be of any real help."

"And if we stay here tonight," Cool said, "we'd have to make up the time we lose here, so we can still meet our pickup powerboat. That would mean skipping the climbing and hiking activities we planned for later in the trip. You folks all paid for those activities, and they're probably why you chose to go on this trip."

And it's why Cool was hired to come along. Mandy detected a note of disappointment in his words.

Betsy, Viv, and Mo all nodded. Their faces bore disappointed frowns, but the women just looked at each other and kept their mouths shut. Mandy decided they probably felt voicing their opinions in the context of the Anderson family's tragedy would be seen as too selfish.

Elsa had no such qualms. "Yes, I'd really be miffed if I couldn't do any more climbing."

And Elsa would be even more miffed when Mandy questioned her about her tryst with Alex, but it was something Mandy planned to do as soon as she could get the woman alone.

"But I've got another question," Elsa continued. "I also signed up for this trip for the whitewater rafting. If someone does appear who can get word out, are you going to cut the whole trip short?"

Mandy hesitated and glanced at Rob. Everyone would want refunds if that happened, and the trip would become a loss—a huge loss. One that would really hurt their fledgling joint outfitter business. Then she felt guilty for her thoughts. They had to do whatever was best for the Anderson family, regardless of the cost.

"We might split up at that point," she said. "Whoever wants to leave can, and the others can continue down the river. Depending on when and if that happens and how many choose to stay or go, we guides would have to do some juggling to make it all work."

"We would already have to do a lot of replanning if we camp here," Cool said. "It would change where we camp every night from now on, so we'd have to scout out new beach locations. The campsites we find might be sketchy."

"Could we just extend the trip by a day?" Mo asked. "Wait here until tomorrow at lunch time, then if no one passes by, continue on with what you had planned for this afternoon?"

Mandy shook her head. "With our radio busted, we don't have any way to reschedule our pickup. And, we don't have enough food and water."

"I could fish for supper," Paul offered.

Elsa pshawed that suggestion. "Yeah, right, like you could catch enough to feed sixteen people. And Tina and I have classes to get back to. We can't extend our vacation time."

Mandy stared at the woman. How could Elsa go on about climbing and her vacation time when her lover was dead? *What a cold-hearted bitch!*

Alice put down her half-eaten sandwich. "Look, the family's talked about this already. We don't think Alex would have wanted us to quit. He was so anxious for all of us to experience the Canyonlands."

Hal nodded and put an arm over his wife's shoulders.

Amy glanced toward the river, where Alex's body lay out of sight, below the edge of the river bank. "I feel like his spirit is still with us," she whispered. "Maybe appreciating the wild beauty of this place is the best way to say good—" She choked up and couldn't continue.

"Oh, honey, maybe you're right." Diana reached for her daughter's hand.

"And, it's not fair to the rest of you if his death ruins your vacations," Alice said. "We should stick with the original plan until we can find a way to get word out."

"I agree," Les said forcefully.

Everyone looked at the older Andersons, who glanced at each other. Finally, Hal breathed out a sigh. "Okay," he said, and the rest of the family nodded in agreement.

"Does everyone else agree with that?" Mandy asked and looked around.

Relief seemed to be etched on most of the faces of those who were not in the Anderson clan.

"Okay." Rob pushed off from the picnic table and stood. "Even though we'll keep moving, we'll also keep trying to find a way to get word out. We guides will search for hikers and other boats along the way. Once the radio dries out, I may be able to get it to work. There's a repeater at the confluence, so I'll try calling there. Our goal will be to arrange for Alex's body to be taken to a morgue as soon as possible."

Diana took Hal's hand and squeezed it. "And Hal and I will go with him."

"Me, too," Amy said.

"No, we want you kids to finish the trip no matter what," Diana said. "As Alice said, it's what Alex would have wanted."

A tear rolled down Amy's cheek. "I don't want you two to have to deal with everything by yourselves when you get back. I want to help."

Les put a hand on her shoulder. "You heard your mom. And besides, it may not happen. We might all be stuck on the river until the end of the trip."

And apparently whatever Les said was golden, because Amy shut right up.

SEVEN

What makes a river so restful to people is that it doesn't
have any doubt—it is sure to get where it is going,
and it doesn't want to go anywhere else.
—HAL BOYLE

AFTER LUNCH, MANDY WORKED with the rest of the guides to re-allocate gear between the rafts, so there was room for two clients to sit in the front again of Mandy's oar raft. With Alex's body bag strapped in the front of Rob's raft, there was no room for others to sit there. That meant he might be oaring solo for the rest of the trip. He and Mandy had made that decision, with the Andersons' okay, because none of the clients—not even the Andersons—wanted to share a raft with Alex's corpse.

During the shuffle, Mandy's emotions wavered between guilt over Alex's death, anxiety about the loss of the radio, their link with the outside world, and doubt about whether she or Rob could have done anything different to prevent either. She was also worried about what might happen to them on the rest of the journey. Since she hadn't been able to speak alone with Rob at the lunch stop to talk about Betsy's findings, she had made do with saying, "We need to talk later."

The Anderson family all opted to stay in Kendra's raft. Tina Norton asked her father to join her in Gonzo's raft along with the three female friends. That left Elsa looking decidedly unhappy. She stomped over to Mandy's raft, plopped down in the front, and crossed her arms.

Cool pushed Mandy's raft off the river bank while she pulled on the oars, then he hopped in next to Elsa. "You look like you could use some cheering up," he said to her with a grin, "so I'm here to delight you with my sparkling company."

Elsa just harrumphed.

Mandy hoped that cheering up Elsa was Cool's only motive—not that he had struck out with the three girlfriends and was going to try his luck with her. He was another one Mandy hadn't had a chance to take aside for a private talk—about his excessive flirting. While she pulled out into the main river current, she wondered if she should divulge Elsa's prior relationship with Alex to Cool when she did talk to him, to get him to leave the woman alone.

No, that relationship was private, and she didn't know Cool well enough to trust him to keep it secret. Besides, he might view Elsa's connection with Alex as a positive sign that she could be lured into a relationship with another younger man.

A morose silence fell over the group during the first couple of hours on the water. The hot sun beat down on them, adding to the feeling of melancholy. Whenever anyone put an oar or paddle in the water, it made a soupy plop in the languid silence. Sweat slid down

Mandy's face, and she batted at a persistent buzzing fly. When they passed the coffeepot formation above them, Rob pointed it out, and the granary ruin underneath it, but it didn't elicit much interest from the group. Mandy saw some heads nodding as people snoozed.

Cool made a few attempts to start a conversation with Elsa, but each time it died after a curt comment from her. He shot a pleading look back at Mandy, as if asking her for help in getting or keeping a topic going, but she just shrugged. She doubted Elsa would ever have anything to do with him, and frankly, she thought they all needed some quiet time.

When they reached the point where Indian Creek fed into the main canyon, Cool perked up and started scanning the shoreline. Mandy figured he was bored and looking forward to a change. A hiking stop at Indian Creek Canyon to see some more ancestral Puebloan ruins and a waterfall that was probably dry at that time of year had been an option on their itinerary—if they were making good time.

Mandy checked her watch. After the long debate at lunch, they weren't making good time.

Before she could say anything to the others, though, Gonzo had directed his paddlers over to scan the canyon entrance. The water was clogged with sand bars and bushy stands of green willows and dying tamarisks. Gonzo's raft promptly got stuck on a hidden sand bar. He and Paul hopped out to push the raft off and sloshed back inside.

"I don't see a good way in," Gonzo hollered to Rob and Mandy.

"We don't have time to stop anyway," Mandy shouted back. Besides, she didn't think their clients could work up any interest in it.

When they floated past the canyon entrance, Cool looked wistfully over his shoulder at it. Then he sat up and yelled at Gonzo. "Hey, since two of you are wet already, how about a water fight? It would cool us all off."

"I'm game," Gonzo yelled back. He ruddered his paddle so his raft floated closer to Mandy's. "Hey, Kendra, come hither!"

Before Kendra could respond, Elsa said, "Well, I'm not game. I don't feel like getting wet."

Cool raised his arms to the clear sky. "Isn't that sun blazing away up there making you hot? Not just hot for me, but hot all over?" He waggled his eyebrows at her and playfully dipped a hand in the river to splash a few drops on her.

"No." Elsa firmly crossed her arms. "I'm not interested in a water fight—or in you either, you little creep. Leave me alone."

A black look passed over Cool's face, and his hands clenched. He glanced at the other rafts. When he realized from their wide-eyed reactions that many others had heard Elsa's comment, his face grew even darker.

"Someone's not in a party mood," Gonzo said lightly, trying to dispel the tension.

"We can't have a water fight unless everyone agrees and all the cameras are protected," Mandy added quickly, trying to draw attention away from Cool and Elsa. "Though it sounds like a great idea to me."

She flipped some water in the air with her oar. Sweat was dripping down the back of her neck and she knew she smelled a little ripe. She longed to cool off. She hoped she could persuade Elsa to change her mind—about the water fight, at least.

"I'm in!" Rob chimed in and flipped an even larger arc of water in the air with one of his oars.

Mandy glanced at Cool. With the attention off him, his embarrassment seemed to be receding. His fists had unclenched.

"Well, I'm not that interested in getting wet either," Alice said from Kendra's raft.

Kendra stopped angling her raft in toward the other side of Mandy's.

"Aw, c'mon gals." Cool moaned. "Yes, we've had a tragedy, and I understand that, but can't we lighten the mood a little?"

Mandy shushed him, but it was too late.

Diana sat up straighter. "No, it's all right. Alex would have wanted us to try to savor this experience even though he's no longer with us." She choked up and covered her mouth with a hand.

That clinched it. No one was interested in a water fight after that.

———

About four that afternoon, the group pulled in at a large stretch of sandy beach on the left side of the river. Gonzo and Cool hid the portable toilet in an alcove among a jumble of hackberry trees, willows, and dying tamarisks upstream. Kendra set up the hand-washing station on the beach and put out some granola bars for snacks.

Mandy and Rob lowered Alex's watertight body bag into the river to keep it cool overnight. Mandy held the bag while Rob secured it to his raft on the upstream side. Rigor mortis had set in, and the corpse was rigid. She could feel Alex's stiff arms and legs through the thick black PVC, but she tamped down the revulsion that turned her stomach. She glanced at Rob, whose lips were clamped shut. They worked quietly by unspoken agreement, trying to show some reverence.

Most of the group deliberately avoided looking in their direction, but Amy and Diana stood nearby watching. Their arms were wrapped around each other's waists and tears slid silently down their cheeks.

After the task was completed and Mandy passed by them, Diana said a soft thank you.

Mandy gave her a gentle nod, then got the group's attention. "We're about a mile upstream from the hiking trail that goes over the saddle of the Loop and down the other side. We'll hike it tomorrow morning and scan the river on both sides from the top to see if we can spot any other rafters or hikers. We had planned to offer the option of climbing and rappelling the cliff on the other side to those who want to, and we'll still do that."

She glanced at Hal and Diana, who stood entwined in a comforting embrace, then continued, "Anyone who doesn't want to do the hike can ride in the rafts on the river around the four-mile loop. So, think about your choice. Right now, the guides are going to take a rest."

That elicited a raised eyebrow from Rob.

"We'll unpack the horseshoe set and some cards," Mandy continued, "if you're looking for something to do. But we don't plan to start cooking dinner for another hour. We'll ask for your help in unloading the rafts then."

"I'm going to do some fishing," Paul announced.

Gonzo helped him dig his rod out of the gear pile, then hunted up the horseshoes. Kendra put some camp chairs around one of their roll-up card tables, then she and the three female friends sat down for a game of hearts. Diana and Hal found a shady spot to sit in. Amy dropped next to her mother and leaned in for a hug, and Alice lowered herself next to her father. Looking dazed, the four of them sat and stared at the river.

Cool seemed to be talking the rest of the group into a game of horseshoes when Mandy pulled on Rob's arm. "Let's go gather some driftwood for a fire."

He followed her along the beach a ways. When they were out of earshot from the others, he turned to her. "What's up?"

She filled him in on her conversation with Betsy Saunders. By the time she finished, they had walked a fair distance from camp and Rob's brow was wrinkled with worry.

"First of all," he said, "can we take everything she said as fact? How much of a bear expert is she?"

"Even if she isn't an expert, her questions make sense to me. Alex should have been fighting the bear and yelling, but nobody heard him *or* a bear. And it didn't make sense for the bear to kill him and leave the remains, no matter whether it was a black bear or a grizzly."

"But jumping from those questions to the conclusion that some-one staged the attack seems like quite a leap to me."

Mandy spread her hands wide. "How else can we explain that all the prints came from one paw?"

"If that's really the case," Rob said, scratching his head. "We're relying on Betsy's judgment there."

"There's a big difference between back and front bear paw prints—and left and right."

"So you think someone brought a preserved bear paw on the trip so they could kill Alex and make it look like an accident?"

Mandy nodded. "And disabled our radio and made it look like the bear did that, too. That means we've got a killer among us—who might be planning to kill again." She rubbed her arms, where the hair was bristling. "Otherwise, why disable the radio?"

Rob let out a long, slow whistle and looked up at the narrow, steep canyon walls. "And we've got no way out of here other than down the river. If that's true, how do we protect ourselves and the others? And who is it?"

"Well, Elsa was the last person who saw Alex alive. That's always who the cops start with."

"But why?" Rob's eyebrows raised. "He was boinking her!"

"It could have been some sort of twisted last goodbye before she killed him. She could have had any number of reasons. Maybe he was going to tell everyone about their relationship, and she wanted to keep it secret. Maybe he was blackmailing her. Or maybe he refused when she wanted to stop seeing him. Who knows?"

"And who else would she want to kill?"

"Someone who found out about them, possibly." Mandy bit her lip. "What gives me the shivers is that Alex could have been dying when Elsa walked past me to camp. Maybe I could have saved him."

"No. Don't go there, Mandy." Rob took her in his arms. "You can't do that to yourself. You have no idea if it's true. Even if it was, how could you have known?" He stepped back. "Come to think of it, how could Elsa have killed him without making any noise? You were right there on the other side of the rocks."

"I didn't hear them finish making love, either, or get dressed. The rocks blocked those sounds."

Rob blew out a breath. "You know what I think? I think being exposed to those other murders this summer may have made you hypersensitive. I really find it hard to believe that Elsa Norton—or any of the others, for that matter—could be a killer."

"We don't know anything about these people!" Mandy had doubts, too. Lots of them. But her intuition was on high alert.

"And the evidence you're basing all of this on is mighty slim."

"I know," Mandy couldn't keep the irritation out of her voice. "And I don't think we should go back there now and accuse Elsa of murder or anything. But we should be on guard, looking for anything else suspicious."

With a nod, Rob said, "Sure, we can do that." He picked up her wrist and checked her watch. "We should head back."

Mandy turned and fell into step beside Rob as they walked back to camp. She jumped when he stopped all of sudden. "What?"

"We don't have any firewood," he said. "That was our supposed reason for this walk."

"Duh!" she said with a smile.

She reached down and picked up a couple of dead tamarisk branches on the sand. They both continued to gather wood on the way back, so when they reappeared, they were each carrying a small armload.

Cool spotted them and put his hands on his hips. "Not much driftwood there, given how long you were gone," he shouted. "I bet that wasn't the real reason for your disappearance, hmmm?" He waggled his eyebrows.

The sexual insinuation was obvious, and Mandy didn't like it one bit. She bit back a retort. *Not in front of the clients.*

"I need to talk to Cool about his excessive flirting," she said quietly to Rob. "Why don't you get the rafts unloaded while I pull him aside?"

"You sure you want to handle that on your own?" he asked.

"Yes." She said it flat and final, so Rob wouldn't argue. He probably saw it as his job to put Cool in his place, but he didn't know the whole story.

To Cool, she shouted, "There's another pile of driftwood back there. Could you help me get it while Rob organizes unloading the rafts?" She dumped her load of wood on the beach and waved for him to come with her.

"Okay, I guess." Cool turned to the other horseshoe players. "We'll start up again where we left off after we all do our chores."

He trotted after Mandy, and she kept up a quick pace until they were out of earshot of camp. Then she turned to him. "There isn't another pile, but we can find some sticks to pick up so it looks like there was one. I needed to talk to you away from the clients."

Cool nervously licked his lips. "What's up?"

Mandy folded her arms. "I know flirting with clients is par for the course, but you're taking it too far."

His jaw dropped. "What?"

"A couple of the women have complained, and I've seen some negative reactions myself."

"You've got to be kidding me!" A red flush crept up Cool's neck. "What negative reactions?"

Sensing his embarrassment, Mandy said, "Well, when you put your arms around some of the women last night, they tensed up and scooted away from you as fast as they could. And when you splashed Elsa today, she didn't like it."

"That's all?"

"Some of your comments have been out of line, too."

"Like what?" Cool fidgeted, his hands clenching and unclenching.

"Like your snarky remark just now when Rob and I came back to camp."

"Oh, c'mon! Wasn't it true?"

"No!" Mandy was getting frustrated. "And that's not the issue anyway. Look, I don't want to make a big deal out of this. And the reason I took you out here to talk about it is that I don't want to make a scene in front of the clients."

"I hope not. You'd be screwing with my tips."

Was that the reason he was doing this? Regardless, it had to stop. Mandy set her jaw. "You just need to tone it down, not be so touchy-feely."

Cool threw up his arms. "That's who I am. No one's had a problem with my behavior on any of the other trips I've been on all summer long."

Mandy couldn't verify that that was the case, but it didn't matter. "Well, we have a problem on this trip."

"Maybe you're the problem," Cool said heatedly. "Maybe you're just wound up too tight." He poked a finger at her. "You should loosen up, you know. We're supposed to give these folks a good time, not let them get all bummed out."

Mandy stood her ground. "It's not just me."

"Hell, I think it is." He thrust his face toward hers. "Why don't we leave it at this? I don't work for you, baby doll. I'm just a loaner on this trip. So you can't tell me what I can or can't do. You earn your tips your way, and I'll earn mine my way. Just stay out of my face." He wheeled and started tromping back to camp.

This hadn't gone at all the way Mandy planned. "That's unacceptable, Cool!" She started after him.

He turned back to her, fists balled up at his side. But before he could say anything, Rob appeared through the willows.

"What's going on here?" he asked.

"Tell your lady friend to get off my back," Cool spat at him and tried to push past Rob.

Rob grabbed Cool's forearm, stopping him. "If Mandy's on your back, it's for a good reason. And that means I'm on your back, too." He looked at Mandy. "What are you asking him to do?"

"I'm not asking him," Mandy said, frustrated that Rob had to step into this discussion. "I'm telling him. Cool, you've got to tone down the flirting and lewd comments."

Rob stared at Cool. "You heard her."

Cool glared at Rob, who even though he stood a few inches shorter, outweighed him by at least thirty pounds of pure muscle.

"Fine," he said between gritted teeth. "I'll tone it down."

Rob released him. "That's all we're asking. It's a simple request."

Glowering, Cool stalked off.

Feeling just as put upon, Mandy folded her arms. "I could have handled him. You didn't need to check up on me."

Rob spread out his hands, palms up. "I wasn't checking on you. I came to tell you it's time to start fixing dinner. People are getting hungry, and it looks like a rainstorm is brewing."

Mandy scanned the western horizon and saw the clouds piling up over the canyon rim. They were white and billowy now, but they could turn gray and angry-looking soon.

"Crap." She bent over to pick up a driftwood log. "Grab some wood."

"Sorry, *mi querida*." Rob reached down for some logs, too. "When I heard you two yelling, I thought you needed help."

And he had done so in his typical macho way, all primed to protect her. Cool knew it and had backed down. She blew out a breath. She knew Rob was like this, and she had accepted his marriage proposal anyway. And he knew she didn't like it and had proposed anyway. They would work this out eventually.

"I'm sorry, too. Sorry I bitched at you. Cool was the one I was really mad at." She walked over to him with her arms full of wood and stood on her tiptoes to give him a kiss. "Thanks."

Yes, she was miffed, but she had to let it go. She did love the big lunk, after all.

EIGHT

It always rains on tents. Rainstorms will travel thousands of miles, against prevailing winds, for the opportunity to rain on a tent.

—DAVE BARRY

WHEN MANDY AND ROB returned with the firewood, the horseshoe game had stopped. Gonzo was now leading the players in an echo contest. They hollered as loud as they could in various directions, then listened to see how many echoes bounced back to them from the looming archways and sweeping curves in the steep canyon walls.

Les puffed himself up and produced a massive bellow.

Gonzo held a cupped hand to his ear and stood still, listening intently. After a few seconds, as the sound faded into the distance, he said, "I counted six echoes. What about the rest of you?"

"Seven," Tina replied. "At least seven."

"I only counted six," her mother replied.

"I'll take the seven," Les said, "and that's the most so far."

When they all clapped, Les took a theatrical bow while Elsa shook her head.

At that moment, Paul appeared, walking down the beach from upriver. He held up what looked to be about a one-pound catfish.

"Caught one," he said with a triumphant grin.

"Congratulations." Rob clapped him on the back. "We'll clean it and fry it up for dinner. But first, we need to unload the gear."

He and Mandy organized a bucket brigade to unload the rafts. Soon the clients were busy pitching their tents on the sand while the guides set up the kitchen. Kendra and Gonzo worked side-by-side chopping vegetables while Cool heated water and studiously avoided getting anywhere near Mandy. Rob buttered bread, and Mandy organized a serving line. The menu was salad, stuffed pasta shells in marinara sauce, and toasted garlic bread.

Dessert would be fixed later—cinnamon apples that Mandy planned to bake in foil packets in the campfire she had built in the metal fire pan. She glanced worriedly at the now-gray clouds looming in the western sky. She hoped the rain would hold off long enough.

"We'd better kick it up a notch," Rob said, following Mandy's gaze, "and get this meal served as fast as we can before the storm moves in."

They all stood straighter and sped up their movements.

"I'll make sure everyone knows that rain's on the way," Mandy said.

She made the rounds. She advised folks to have raincoats handy. She also told them to stake down the corners of the tents or put large rocks in the corners, since wind would come with the storm.

The only indication of that so far was the open flap of the Anderson family's 4-man tent gently undulating in a slight breeze.

Les and Amy were sitting at one of the camp tables and drinking beer when Mandy stopped to warn them. Amy made a move to get up, but Les stopped her with a hand. "There's plenty of time. Stay and finish your beer with me."

She sank back down in her chair but shot a worried glance at their tent.

"What about your tents?" Paul asked Mandy. "You guides haven't had time to pitch yours yet."

"We'll pitch them later." Mandy wondered if they would be doing it in the rain. It wouldn't be the first time.

"I'm not doing anything now," he answered. "I can do it."

"That's awfully nice of you," Mandy said. "Thank you."

"Hey, you're cooking my catfish," he answered jauntily and started unrolling Rob's and her tent.

Catfish. Right! Mandy rushed back to the kitchen area, found Paul's fish in a pail of river water and went to work gutting and filleting it. She tossed the offal into the river so the catfish's mates could eat it. Then she laid the fillets on the grill pan next to the garlic bread Rob was toasting. She took another glance at the darkening sky while washing the fishy smell off her hands.

Suddenly a strong gust of wind blew into camp, a harbinger of the dark storm on its heels. The wind whirled along the beach, lifting puffs of sand, while clouds raced overhead, blotting out the sun. The air temperature instantly dropped. Sand-clogged air swirled toward the kitchen.

"Cover the food," Mandy yelled while grabbing a couple of skillet lids to clamp over the bread and fish.

Kendra threw a towel over the huge salad bowl and held it on. Cool dropped a lid on the stuffed shells and marinara sauce. Gonzo laid his arms across the serving table, holding down the red-checked plastic tablecloth and the plates and silverware stacked on it. Rob chased after the trash bag that was rolling along the beach, spilling onion skins and other cuttings as it tumbled.

Damn it! Mandy knew they would have to pick up every scrap of food later. It was a park regulation, to avoid training wild ravens and squirrels that human campgrounds were a source of food. Before she could think about what to do next, another powerful gust flung grit in their faces. Mandy and the others all squinted and turned away, holding on to whatever they could grab.

Paul tossed gear into Cool and Gonzo's tent before the wind could carry it away. The table Les and Amy were sitting at fell over, spilling their beers and eliciting a stream of curses from Les. The cans skittered past Mandy. She hollered at Rob to catch them, too. Smelling burned toast, she risked releasing one of the lids on the grill to quickly turn off the gas before clamping her hand back on the lid.

Then Les and Amy's tent blew over. He ran for it, yelling, "God damn it!" and pushed Amy ahead of him. Alice had ushered her parents into their tent and was zipping the fly. Betsy, Viv, and Mo also dove into their tent, but Elsa and Tina were running around after camp chairs and other loose gear tumbling in the wind.

Thank the river gods for helpful clients. Mandy yelled to them, "Thanks, gals. Dump anything that won't stay lying down in the sand in Rob's and my tent!"

Paul came running up to her, the wind flapping his rain jacket as he struggled to zip it. "Should we eat before the storm rolls in?"

Rob had rejoined them and was tying the trash bag to a leg of the kitchen table. "If we tried to serve the food now, this wind would blow sand into all of it."

"But if it starts raining, the food will get all wet," Paul shouted above the wind.

"Better wet than gritty," Rob replied with a half grin.

As if on cue, fat drops started plopping on their heads and splashing off the metal pan lids.

Paul covered his head with his jacket's hood. "Anything I can do to help?"

Rob looked at the other guides, who were all too busy protecting the food to protect themselves from the elements. "Where're your jackets stashed?" he asked.

After they replied, he sent Paul to Cool and Gonzo's tent. He went to Mandy's and his tent to retrieve their coats, then to the gals' tent, telling them through the flap where to find Kendra's jacket.

By the time he and Paul returned with the coats, the rain was pouring down in sheets angled by the wind. Mandy was soaked and chilled to the bone, and both she and Kendra were shivering. Rob and Paul helped everyone on with jackets as best as they could while they kept the food covered.

Rob sent Paul back to his tent to stay sheltered. The guides, however, were stuck with standing by the food and covering everything as best as they could while waiting out the squall. Mandy hoped it would be a short one while she stood there shivering with water dripping a steady stream off her nose. She could tell the others were equally uncomfortable, but they knew this was a river guide's lot.

Finally, after about fifteen minutes, the rain slowed to a drizzle and the wind returned to a light breeze. Mandy looked at the sky, which showed a lighter gray color overhead. The dark band of clouds that had just passed over them lay to the east. Another dark band was headed toward them from the west.

"It's now or never," she said. "How about if we suggest they grab their dinners and eat in their tents?"

"Let's do it," Rob said. He called out, "Dinner! Get it now while it's still hot!"

The clients tumbled out of their tents, bundled up in rain jackets and hats, and quickly formed a double buffet line. While Rob suggested they all return to their tents to eat, Mandy realized Alice, Diana and Hal weren't there yet.

She went to their tent and asked, "Are you folks going to come eat dinner?"

"Could you bring it to us?" Alice replied. "We don't want to get wet."

Well, neither did anyone else, Mandy thought as she wrung out her drenched ponytail. But she held her tongue. After all, the Anderson family was suffering a great loss. "Okay."

She trudged back to the serving table and filled three plates, then asked Kendra to help her carry them to the Andersons' tent. While they walked over, Kendra smirked and said, "There's always one—or three in this case."

Mandy shook her head. "They *are* grieving."

Alice opened the tent flap just wide enough to pass the plates through.

"We'll come back for them later," Mandy said to her and returned to the outdoor kitchen. She and the other guides ate standing up, since there was no dry place to sit. Unfortunately, some sand had gotten into the salad, giving it extra crunch, and the garlic bread had burned. Rob tossed the blackened pieces in the trash bag.

Paul stayed with them and happily chewed his catfish. "Nothing tastes as good as fresh-caught fish, though I prefer trout to bottom feeders. Say, do you think this storm will raise the level of the water in the river?"

Being the local, Cool answered, "Nah, the Colorado's too big a river for this storm to have much of an impact. We might see some muddier flows coming in from the side canyons tomorrow. They can flash flood in small rainstorms like this. Take a look at Salt Creek when we pass it right after the Loop, and you might see some debris coming out."

"Flash flood, huh." Paul's eyes widened. "Can they be dangerous?"

"Hell, yeah, if you get caught in one," Cool replied. "And they can come from a rainstorm high up on the plateau that you don't even see or feel down here at river level. One of our J-rig boatmen told me a story about beaching at Range Canyon, which empties into Cataract Canyon. It was a bright sunny afternoon. He was unloading gear when a little boy in the group said, 'Wow, look at that.' He was pointing at water pouring over the rim of the canyon at the other end. The boatman said it looked like Niagara Falls."

Paul gave out an appreciative whistle.

Cool nodded. "He grabbed the boy and hollered for everyone to run for the boat. He tossed dry bags on the boat while his clients came running, then high-tailed it out of there. He said thank goodness the engine started on the first crank, because they missed the floodwaters by only about thirty feet. Everyone had to hold on while the gush rocked the boat as it poured into the Colorado. He lost his kitchen box to the flood."

"Man, oh man." Paul eyed the canyon rim above them. "Are we in any danger here?"

Cool laughed. "No, but I bet we can see some waterfalls."

"Great! Where?"

"I'll show you." He dumped his empty plate in the dishwater and gestured for Paul to follow him. After Paul joined him, Cool glanced over his shoulder at Mandy, as if to say, "See? I know how to butter up the clients, men included."

Mandy nodded back at him. Yeah, he was entertaining Paul, but now the clean-up crew was one short. She made the rounds of the tents with Kendra, collecting dishes and utensils. Rob and Gonzo dumped the uneaten food in the trash and started packing up. The second squall moved in while they were washing dishes, quickly soaking them all again.

Kendra started shivering so hard she dropped dishes twice in the sand while transferring them to the dishnet. Mandy peered at Kendra's face. Her dark lips definitely showed a tinge of blue.

"We can finish up here," she said to Kendra. "Why don't you go put on some dry clothes and entertain your tent mates?"

"You sure?" Kendra asked reluctantly.

Rob waved the back of his hand toward the gals' tent. "We're sure. Go!"

She gave them a grateful smile, then trotted off and crawled inside the tent. Soon, Viv came out and loped over to the cooler. She pulled out a box of white wine.

"Our Kendra's going to need this to warm up," she announced before hurrying back to the tent.

Within minutes, peals of laughter could be heard coming from their tent.

"Likely excuse," Gonzo said to Rob with a wink. "They all needed some warming up."

"I bet that box is empty by morning," Rob replied with a grin.

Gonzo looked wistfully at the tent. "I wish I was sleeping with her instead of with Cool, but I can't complain too much. Those women are taking good care of her."

Cool returned with Paul, who promptly dived into his solo tent to get out of the rain. It was pitched on the opposite side of the kitchen area from the other tents because of his snoring. By then, the cleanup was done, so Rob sent Cool and a bedraggled-looking Gonzo off to their tent. Then Rob pointed at the fire box and started laughing. Mandy's carefully laid firewood was floating in a two-inch-deep puddle of water.

With a smile, Mandy said, "I hope none of our clients misses having dessert."

"I'm sure they're happy to be warm and dry," Rob lifted Mandy's arm to check her watch. "Even though it's only eight, I doubt we'll see anyone until tomorrow morning."

Mandy helped Rob stow the trash and food back on the rafts, then crawled into their tent with him. They stripped off their wet clothes and climbed into their sleeping bags which they zipped together. By then, Mandy was shivering again, too, and Rob held her close until she was warm again.

Then things really heated up.

———

An hour later, snuggled next to Rob, Mandy felt as sated and content as a fat cat who had lapped up a dish of heavy cream. But her bladder wasn't content. It urgently needed to be emptied. She sighed and sat up.

"Problem?" Rob murmured, almost asleep.

"Gotta wee. I'll be back soon." She dug some sweats and a fleece jacket out of her dry bag, pulled them on, then scooted to the end of the tent. She unzipped the flap and stepped into her cold, wet river sandals that she had ditched outside earlier.

"Ugh."

The storm front had moved east, leaving just a few wispy cloud tails behind, so there was enough moonlight and starlight to dimly light Mandy's path. She made her way to a stand of willows past Paul's tent. His sonorous snores were indeed loud and irregular, punctuated by sighs and grunts. There was a good reason for him to sleep alone.

While picking her way back to her tent, Mandy had an idea. She still had Betsy's guidebook, because she had kept it to show Rob the differences in grizzly and black bear prints and claw marks. She wanted to compare the marks on Alex's body with those in the book. Now, when no one else was around, seemed like a good time. She returned to their tent, quietly dug out the book and her headlamp, slipped them into her coat pocket, then walked toward the water. As she approached Rob's oar raft, she heard the sound of quiet weeping.

But it wasn't one of Alex's family members. The weeper was Elsa Norton.

She was kneeling in the raft with her hand on the body bag. She looked at Mandy and hastily tried to dry her tears.

"Sorry to intrude," Mandy said softly, then realized Elsa was probably wondering why she was there. "I just wanted to check that the bag's secure. You mind?"

"No, it's okay."

Mandy climbed into the raft. She gave a little tug on each of the lines tied to the body bag and scanned the knots. "Everything looks fine."

"You don't sound surprised to see me here." Elsa peered at her. "Why's that?"

Mandy sat on the inflated tube next to Elsa and debated what to say. The woman was still waiting for an explanation. Mandy chose the truth.

"Last night at Little Bridge, I went to check on Alex after everyone was settled."

Elsa drew in a sharp intake of breath.

Mandy nodded. "I saw you two together." She hastened to add, "As soon as I realized what I was seeing, I left. Sorry."

Elsa ran her hand over the body bag in a gentle caress. "Despite the difference in our ages, I loved him. Still do. He had such a zest for life, such an inquiring mind, such potential. And now it's gone. Snuffed out way too early. I just can't believe it!" A thin wail escaped her lips and her shoulders shook with sobs again.

Mandy did the only thing she knew to do. She rubbed Elsa's shoulders as the woman silently wept. This behavior was totally at odds with the cold-hearted comments Elsa had made earlier that day. Maybe then she had been trying to mask her true feelings.

Before Mandy could ask Elsa about her comments, a branch cracked in camp. A quiet voice called out, "Mom?"

"Shit," Elsa whispered, sitting up straight. "That's Tina. I thought she was sound asleep when I snuck out."

She sniffed and wiped her eyes on her sleeve. "What do I tell her?"

With a shrug, Mandy said, "I don't know."

Tina approached the raft. "Mom? Mandy? What are you two doing out here?"

Mandy looked at Elsa and started to rise. "I should leave."

Elsa shook her head. "I'd rather you stayed. Please."

Mandy hesitated, then resumed her seat and moved over to leave room next to Elsa for Tina to sit. "Join us," she said to Tina.

Tina climbed on the raft.

As she neared, Mandy could see that her expression showed deep puzzlement and concern. *Wait until she hears what her mother has to say.*

"I'm, um, mourning Alex," Elsa began haltingly.

Tina glanced at the body bag and gave a little shudder. "Was he one of your students?"

"Yes, and more."

"A teaching assistant?"

"More than that." Elsa gritted her teeth and plunged in. "Alex and I were lovers."

Tina reared back like she had been slapped. "What? You and a student? No!"

Elsa told her how she and Alex had met when he enrolled in one of her classes, how they had clicked over common interests. Then they started getting together for long talks that led to more. Mandy just sat and listened and observed mother and daughter.

Elsa seemed to gain courage from her presence, courage to confront her daughter's obvious disapproval.

The woman's grief over Alex's death seemed genuine, since she had been crying alone, without observers, when Mandy discovered her. So, Elsa wasn't trying to hide a murderous deed with false mourning. But could she have killed her lover in a jealous rage or while under the influence of some other strong emotion and now be regretting it?

Or was Tina the one who was being disingenuous? Had she really found out about her mother's affair before the trip and wanted to get rid of her father's rival?

As if to confirm Mandy's assessment of how she felt about her mother and father's split, Tina said to Elsa, "But I was hoping you and Dad would get back together. That you would realize how stupid this whole divorce is. That's why I organized this trip. So you could see how much you still have in common with Dad, not some hot young guy who was probably just screwing you to get a good grade!"

"Don't speak ill of the dead," Elsa hissed. "Alex did no such thing. He was a brilliant young man who was going to become a great geologist."

"Does Dad know about this?"

"I doubt it," Elsa said. "And frankly I don't care if he does. We're leading separate lives now, Tina. I'm sure he knows I haven't been celibate since we separated."

"Well, I care if he knows, and I can't believe he doesn't care," Tina rose, her face flushing. "I'm going to tell him about you screwing a student. He's got to know that it's because Alex seduced you that you haven't been interested in him lately. Not because you don't love him." She started climbing out of the raft.

"But I don't love your father. Not anymore."

"You're just saying that. Look at you. Just look…" Sputtering, Tina gestured at her mother's hand, still lying on Alex's body bag. "You're still in shock. Once you get over that babe magnet, you'll see that Dad's the one you really love." She stomped off toward her father's tent.

Sadly, Elsa shook her head. "You see how unreasonable she is? Neither Paul nor I can get through to her that our marriage is over. It can't be resurrected. It's as dead as Alex is." She bit her lip.

"Maybe she just loves you both so much that she can't bear to see you apart," Mandy offered.

"What can I do?"

Mandy felt awkward giving advice to a woman with many more years of life experience than her, but somehow the wise words came. "I think all you can do is keep on loving her, even though you can't give her what she wants."

She wondered what Paul would do when his daughter woke him to give him the news. Or would his ex-wife's affair with Alex be news to him? Maybe he already knew about it and felt the same way Tina did about his failed marriage—that it could still be saved. Mandy stared at the black body bag floating in the water that was Alex's temporary tomb.

Maybe Paul Norton had eliminated his competition.

NINE

*Identifying and overcoming natural fear is one
of the pleasing struggles intrinsic to climbing.*
—ALEX LOWE

WHEN MANDY WOKE THE next morning, fuzzy-brained and fuzzy-mouthed, Rob wasn't in the tent. She realized when he called "Coffee!" from outside that his first call was what had woken her. She quickly dressed and exited the tent. The storm had completely blown through, and the sky was clear blue again. The air still held a damp chill, though, because the sun hadn't breached the east canyon rim yet and the camp lay in shadow. Sunlight bathed the upper half of the western rim, making it gleam like polished bronze.

Cool was busy putting out bananas, syrup, utensils, mugs, and plates. Kendra stirred a huge bowl of pancake batter while Gonzo fried rows of sausage and bacon on the griddle. The meaty aroma made Mandy's mouth water.

She gratefully accepted a mug of coffee from Kendra, then walked over to Rob, who had the radio partially dismantled on the table in front of him. "Why didn't you wake me? I feel guilty that I didn't help with breakfast."

"You looked bushed," he said, "and I know you were up for a while last night." He lifted a questioning brow at her.

The clients were crawling out of their tents and lining up for coffee, so Mandy said, "I'll tell you about it later." She faced the rest of the crew. "Thanks for letting me sleep. I'll wash the dishes."

"We kinda expected you would," Cool replied with a smirk.

The comment irked Mandy, but when she saw Gonzo and Kendra nodding along with Cool, she kept her mouth shut. Instead she focused on the radio. "Think you can get it to work?" she asked Rob.

"Don't know yet," he said. "The parts are all dried out now. I'll try it after I get it put back together."

During breakfast, Mandy noticed that Tina Norton pointedly sat with her father, not her mother. Both stole disapproving glances at Elsa. When the sun breached the canyon rim and bathed the campsite with bright rays, Betsy, Viv, and Mo winced and passed an aspirin bottle among themselves, probably battling hangover headaches. Mandy glanced at Kendra, but she looked like her normal, serene self. That gal sure could hold her liquor. After all of the nights the two of them had spent at the Victoria Tavern in Salida, drinking beer and playing pool with other river guides and rangers, Mandy had never seen Kendra looking hungover the next morning.

As soon as she finished eating, Mandy dumped her plate in the dishwater and went to work washing the dishes that were already there. When Diana arrived with Hal's and her dishes, she leaned over to Mandy and said, "I apologize for last night."

Surprised, Mandy took the dishes and asked, "Last night? Why?"

"For making you wait on us—in the rain. Hal and I felt guilty about it, but Alice said that's what we paid for, to have you guides do whatever we need."

"Alice was right," Mandy said. Technically, at least. She dunked a dish in the bleach water and slid it into the dishnet.

"And you're dealing with a huge loss under awful circumstances," she added. "I'm glad to give you what little comfort I can. I just wish I could do more." She wiped her hands on a towel and reached over to squeeze Diana's hand. "So, no need at all to feel guilty."

"Still, it was too much to ask." Diana pursed her lips. "Sometimes I wish we'd deprived our kids just a little more. We should have made them work harder, do more chores, even though we could afford to hire a housekeeper and gardener. Unfortunately, I think they grew up with a sense of entitlement, like hard work is beneath them. Alex was the exception." She sniffed and dabbed at her weepy eyes with a balled-up tissue.

Mandy just nodded. Yep, she agreed that the whole Anderson family seemed to feel entitled, but she wasn't going to say so. Especially after the terrible tragedy they had experienced.

Diana looked at Alice, chatting animatedly with Les, while Amy just listened and picked at her food. "Alice especially. Being the firstborn, I'm afraid we spoiled her." She seemed to realize that she was sharing too much and stood straighter. "Well, I just wanted you to know that I appreciate you running back and forth to our tent in the rain last night."

Mandy smiled. "Thanks. Again, I was glad to do it, but I appreciate you telling me."

Rob came up to them, hefting the reassembled radio. "No dice," he said to Mandy. "This might as well be a brick. It's completely dead." Then he turned to Diana. "Did you and Hal decide if you want to do the hike this morning?"

Given Hal's difficulties hiking to the Lathrop ruins, Mandy didn't think he should attempt the hike over the Loop saddle. "It's very steep and rocky," she said to Diana. "While the hike's not that long, it can be pretty difficult, especially for folks who aren't used to hiking—or to our altitude."

"Maybe Hal and I should ride in the rafts, then," Diana said doubtfully, "though if the girls are going, he might want to go with them."

"I think you'll both prefer the raft ride," Mandy said. "You won't get all hot and sweaty and run the risk of falling. And, Cool said that the guides often spot bighorn sheep on the canyon walls while they're taking the rafts around the Loop."

"I'd like to see some bighorn sheep," Diana said. "I remember Alex telling us how majestic the males look with their heavy round horns." She blinked back tears. "I'll tell Hal I want us to go with the rafts."

After she left, Rob asked, "Why'd you work so hard to convince her to go on the rafts?"

"I'm concerned about Hal's health." Mandy filled him in on what she had seen at the ruins.

Rob pursed his lips and nodded. "We should try to talk him out of the Doll House hike tomorrow, then, too, though that's going to be harder to do. The scenery up there is spectacular. Speak-

128

ing of that, Kendra, Gonzo, and I all hiked the Loop trail during our scouting trip. You should go with the group. There's a great view of the river on both sides from the top. Kendra and I can handle the rafts."

"All right, if it's okay with Kendra."

"I already checked." Rob grinned. "We've been plotting behind your back."

Mandy splashed him with dishwater.

The next hour was spent cleaning and packing up. As always, the chemical toilet was last. Mandy hollered to the group, "Last call for the toilet!"

There were no takers, and the key, the roll of toilet paper in a plastic bag, still sat on the ground. Mandy snatched it up to use herself and walked along the beach to the alcove where the toilet was hidden.

She was surprised to see Amy there, sitting with her pants pulled down to her knees. In that brief moment, Mandy noticed green and yellow bruises all over the tops of Amy's thighs—too old for Amy to have gotten them on the trip.

Amy saw her and gasped. "Oh!"

Mandy shielded her eyes. "Sorry, but you left the key on the beach. I thought no one was here." She held out the roll to Amy. "I'm sure you're going to need this."

Amy tried to cover herself when Mandy approached, but the old bruises showed through her fingers splayed across the tops of her thighs. Mandy averted her eyes, but Amy had seen where her gaze had been and looked stricken. She didn't say anything other than "Thanks," though, and snatched the roll from Mandy.

Mandy turned and walked away, out of sight of the alcove. While waiting, she wondered what had caused Amy's bruises. Was Les hitting his wife? Her gut started a slow burn, but then she checked herself. There could be other causes for those bruises. She knew from her first-aid training that some possibilities included hemophilia, autoimmune disorders, and leukemia. Any of those they should know about.

Clothes back in place, Amy came skittering out.

Mandy stopped her before she could head back to camp. "Sorry, Amy, but I have to ask you this. I saw your bruises, and I need to know if you have some kind of medical condition that would cause them. It could affect how we treat you if you get hurt. Of course, I'll keep it totally confidential."

Amy's cheeks pinked. "Oh, no, no. I don't have any special medical condition."

Mandy waited for an explanation, but Amy clammed up, her gaze darting around and not meeting Mandy's, until finally she said, "Darn, I left the TP!"

She turned to go back, but Mandy said, "That's okay. I'll need it next," and smiled, trying to put Amy at ease.

"Ah, all right then. Well, I'll go back to camp," Amy stammered, then rushed off.

Amy's reaction made Mandy sure that Les was the one responsible for her bruises. She clenched her fists. *The scumbag!* Still fuming, Mandy used the toilet then took the seat off and screwed on the cap.

"You decent?" Rob yelled from up the beach. "I came to help you carry the box."

"Great! Yeah, you can come."

While they lugged the box back to camp, Mandy told Rob what she had seen. "If Amy got those bruises from something other than Les hitting her, I think she would have told me."

Rob nodded. "Probably. Man, that guy is scummier than a snail's slime trail. Maybe at least we can keep him from whacking his wife on this trip. Though I'd love to catch him at it and whack him right back."

And Mandy knew her protective macho-man would do just that. She grinned at him.

He drew back. "What? What are you smiling at?"

"You. I'm happy I have you and not someone like Les. You know I love you, don't you?"

Rob smiled back. "Yeah, but I don't think I'll ever get tired of hearing you say it."

———

After a short float down the milk chocolate–colored waters of the Colorado River, the group arrived at the trail head for the hike over the saddle of The Loop. The wide notch in the steep canyon wall looming over them cut out almost half of the approximately 800-foot height. At the top, it gave hikers a view of the river flowing north-to-south on one side of the narrow pink sandstone ridge and flowing south-to-north on the other side, after making a four-mile loop.

Mandy was disappointed to see no signs of activity on the trail or at the sandy ledge where Gonzo had nudged his raft to disgorge his passengers. She knew the hike was a popular stop on summer rafting trips. She had hoped to find someone there who could get word out about Alex. But, as had been the case since they got on the river, they were alone and isolated in the canyon.

She and Kendra had swapped rafts, so Mandy let off her passengers from her paddle raft next. While Cool and Gonzo gathered the climbing gear and passed out helmets and water bottles for folks to carry with them, Mandy helped Kendra and Rob tie the two paddle rafts to the backs of the two oar rafts. Diana and Hal sat quietly in Kendra's raft and gazed sadly at Alex's body bag in Rob's raft beside them.

"I'm sorry we didn't find anyone here," Mandy said to them. "We'll look again at the top, and you four can look for other rafters while you go around the Loop."

"We know you're doing your best," Hal said. "We can't ask for anything more."

"See you on the other side," Rob said to Mandy, as he and Kendra pulled away.

"Try to spot some sheep—for Diana," Mandy reminded him.

Diana and Hal waved goodbye to their daughters from the front of Kendra's oar raft, and Diana yelled, "Take lots of photos."

"We will!" Les held up his small knapsack, from which Mandy had seen him pull out a camera and lenses during the trip.

"Let's move out." Cool said, taking the lead in front of the hiking group.

Gonzo positioned himself in the middle of the group, and Mandy brought up the rear, carrying a first-aid kit and extra water in her backpack. Cool set a slow, steady pace up the steep trail with stops every fifteen minutes or so to drink water and encourage others to do the same. A couple of times he pointed out lizards sunning themselves on the rocks—a whiptail and the colorful collared lizard with its yellow head, green body, and black collar. Les zeroed in on that one with his camera and snapped away.

About two thirds of the way up, after climbing around a boulder fall, Amy stopped and said, "Boy, I'm glad Mom and Dad didn't try to do this." She was panting herself.

Mandy took the opportunity to make a suggestion. "Maybe you can talk them out of doing the Doll House hike, too. It's just as steep and even longer because it goes all the way to the top of the plateau."

"That's going to be tough," Amy said. "Dad's been talking a lot about wanting to see the rock spires in the Doll House. Alex said it was the best feature of the trip."

"And who are we to stop your dad if he really wants to do it?" Les said over his shoulder from in front of her. "C'mon, Amy, you need to step it up. You're falling behind. We're already last." He turned and strode ahead.

"Do you need to rest?" Mandy asked Amy. "I can stay with you."

"No, I'm fine." She wiped her sweaty brow and scrambled after Les.

When they reached the top of the ridge, Amy sank onto a boulder and drank heavily from her water bottle. Mandy noticed Amy's flushed complexion, but she seemed likely to recover. She had probably just pushed herself a little too hard to keep up with Les and the others.

Cool pointed out the views of the river on both sides, then he and Gonzo headed north to where the cliff face made a sheer drop of over a hundred feet. They started rigging rappelling and climbing lines. Meanwhile, the Nortons and the women friends took photos of each other with the river in the background, first on one side of the ridge then on the other.

Mandy searched for rafts for as far as she could see in either direction, but she saw only Kendra and Rob's tiny flotilla. Then she searched the sky for small planes and the canyon rims for hikers. She saw nothing but a couple of hawks making lazy circles in the thermals high over the river, hunting for their next kill. *Damn!*

When Cool hollered, "Ready for climbers!" Mandy asked if anyone did not want to rappel, but everyone seemed to want to give it a try. They lined up behind Cool, who stood at the top of the cliff. Mandy looked down and spotted Gonzo perched on boulders at the base of the cliff below.

"First, we'll give everyone a chance to rappel down," Cool said. "Then those who want to can climb back up and either hike down or rappel down again."

"How can I help?" Mandy asked.

"After Gonzo ties rappelling harnesses on that other line," he said, "you can pull them up and hand them to me."

She noticed that he seemed to relish the idea of bossing her around for a change, but she gave a nod and took up her position at the top of the second line.

They spent the next hour sending all of the clients down one at a time. Before each person came down, Gonzo would take the harness off the previous rappeller and send it back up to Mandy. Then when it was the next person's turn, the second harness would be waiting for them. Betsy, Mo, and Viv took their turns first and each of them whooped the whole way down. That set the mood for the rest of the group.

When it came time to climb back up, Amy opted out and found a place to sit out of Gonzo's way to watch the others. Les went first, then took out his camera to take photos of Alice climbing. The Nortons and the three women friends followed, then it was time to rappel back down. Mandy had been scanning the river for boats the whole time and noticed Rob and Kendra pulling up to the river bank below them.

"The rafts are here, so we should wrap this up soon," she told Cool. It was also approaching lunchtime, according to her watch and the position of the blazing sun. She knew Kendra and Rob would start preparing the food as soon as they secured the rafts.

"Okay, folks," Cool said to the clients standing with him at the top, "we need to finish up here. This rappel should be quick, since you've done it before. Then it's a short hike to the river."

"Rob and Kendra should have lunch waiting for us by the time we get there," Mandy added.

Cool asked Paul to help him strap harnesses on people, to make the process go quicker, and Les offered to carry harnesses from Mandy to Cool. Amy stood up so she could help Gonzo at the bottom of the cliff by attaching harnesses to the retrieval line for Mandy

Alice, Betsy, Viv, and Mo rappelled down quickly, then started hiking on their own to the rafts. With Amy and Gonzo watching from below, Paul and Cool buckled Elsa into her harness.

Les snapped a photo of the process, and Tina said to him, "Would you take a family photo for us?"

Elsa frowned but put up with Paul and Tina flanking her. Tina tugged at her mother's harness to smooth out the wrinkles in her pants so she would "look less dorky." After smiling for the camera, it was time for Elsa to ease backward off the ledge. She fed rope with one gloved hand through the belay tube fastened to her harness with a locking carabiner. With her other hand, she held the rope below her away from her feet and body. Her technique looked proper to Mandy.

Cool yelled, "Looking good, Elsa!"

Elsa was less than halfway down the hundred foot cliff when the waist strap on her harness snapped, releasing the hardware and the rope. Mandy gasped.

Screaming, Elsa clutched the rope, one hand above the belay tube and one below it, while her body dangled free.

"Oh shit! Hang on," Cool shouted to her over Tina's screams. "I'll lower you."

He started playing out the rope from above.

"Go get help," Gonzo yelled to Amy, and she took off down the trail.

Sucking in a breath, Mandy watched Elsa in horror. She prayed that the woman was strong enough to hold on until Cool could lower her to a safe distance. She had over fifty feet to go.

Gonzo shouted from below, "Hold on, Elsa! Squeeze your hands as hard as you can."

Elsa dangled precariously for a few seconds. Forty feet left. Then she lost her grip with the hand above the belay tube. With nothing left to brake her, she started sliding one-handed down the rope. "Help!"

Les and Tina gasped, and Paul yelled, "No!"

Legs kicking frantically, Elsa managed to grab the rope again with her other hand. But with nothing still to stop either hand, she continued to slide.

The grimace on Elsa's face showed her palms were being abraded inside the gloves from the friction. The woman wasn't going to be able to hold on much longer.

Thirty feet. Mandy glanced at Cool, whose face was grim, but he couldn't seem to play out the rope any faster.

Time slowed. Mandy's hands clenched and unclenched as she stood there unable to do anything to help. The tension was excruciating.

About fifteen feet from the bottom, Elsa finally lost her grip and fell. She landed hard on her feet and tumbled over onto loose boulders. She let out a yelp of pain.

Tina screamed, "Mom!"

Gonzo ran to Elsa. "Don't move! Let us check you first."

"Get me down there," Mandy said to Cool. "I've got the first-aid kit."

He and Paul helped her into the other harness. Nervous after the break in Elsa's harness, both she and Cool quickly double-checked the gear. They rigged another belay line, then Mandy went over the cliff. She rappelled down as fast as she could, unbuckled and joined Gonzo and Elsa, who was now sitting up and holding an ankle.

"No signs of concussion," Gonzo said to Mandy. "Good thing she was wearing a helmet."

"Where do you hurt?" Mandy asked Elsa.

"My palms are burning, and my ankle is killing me. I think that's all."

"She can move her toes and knees," Gonzo said.

Mandy was thankful for that. She eased Elsa's sock down and gently probed around the ankle. All of the bones seemed to be in place.

"Can you flex it, Elsa? Go slow."

Elsa did, with a grunt of pain.

Mandy nodded. "I think it's a sprain, not a break." She turned her face toward the top of the cliff, where Tina and Paul stood clutching each other and staring down at them. "She's going to be okay."

"Thank God!" Paul shouted back. "We'll hike down as soon as we can." He released Tina and turned away from the rim to help Gonzo and Les pack the rest of the climbing gear.

Mandy took a chemical cold pack out of the first aid kit and massaged it to get the reaction started that would cool it. She placed the pack on Elsa's ankle and wrapped an ace bandage around to hold it in place. Then she pulled off Elsa's gloves and cleaned the abrasions with an alcohol wipe.

When Elsa hissed, Mandy said, "Sorry! I hate adding to your pain." She gently spread on some antiseptic and covered Elsa's palms with taped-on gauze pads.

By then, Rob had arrived, out of breath after running up the trail from the river, to ask how Elsa was and how she fell. While Gonzo filled him in, Mandy glanced at the top of the cliff. Cool was leading Tina, Paul, and Les down the steep hiking trail that wove back and forth across the rocky hillside beside the cliff.

"Gonzo and I will carry you to the raft," Rob said to Elsa. "We'll take it slow and gentle."

"I think I can stand on the other foot," Elsa said. "It might be better if I just lean on one person while I hop down. But can we get this stupid harness off me?"

"Sure." Gonzo moved in to loosen the thigh straps. "I want to find out what happened to it, too. These things are tough. They just aren't supposed to break, even with a three-hundred-pound guy in one."

He worked the harness off of Elsa's legs. Then he and Rob helped her stand on her good foot.

Rob pulled her arm over his shoulder and put an arm around her back. He studied her face. Mandy knew he was checking for signs of dizziness or shock.

"You good?" he asked.

"I'm good," Elsa replied, and they slowly started a three-legged walk down the trail.

Gonzo had been examining the harness. He let out a long whistle and held up the waistband strap for Mandy to see.

"It was cut almost all the way through. The extra strap that allows the waistband to be loosened for a big person was lying over the cut, so it couldn't be seen."

Mandy fingered the jagged edge beyond the cut where the waistband had ripped loose. "How was it cut? There was nothing sharp in the pack with it."

"A pocket knife would do it."

They exchanged a meaningful glance. Pocket knives were such useful camping gear that almost everyone on the trip was carrying one.

"When do you think the cut was made?" Mandy asked.

Gonzo thought for a moment. "I think it must have been cut right before Elsa's turn."

"How long did it take for the waistband to rip the rest of the way?"

"As soon as any weight was put on it, it would start to rip."

"Then the question is who cut it." Mandy's grip tightened on the harness waistband. She looked up at the four hikers working their way down the trail. Besides herself and Gonzo, they had all touched the harness—as had Amy—before Elsa went over the cliffside.

Which one of them wanted to hurt—or kill—Elsa?

TEN

*The water is your friend. You don't have to fight
with water, just share the same spirit as the water,
and it will help you move.*

—ALEKSANDR POPOV

WHEN MANDY AND GONZO reached the rafts, she saw that Rob's raft with Alex's body inside was tied off at a respectful distance downstream from the others. Diana and Hal and the clients who had already hiked down were sitting on the pontoons of the other rafts and munching on tortillas rolled into cones that held teriyaki chicken salad. Whole apples and oranges completed the lunch that could be eaten easily by hand. Mandy had planned that because Rob had told her before the trip that there was only enough room on shore here for the handwashing station and a small card table for food preparation.

Contrary to the anxiety churning Mandy's gut, the scene looked peaceful and absolutely normal. After Cool, Les, Tina, and Paul arrived, Mandy quietly observed them and Amy, and how they interacted with Elsa. After a cursory "you okay?", Les grabbed his lunch and sat next to his wife to eat.

Cool hovered around Elsa, babbling about how that had never happened before, he couldn't imagine what had gone wrong and so on. To Mandy, he seemed more concerned about Elsa blaming him for the accident and reporting it than about her welfare.

Both Tina and Paul asked if Elsa was in pain and seemed to genuinely care about her well-being. However, either one of them could have been putting on a great show.

Once all of the clients had food and water, Mandy signaled to Rob to walk up the trail a way with her so they could talk. Gonzo asked Kendra to follow him downstream to "check on the current." Mandy and Gonzo had arranged this on the way down, so they could relay their suspicions to Rob and Kendra. She had decided not to reveal the harness was cut to the whole group, because she didn't want the clients to panic.

"Five of them had access to the harness," Mandy said to Rob, after telling him about the cut waistband. "Amy took it from Gonzo and put it on the line for me, Les passed it from me to Cool, Cool and Paul put it on Elsa, and I remember Tina tugging on it before Les took their photo. Any of them could have cut the waistband with a knife hidden in their hand without the rest of us noticing."

Eyeing her, Rob said, "You and Gonzo think one of them tried to kill or hurt Elsa?"

"Yes, we do. And that's why we've got to keep an eye on all of them."

Rob thoughtfully chewed the last bite of his chicken salad cone and swallowed. "What reason would any of them have to hurt her?"

"She was pretty blunt rejecting Cool yesterday when he tried to get that water fight going. He was really embarrassed and he's pretty hot-headed. Maybe he was trying to get back at her."

Shaking his head, Rob said, "I just don't see it. Yes, he was mad at her, but cutting her harness seems like an over-the-top reaction. And if word got out that he did it, it would not only land him in jail, it would ruin his career. No one would hire him. It's crazy!"

"Precisely," Mandy replied. "We don't know him that well. Maybe he *is* a little crazy. And he knows climbing gear well enough that he probably figured it wouldn't break until she was partway down and she'd just be hurt, not killed."

"I still think it's far-fetched." Rob took a bite of apple. "What about one of the others?"

"There's no connection between Les or Amy and Elsa that I can figure out," Mandy said.

"Elsa was screwing Amy's brother, Les's brother-in-law."

"I doubt either one knew that, and if they did, why would they care? How did Amy react when you brought Elsa down?"

"Just like the others," Rob said. "Everyone gathered around Elsa, asked her how she was, said how lucky she was that she wasn't hurt worse. Amy was right there in it, even helped Elsa to her seat."

Mandy bit into her chicken cone and mulled over the problem while she chewed. "Elsa's affair with Alex makes me suspect Paul or Tina more, and it links her fall with Alex's death. One of them could have found out about the relationship before the trip. Maybe they got so upset about it that they killed Alex to eliminate him as a rival for Paul, then hurt Elsa to make her pay for betraying them."

Rob scratched his head. "Shit, just yesterday, you thought Elsa killed Alex, and I didn't agree. It's just as hard to believe that either

Paul or Tina is a killer. And you said Tina acted like she didn't know about the affair last night and ran to tell her father."

"Acted is the key word here. Whoever did this is acting now, so she or he could have been acting last night, too."

"This is like a damn soap opera!"

"It's a lot more serious than that." Mandy's stomach turned. She looked at her cone and suddenly couldn't eat anymore. "We've got one dead client and one injured one."

"And both look like they were accidents. Not a good track record at all for this trip. If word gets out, this could seriously hurt the reputation of RM Outdoor Adventures."

"Not if we can find out who's doing this and get them arrested once we reach Hite Marina. But I'm more concerned about what she or he is planning for the rest of the trip. What's going to happen next?"

Looking worried, Rob asked, "Do you think whoever cut the harness is going to go after Elsa again? Should we warn her?"

"Against who? And against what? Maybe nothing, if all the person wanted to do was scare or hurt her. They've accomplished that." Mandy bit her lip while thoughts swirled in her head. What should they do?

"Until we have something definite, we can't accuse anyone," she finally said. "If we're right, the killer will just deny it."

"And will know we're suspicious and might decide to come after us next," Rob added.

Mandy's heart gave a lurch and started racing with fear. Fear for herself, yes, but fear for Rob's life even more. "And if we're wrong, we've pissed off someone, and the killer will think he or she got away with it."

"And everyone else will panic."

Mandy nodded. "I'll try to get Elsa alone later, say I want to check her ankle. I'll tell her the harness was cut so she can be on the alert, and I'll ask her to keep it secret."

"Do you really think she'll do that? She might flip out."

"From what I know of Elsa, I don't think she will, not if I explain the danger if she does. Then I'll feel her out, see if she thinks Tina or Paul might be capable of hurting her."

After finishing his apple, Rob stared at the browning core. "I'm concerned about what might happen when we camp tonight. Maybe we should organize guard shifts through the night, between you, me, Kendra and Gonzo, to watch over Elsa—hell, to keep an eye on everyone."

"Good idea. I think that's the best we can do for now. We really can't accuse anyone and tie them up without proof."

Rob slapped his thigh. "Damn, I wish we'd found someone here and could have gotten word out."

"We knew it would be quiet on the river in October, but I didn't expect to be *totally* isolated."

"By the way, Cool asked if he could take a crack at fixing the radio, so I gave it to him and told him to have at it."

Suspicious, Mandy asked, "What's he know about radios?"

Rob shrugged. "He can't know much less than me, and given that I couldn't get it to work, what's the harm in letting him try? Hey, you gonna eat that?" He pointed at Mandy's unfinished cone.

"No, here." She handed it to him. "I think we're going to be stuck with having to figure this whole mess out on our own—"

Gonzo called to them from the rafts, "Rob, Mandy, we're ready to go!"

"Enough nookie nookie," Cool yelled out. Laughter followed.

Mandy frowned and Rob rolled his eyes.

While they walked back along the trail and Rob wolfed down the rest of Mandy's lunch, she said, "I asked Gonzo to hold on to the harness for now and not show it to anyone or give it back to Cool. And I asked him to buddy up to Cool and find out what his feelings are toward Elsa. Why don't you try to get some time alone with Paul and talk to him, while I do the same with Tina? We can compare notes with Gonzo tonight."

"And hopefully we'll spot someone at the confluence or Spanish Bottom," Rob said. "I'd love to drop this whole problem in someone else's lap—get the cops involved."

When the rafts came back in view, Mandy scanned the people in them. Who knew what was going in any of their heads? The only people she felt she could really trust were Rob, Gonzo, and Kendra. She rubbed her suddenly clammy hands on her nylon river shorts.

"In the meantime, we're stuck in this canyon with a killer."

———

Kendra and Gonzo took all of the clients and Cool in their rafts that afternoon, so they could give them some final lessons in paddling technique and make sure they were prepared for the rapids. Mandy and Rob hung behind in their oar rafts, partly to keep Alex's body out of direct view of the others and partly to give the paddle rafts room to maneuver. While they watched, Kendra and Gonzo sent their rafts spinning and slipping sideways with different commands issued to their paddlers. After everyone had learned the commands and their techniques had improved, Gonzo organized a couple of competitions between the paddle rafts to seal the lessons in everyone's mind.

Mandy had quietly observed the practice session, but everyone acted normally—or as normally as could be expected given Alex's death. There were no signs of revengeful gloating or sly glances at Elsa. By the time they reached Salt Creek, everyone was ready for water and a rest, so Mandy called a halt to the competitions.

She and Rob pulled in closer to the paddle rafts, then she pointed out the debris and heavily muddied waters pouring out of Salt Creek. "The darker water shows this side canyon flash flooded during the rainstorm last night."

"That's why we avoid camping at canyon entrances when there's any hint of rain." Rob pointed at another dark stain in the water as they reached it. "Elephant Canyon flooded, too, though not with as much water, since it's smaller."

"Where's all this silt go?" Paul asked.

"Lake Powell," Mandy answered. "It's slowly filling up with mud, which will eventually cause problems at the Glen Canyon Dam." And was a concern of environmental groups worried about the impacts of a monumental flood downstream in the Grand Canyon.

Paul nodded vigorously. "I've heard about that."

Before he could say more, Rob smoothly moved away from this potentially touchy topic. "Now, in about a mile and a half, we'll reach our first rapid, The Slide. An old landslide narrowed the river there, creating a little class II riffle." He mimed an evil grin. "Just a small taste of coming attractions in Cataract Canyon."

"Yowser," Cool shouted and hefted his paddle overhead. "Rapids today!"

Diana's eyes went wide.

Sweat dampened Mandy's palms. Yes, rapids could be dangerous, and Cataract Canyon was known as the graveyard of the Colorado because of the dozens of drownings that had occurred there. But she was worried about a much worse threat to their collective safety. With a hidden killer in their group, she prayed that they would all make it through the rest of the trip alive.

The Slide was a wide-open bumpy water ride with no technical features. All of the rafts ran it cleanly with just a few squeals from Tina and the women friends and a couple of whoops from Paul and Cool. The Andersons were all quiet. Hal shot a worried glance back at Rob's raft, but Alex's body bag was securely tied down and wasn't jostled much by the rapid.

Soon after the Slide, they reached the confluence with the Green River. Mandy and the other guides scanned all of the potential camping spots along the river banks for canoes, kayaks, or rafts.

Nothing.

Then Gonzo and Kendra encouraged their passengers to paddle hard so they could reach the beach on the other side of the junction as planned. Mandy and Rob grunted and hauled on their oars. They had to cross the width of the current pouring in from the Green to do it, and the effort strained everyone.

When they finally beached the rafts, Gonzo yelled, "Rest stop!"

"We need it after that." Hal wiped sweat from his brow. "Why'd we go to all that trouble to get here?"

"This long beach is a popular camping stop," Mandy said. "We'll search for other parties and try to get word out about Alex. This is also a good place to take photos of the confluence, looking upstream at both rivers. Anyone need a snack or some water?"

While Kendra and Rob pulled food and drinks out of the supply rafts, Mandy took Gonzo and Cool aside. "I want you two to go
as fast as you can to the upstream end of this beach on the Green,
looking for campers. If you find someone with a radio, or who's
going to be picked up by a powerboat today, tell them we need
help. Have them send a powerboat to Spanish Bottom to meet us
this afternoon. But whether you find someone or not, be back in
an hour, so we can keep moving and set up camp at Spanish Bottom before dark."

They nodded and took off at a trot along the beach to where it
curved out of sight. In addition to looking for help, Mandy hoped
that Gonzo would be able to get some useful information out of
Cool during the errand.

Speaking of which, it was her turn to try to get some useful information. She walked to where Elsa was sitting in the shade of
some hackberry trees. "How'd you get here?" she asked.

"Rob and Paul helped me hop over, before they took off downstream. Said they were going to look for campers at that end of the
beach."

And Rob would have a chance to quiz Paul in the process.
Mandy looked around and saw that Tina and Kendra were taking
group shots of the girlfriends. They had somehow convinced the
Andersons to pose in front of the confluence, too. Mandy wondered
if they would later look on those photos fondly, as a tribute to Alex's
wish for his family, or with abhorrence. At least his body bag was
out of photo range. She seized the opportunity to talk alone to Elsa
and sat next to her.

"I'm going to check on your ankle." She started unwrapping the
Ace bandage. "While I'm doing that, I need to tell you something

that will shock you. And you have to keep it a secret. You can't tell anyone or react to the news or make any loud noises. Can you do that?"

Looking puzzled, Elsa nodded. "What's going on?"

Mandy took a deep breath and plunged in. "Your climbing harness was deliberately cut. That's why you fell."

Elsa's eyes went wide and she hissed in a lungful of air, but as Mandy shook her head, Elsa clamped her lips shut. After she recovered, she said, "Are you sure someone cut it on purpose, that it wasn't an accident or defect?"

"I'm sure. It was a clean slice done with a knife almost all the way through, so once any weight hung on it, the harness would break. It must have been done just before you put it on."

"Who would do that?"

"That's what I need to ask you. The people up there besides you and me were Cool, Les, Paul, and Tina. I'm sorry to say that the obvious suspects are your daughter and your ex-husband."

"What? Why?"

Mandy shrugged. "That's what I'm asking you. Maybe Tina—"

"No, Tina would never hurt me!" Elsa said vehemently.

"Even if you sabotaged her plan to get you and her father back together by having an affair with Alex?"

Elsa started to shake her head, paused for a moment, then said, "Yes, she was upset about that, but she wouldn't get back at me by making me fall. I mean, I could have been killed!"

"Maybe she just wanted to hurt you after you hurt her."

"It's too unbelievable."

Mandy was still skeptical, but she decided to move on. "What about Paul?"

"That wimp? Yes, Paul and I have our differences. We've had some shouting matches, but he's never gotten violent with me. He wouldn't dare! And he wouldn't have the guts to pull off something like this." She swept a hand toward her ankle.

The ankle was swollen and starting to purple. Mandy felt the cold pack. It was still chilled. "We'll need to keep your ankle cool and wrapped for awhile longer."

Mandy started rewrapping Elsa's ankle and thought again about Paul. If the man had been too afraid to confront Elsa directly, it made sense that he might choose this indirect route to send her a message. She studied Elsa's face.

"Are you absolutely sure neither Tina nor Paul knew about your affair with Alex before the trip?"

"I really doubt it. Neither one of them is living with me now. Tina's in the dorms and Paul has his own apartment. Alex and I were discreet, too, because we didn't want anyone in the department knowing." Elsa paused. "But why are you asking that? What difference does it make when they found out, whether it was before the trip or last night?"

"Well, there's Alex."

Elsa's eyes went wide. "I thought he was killed by a bear!"

"Possibly," Mandy said. "But there are signs that make us think it may not have been a bear."

"What signs?"

"Sorry, I don't think I can share that information with anyone yet."

"You think Alex was murdered?" Elsa said incredulously in a loud voice.

Mandy shushed her and glanced at the others to see if anyone had heard. Thankfully, no one was looking at them.

"And murdered by Tina or Paul?" Elsa continued more quietly. She shook her head violently. "No, no way."

Then she paled and clutched Mandy's arm. "Maybe there's some sick maniac on this trip who's killing people randomly." She stared at the others on the beach and whispered, "Trying to pick us off one by one."

The hair on the back of Mandy's neck rose, as if she was being watched. She jerked her head and scanned the other clients. None of them seemed to be paying any attention to Elsa or her, so she faced Elsa again, who now looked terrified.

"Rob and I haven't ruled that out," she said to Elsa, "but we're thinking this person is choosing victims for a reason, and that if we figure out the reason, it will help us figure out who it is. In the meantime, we're trying to play it cool, not let on what we know. I need you to do the same thing."

Elsa's palm on Mandy's arm grew sweaty. "Okay, I will. But what's to stop him from coming after me again?"

Nothing. But Mandy wasn't going to say that and alarm Elsa. "The guides are watching everyone during the day, and we're going to organize guard shifts at night. We'll protect you the best we can." She paused and locked her gaze with Elsa's. "But if it's Paul or especially Tina, who is sharing a tent with you, that will be hard, since they have good reasons to approach you."

Elsa let go of Mandy and waved her hand dismissively. "I can't believe one of them tried to hurt me. It's got to be someone else."

Rob and Paul reappeared from around the bend downstream. Hopeful, Mandy stood and waved to them.

When Rob spotted her, he signaled with arms crossing low in front of him that they had found nothing, no other campers.

"Damn, no luck." Mandy put her hands on her hips and looked back at Elsa.

The woman was staring at her ex-husband and murmuring, "Absolutely no way..."

———

After the confluence, the water volume in the Colorado River doubled, with the flow from the Green River added in. Mandy had checked the water gauges before they left and knew the combined total was a moderate 12,000 cubic feet per second (cfs). That would be enough to give their clients a fun ride, but hopefully none of the rapids would be truly life-threatening. They were already carrying one body with them, after all, and Mandy didn't want the river gods adding any more.

Also after the confluence, a park regulation requiring all boaters to wear personal floatation devices (PFDs) went into effect. So everyone in the four rafts, guides included, now wore a tightly cinched PFD even though they planned to pull out for the night at lower Spanish Bottom. The campsite was just upriver from Brown Betty, the first of over two dozen rapids in Cataract Canyon. The exact number was dependent on the water level in Lake Powell, and how far it backed up into the canyon.

Cool explained to the group that Brown Betty was named for the cook boat, which got its name from the popular dessert, in the disastrous Brown expedition that went through the canyon in 1889. The cook boat lost valuable provisions and kitchen gear in the rapid.

While he was telling the story, Mandy glanced at Alex's body bag in Rob's raft and at Elsa in Gonzo's raft. She sent up a silent prayer that their body count would not go as high as the three men that expedition had lost, including Brown himself.

About two miles downriver, the four rafts pulled out at the huge, red-lettered "DANGER, Cataract Canyon, Hazardous Rapids" sign on river left. It was a good photo stop for groups, but it was also where campers registered for campsites in the canyon, on a clipboard in the waterproof metal box below the sign.

Mandy went with Rob to look over the registration sheet. It was totally blank for that day and the next day, so they were the only group, so far, going through the canyon those days.

"What about yesterday?" Mandy asked. "Maybe we'll catch up to a group that's taking its time."

Rob flipped the page. It was empty, too. "There's still a chance there's a group in the canyon that didn't bother to register."

"Which means they're not with an outfitter and probably don't have a radio."

They moved aside to let Betsy, Viv, and Mo take a group shot in front of the sign, their grins wide and just a little twitchy with nervousness. The Nortons waited for their turn, Elsa sitting on a rock after she had limped over with Gonzo's help. Tina was chattering excitedly with her father about the upcoming rapids.

Rob put an arm over Mandy's shoulder while they watched the photo-taking. "We knew the river would be almost deserted in October. That was part of the appeal of this trip, after all."

Mandy looked at Diana and Hal Anderson, who were gazing worriedly downstream. She had a sudden scary thought.

"I wonder if that was the appeal for our killer, too. Knowing that after the radio was destroyed, we'd probably be stuck with no way out of the canyon and no way to call for help."

ELEVEN

*(The river) communicates in extremes ranging from placid
to enraged, and its message may dip beneath the surface
of consciousness, telling us things
we don't even know that we've heard.*

JEFF WALLACH—*WHAT THE RIVER SAYS*

AFTER ANOTHER MILE AND a half float, the group reached the huge flat expanse of Spanish Bottom in the late afternoon. The red-and-white striped pinnacles of the Doll House formation lay jumbled across the top of the canyon rim that overlooked the half-mile long, half-moon-shaped sandy bottom below. Dying tamarisks and native willows and cottonwoods formed a thin band of riparian greenery along the river bank, while the sparse vegetation on the bottom consisted more of cactus, yucca, and other desert-adapted species.

The screech of a hunting raptor high above them was the only sound that broke the silence of the deserted and desolate scene before them. There were no signs of human activity.

As they neared the far end of Spanish Bottom, Mandy scanned along the edge of the four-foot shelf of packed sand along the river, looking for a good landing spot. Rob had said they would camp at the downriver end of the bottom, right before the Colorado River made a sharp left turn to enter the narrower Cataract Canyon.

The base of the Doll House trail was near there. It was likely their last chance of finding people before reaching the end of Cataract Canyon. This trail and the Lathrop Canyon trail were the only two that zig-zagged down from the canyon rim to the river along the whole expanse of their 100-mile river journey.

The group would hike up the trail the next morning before hitting the rapids after lunch, but Mandy was anxious to spot somebody, anybody, on the trail or the rim right then and there. She kept glancing up high as well as at the river bank.

Rob, Kendra, and Gonzo searched, too, for both a good landing and human activity. Kendra was the first to say, "How about there?" She pointed at an alcove in the bank. A collapsed shelf of firm sand provided a stepping-up point to a small break in the thicket of brush lining the bank.

"Looks good to me," Mandy replied.

Kendra paddled her raft in and jumped out to tie it to a large cottonwood trunk. "I'll do a quick scout."

She trotted into the brush while the other rafts jostled in next to hers. Gonzo hopped out to tie his raft to the same tree that Kendra had. Then he took ropes tossed from Rob and Mandy and tied their rafts to a thick tamarisk trunk a dozen feet upstream.

Kendra returned as he finished the last knot. "It's just a short walk to a nice open sandy area on the other side of these willows."

"Okay, let's set up the bucket brigade, then," Rob said.

While Rob and Mandy unlashed gear, Cool hopped out. He and Gonzo gave all of the clients a hand-up onto the bank. Rob and Mandy lifted Elsa to them, so she wouldn't have to put weight on her injured ankle. Then Kendra helped her hobble to a shady spot to rest in. Familiar with the routine, the other clients formed a line to the campsite to pass gear along, with Rob and Mandy doing the hard part of hoisting the gear up to Cool and Gonzo from river level to sand bank level.

After the unloading was complete, everyone but Mandy and Rob scattered to pitch tents. The two of them lowered Alex's body bag into the river again to keep it cool overnight. The corpse's arms and legs were less stiff, indicating rigor mortis was receding. Mandy knew that meant bloating was not far behind, and with it the stink of decomposition. She fervently hoped they would be able to hand off the body soon.

When she jumped onto the bank after the job was done, she noticed that Hal had returned. He was watching them with an anguished expression.

"I'm sorry we haven't been able to find a way to get him out of the canyon yet," Mandy said.

"I understand," Hal replied. "I've seen all you guides scanning the river and cliffs for people. I know you're trying." He gulped hard and blinked. "In the meantime, you've been very respectful of his body. I want to thank you for that."

Mandy did what came naturally. She hugged him. The poor man had lost his son and was stuck with the body in the wilderness, with no way to properly mourn his son or honor his life.

She released Hal and gazed into his hang-dog eyes. "I wish we could do more."

He patted her arm. "You're taking care of him the best you can. That's all I can ask." He turned and walked back toward the campsite, his head lowered and his hands jammed in his pants pockets.

Rob joined Mandy and silently watched Hal go. "Unfortunately, I think we'll be doing this again tomorrow night."

They walked to the campsite, quickly pitched their tent and threw sleeping bags inside. Then they rolled up their sleeves and went to work on dinner preparations with the other guides. The menu was grilled squash and Spanish rice with shrimp and leftover breakfast sausage. Dessert was an assortment of large soft cookies from the City Market bakery in Moab, including Mandy's favorite, peanut butter. She hoped that the menu would tempt the Anderson family's appetite. She was especially worried about Diana and Amy, who had only managed to pick at their food since Alex had been killed.

Mandy scanned the campsite while she chopped onions, wiping tears from her eyes. Hal and Diana sat with Paul and Tina at one of the camp tables, talking quietly. All four were sipping wine, but only Paul and Tina were snacking on the tortilla chips and guacamole that Kendra had set out. Betsy, Mo, and Viv had enticed Amy into joining them in a game of bridge at another table.

Elsa was resting in Tina's and her tent, which Mandy noticed was pitched right next to Cool's and Gonzo's. Mandy knew it was a cautious move on Elsa's part to put herself right next to two guides. However, it also put her next to one of Mandy's suspects, Cool, though while he may have had a motive to hurt Elsa, she hadn't found any reason for him to go after Alex.

Les and Alice approached the kitchen with beer cans in their hands. "We're going to reconnoiter," he said and held up his camera pack that was always with him. "And I want to get some photos of that field of big white flowers near camp. What are they?"

"There're multiple names for them," Cool said. "Moonflower, jimson weed, locoweed, or sacred datura are some of them. The plant's hallucinogenic. Native Americans would smoke it for ceremonies."

"How appropriate," Alice said with a nod. "All those flowers reminded me of the poppy field scene in the *Wizard of Oz* movie."

Cool cackled like the Wicked Witch of the West. "Poppies will put them to sleep!"

With a grin, Rob said to Les, "Just plan to be back in about forty-five minutes. Dinner will be ready then."

Les saluted him with his beer. "Will do. Don't want to miss one of your great meals."

Alice looked at the dinner preparations and made a face like she didn't agree with that assessment, which raised Mandy's hackles. She sank her knife in another onion. Here she had been slaving away to make an appealing meal for the grieving family.

When Tina stood a few minutes later and headed off in the direction of the portable toilet, Mandy whispered to Rob, "Now's my chance to talk to Tina alone. I'll catch her on the way back."

He nodded, and she waited a couple of minutes. Then she headed through the thicket, stopping about halfway along the path from the camp to the toilet to wait for Tina to reappear. When she did, carrying the key, Mandy waved to her and said, "I'm next."

"Here you go, then." Tina handed her the plastic bag containing the roll of TP.

Tina started to pass, but Mandy stopped her with a hand on her arm. "Wait. I wanted to talk to you, alone, and I haven't had a chance to until now. You seemed pretty freaked out about your mom and Alex last night. Are you okay?"

Tina put her hands on her hips. "Not really. I still can't believe Mom was sleeping with Alex. I mean, he was young enough to be my brother!"

Mandy nodded, trying to look sympathetic. "I guess the news was pretty hard to take."

"Damn right!"

"How'd your dad react when you told him?"

Tina pursed her lips. "He took it better than I thought he would, said Mom wasn't married to him anymore, so she could sleep with whoever she wants. I can't believe he wasn't more upset!"

"Do you think he already knew about it?"

Shaking her head, Tina said, "I asked him if he did, and he said no, that last night was the first he'd heard about it."

"And you didn't know about it before either?"

"Hell no! If I did, I sure wouldn't have brought Dad on this trip, knowing her boy toy was coming, too. And, I would have told Mom how pervy it was that she was screwing one of her students." Tina threw up her hands. "Think of the trouble she would have been in if the department chair or university administration found out!"

Mandy was sure professors had had affairs with students before, and Alex was over twenty-one, an adult, so she didn't agree that Elsa would have been in trouble. But, she wasn't going to say that to Tina. Instead, she flung out something provocative to see how Tina would react. "I bet you were ready to wring her neck."

With a laugh, Tina said, "I guess that's one way to put it. I'm still not talking to her."

"I noticed."

Tina's brow furrowed and she worried her lip for a moment. Finally she spoke. "I guess I should apologize to her. That's probably what you came out here to ask me to do, because our fight is yet another downer on the whole group." She sighed. "I'll go talk to her now." She turned and walked away before Mandy could say anything else.

Suddenly shouts rang out from camp.

Tina looked back at Mandy, her eyes wide.

What the hell is going on?

Mandy took off running toward camp, and Tina turned and followed her. When they broke through the thicket, Mandy saw that everyone was standing and shouting and waving their hands toward the top of the canyon wall, where the Doll House formation sat.

Mandy shaded her eyes and searched the formation. *There.* She saw two tiny figures dressed in blue and green clothing, so they stood out against the red, pink, and white backdrop of the wind-carved sandstone. They were waving, too, but if they were shouting something back, the sound wasn't carrying down to them.

The people in camp were yelling, "Help!" "Come down!" "Do you have a radio?" and other phrases, all jumbled into a mishmash of incoherent noise.

Mandy ran to Viv. "Where are your binoculars?"

"Good thinking." Viv ran to her tent to get them and Mandy followed. After taking the powerful binoculars from Viv, Mandy trained them on the two figures. They were a young Asian couple with black hair, wearing backpacks. They had wide grins on their faces and waved gaily at the group far below them.

"They can't tell what we're saying," Mandy yelled to Rob.

Rob shouted, "Hush, everyone! Quiet!" until he had everyone's attention. "Now, on the count of three, we'll all yell 'help us' at the same time."

He counted and they all yelled while Mandy watched the couple through the binoculars. The couple laughed and waved back again. Either they couldn't make out the words of their shouts, they thought the group was joking, or they didn't understand English.

"They aren't getting it," Mandy said. "Someone needs to go up there."

"I'll go," Cool said, grabbing a bottle of water. "I know the trail best."

As he took off running, Rob yelled to him, "If you don't see them when you get to the top, come back. Don't run around up there in the dark!"

Mandy looked at the sky and realized the sun was dipping below the canyon rim. They would be losing the light soon. She focused the binoculars on the couple again. They had turned away from the rim and soon disappeared from sight. If they were heading back into the Doll House formation, or somewhere else in The Maze district of the Canyonlands up there, it would be impossible for Cool to spot them after he reached the top. Even scrambling up the trail as fast as he could, it would take him almost an hour.

She crossed her fingers and said to Rob, "Hopefully they're coming down the trail to Spanish Bottom and Cool will run into them on the trail."

He nodded. "And hopefully they have a radio."

Almost two hours later, Cool returned, dragging himself into camp and looking dejected. He slumped into a camp chair at one of the tables. Mandy was glad to see he had made it back okay but was not glad to see his expression.

"Gonzo and I were just about to form a search party and go after you," Rob said to Cool. "I wasn't sure you could make it back in the dark." The last bit of twilight had just faded.

"Bummer, dude. No sign of 'em, huh?" Gonzo said from the next table, where he had most of the clients ensconced in chairs with their heads tilted back. He had started another session of stargazing, since the night sky was clear and the Milky Way was blanketing the sky with brilliant stars. Diana and Hal peered hopefully at Cool.

"No, never spotted them. I ran out of water, so I figured I should head back." Cool held up his empty water bottle.

Looking disappointed, Diana and Hal turned away. Mandy took Cool's water bottle and refilled it from the fresh water jug while Kendra brought him a plate of food.

"We kept it warm for you," she said as she handed him some utensils.

"Thanks, I'm starving." He dug into the Spanish rice and took huge gulps of water while Kendra kept him company.

"We need to talk," Mandy said to Rob. She pulled him into a willow thicket, well out of earshot of the clients and Cool. She filled him in on her conversation with Tina Norton. "It sure seemed like neither she nor Paul knew anything about Elsa and Alex before last night."

"That's the story I got from Paul when we searched the confluence beach together."

"Did he seem upset or angry about Elsa and Alex?"

Rob shook his head. "Not really. He seems like a pretty laid-back guy to me, not one to get hot-headed, like his ex-wife."

"Or his daughter," Mandy added. "Do we know if Gonzo was able to get anything out of Cool when they searched the other end of the beach?"

"When you went after Tina, Gonzo and I walked to the rafts together to fetch the dinner stuff. I asked him then. He said he brought up the subject by asking Cool if he was having any luck with any of the women, Cool said it looked like he wasn't going to get any tail on this trip." Rob held up his hands. "His words, not mine."

"That slimeball," Mandy spat out. "He has absolutely no respect for women."

Rob smiled and smoothed a thumb across her cheek. "That's why the fool will never be lucky enough to find a little spitfire like you to marry him." He kissed her on the nose before continuing. "Gonzo said that comment opened the door for him to ask Cool if he was mad at any of the women for turning him down."

"Let me guess." Mandy put her hand on her hip and stared between willow branches at Cool as he pointed out a star formation to Tina, his arm around her shoulder. He had finished his meal and joined the stargazers. "He can't figure out why they're all turning down God's gift to womankind."

"Something like that," Rob said with a smirk. "The gist of the conversation, though, was that Cool didn't seem to feel any more anger toward Elsa than he did for the other women."

"Or he was very good at hiding it from Gonzo." Then a sinking thought hit her. "Do you think he was really looking for the hikers? Maybe he didn't *want* to find them—or us to either. Maybe that's why he volunteered to go."

Rob quirked an eyebrow at her. "You're quite the suspicious one, aren't you?"

"We have to be—until we find out who's doing this!" She stared at the people in camp. "But Cool's not the only one I'm suspicious of. Tina or Paul could have been hiding their true feelings from us, too. Just because we haven't found a good reason for any of them to kill Alex or sabotage Elsa doesn't mean one doesn't exist."

Rob cocked his head to one side. "You don't think we have more than one killer in our group, do you? That one was after Alex and the other after Elsa, for different reasons?"

"I don't know what to think," Mandy said with exasperation. "It's creepy enough to believe we have one killer among us. But Alex is dead, and it sure doesn't look like a bear did it, given what Betsy said."

"You never got a chance to compare the claw marks on his face with those in her guidebook, did you?"

"No, not with Elsa and Tina there last night."

"We should try again tonight," Rob said with some reluctance, "after everyone's asleep."

Mandy gave a nod. "We should, and maybe we'll find something else, now that we're looking for evidence of murder." She shuddered. She had seen more than her fair share of dead bodies the past summer working as a river ranger. "But his body's going to be gruesome—and smelly."

Rob wrinkled his nose. "There aren't any cops here to help us, so I don't see any alternative. We need to look for clues ourselves."

"Very carefully, though," Mandy said, "because if the killer finds out what we're doing before we find out who he or she is, we'll become targets." A shiver of dread crawled up her spine and tapped her on the shoulder. She wheeled to search the dark willows around them to make sure no one had crept up on them.

With a nod toward camp, Rob said, "I counted heads. They're all there, except Kendra."

Mandy blew out a breath, trying to slow her racing heart. "We'll have to be on constant alert if we're going to protect ourselves and the clients."

"Especially at night. We need to set up guard shifts. Frankly, we should have done it last night."

Kendra had just returned to camp after throwing out the dishwater from washing Cool's plate and silverware. Rob walked toward camp and called out, "Kendra, Gonzo, could you come over here for a minute?"

When Cool glanced at him, looking puzzled about why he wasn't included in the summons, Rob said, "You're the stargazing expert, so keep on doing what you're doing."

After Kendra and Gonzo joined them, Rob and Mandy explained that they were going to organize guard shifts.

"Crapola," Gonzo said, his eyes wide with worry. "So you think this killer's going to strike again?"

"We really don't know," Mandy said, "since we don't know who killed Alex and hurt Elsa, or why."

Gonzo put an arm around Kendra. "Well, I sure don't want Kendra sitting out there alone at night, especially if a killer could be stalking around."

"We don't think anyone's after any of us," Mandy said, thinking *yet*, "just Elsa, potentially. Still, having two guards per shift is a good idea. And we don't want anyone to know we're suspicious. You've got to keep all this secret from the clients and Cool."

Kendra gave a somber nod. "We promise."

"That's going to be tough," Gonzo said, "since I'm sharing a tent with the guy."

"Here's a solution to both of your problems," Rob said with a grin. "Tell Cool that you and Kendra are going to sleep outside together tonight, since there's no threat of rain."

"Great idea!" Gonzo grinned at Kendra, and she returned his smile. "We'll take the first shift. I'm sure we can find a way to keep each other awake."

———

The alarm on Mandy's wristwatch beeped in the middle of the night, waking her from a troubled dream. She had been fighting off an attack from a grizzly bear, who seemed to have an almost human form. She roused Rob and dressed quickly. They crept out of their tent and used the dim illumination from their headlamps to locate Gonzo and Kendra sitting at one of the camp tables.

"Anything?" Mandy whispered.

Gonzo shook his head. "All quiet."

"We'll take over," Rob whispered. "Want to use our tent for the rest of the night?"

"Yeah," Kendra replied while huddling in her fleece jacket. "I don't want to wake the gals, and it's gotten pretty chilly out here."

Mandy did feel a definite nip in the air. She pulled a fleece headband out of the pocket of her jacket and put it on. "Where are your bags?"

Gonzo pointed to their sleeping bags, in the shadow of a few willows on the other side of the kitchen area. It was a somewhat private hideaway that still afforded them a good view of the tents in camp. "If you need to bundle up, feel free to use them."

He and Kendra left and crawled into Mandy and Rob's tent. After listening to mostly silence for about fifteen minutes, except for Paul's irregular snores coming from the other side of the willows behind Gonzo and Kendra's bags, Mandy leaned in close to Rob.

"All's quiet. Think now's a good time to look at Alex?"

Rob nodded and held up Betsy's wildlife tracking guidebook.

Mandy took one last glance around the slumbering camp, then followed Rob to the rafts. They climbed into Rob's raft and positioned themselves at the top and bottom of Alex's body bag. On the count of three, they hoisted it out of the water and inside the raft. After Rob removed the ropes, Mandy knelt beside the dripping bag and turned on her headlamp.

She put on latex gloves from their first-aid kit, and he did the same. She laid her hand on the zipper and looked at Rob. "Ready?"

"Ready." He opened the guidebook to the place he had marked and trained his headlamp on the page.

Mandy unzipped the bag a third of the way, figuring they only needed to look at Alex's head. She pulled back the flaps over his face. The sick smell of flesh beginning to rot rose out of the bag and made her gag. She turned her head to suck in a breath of fresh air, then glanced at Rob.

His face looked green, and he swallowed convulsively. When Rob clamped a hand over his nose, she did the same. The smell of the latex glove helped mask the odor of death a little. At least enough to keep her from losing her dinner.

Training her headlamp on Alex's bloated face, she examined the vertical claw marks that raked one side of his face and along the neck, where he had bled out. Five distinct lines split the flesh, the three inside ones starting slightly higher on Alex's forehead than the two outside ones.

"The book says tracks from both bears are about three inches wide," Rob said, "but that grizzly tracks are longer. And the toes of a grizzly are more separated and less curved than those of a black bear."

"We've only got claw marks," Mandy said. "What's it say about claws?"

"The claw mark pattern would be different, too." Rob pointed to the illustration in the book. "See here, on the black bear, the little toe claw is a lot lower than the others." He looked at the deep scratches on Alex's head and back at the book. "I'd say those match the grizzly claw description better."

Mandy studied the illustration then Alex's face. "I agree, but it's not a big difference."

"Here's something else. Grizzly claws are two to four inches long and black bear claws are only one to two inches long and fatter."

"That means we should measure how deep these gashes are," Mandy said, then shuddered at the thought of poking something in Alex's dead flesh. But it had to be done. "Got anything I can use?"

Rob pulled out a pocket knife and fiddled with it until he found the tool he wanted, then handed it to Mandy. "Believe it or not, this has a ruler on the edge of the nail file."

Mandy held it over Alex's face, gritted her teeth and breathed through them. "You okay with me sticking it in him?" She almost wished he would say no.

"I'll dump it in boiling dishwater in the morning," Rob said. "Do it."

Gingerly, Mandy probed in various places along each of the gashes, swallowing down bile as she worked. For the inside gashes, she was able to go about three inches deep in many places. "I'd say that cinches it. A grizzly paw did this."

"But how did Alex sit still for this?"

Mandy unzipped the body bag farther and gingerly lifted Alex's arms out of the bag. She examined each wrist in the light of her headlamp. "It doesn't look like he was tied up. Maybe he was choked first." She tilted his head back to examine the neck, then sucked in a breath. "Look at this!"

A red mark appeared around a tiny pinprick hole in the side of Alex's neck opposite the side that had been shredded by the claws.

Rob bent in for a closer look. "Is that a needle mark?"

171

TWELVE

*Nature reserves the right to inflict upon
her children the most terrifying jests.*
—THORNTON WILDER

BLEARY-EYED AND DRY-MOUTHED THE next morning, Mandy poured a cup of hot coffee and drank a large gulp, scalding her tongue. She grimaced but took another, smaller sip. She needed the caffeine after losing half a night's sleep. After discovering the needle mark on Alex's neck, she and Rob had argued quietly for hours while bundled in Gonzo and Kendra's sleeping bags.

They had both changed their minds, at different times, about whether they should tell everyone that a killer was among them or keep it secret. The first choice would create widespread panic and suspicion and alert the killer that they were on to him or her. The second choice would allow the killer to come after Elsa again or target a third victim, if there was one, in secret. And if anyone else was killed, Mandy and Rob would feel responsible for the death.

But keeping quiet would also allow Mandy, Rob, Gonzo, and Kendra to observe all of the others on the sly to try to ferret out which one was the killer.

Finally as the eastern rim of the canyon was lightening far above them, they had roused Kendra and Gonzo. While quietly brewing a pot of coffee so as not to wake the others, Mandy and Rob pulled their two trusted guides out of earshot of the rest of camp and filled them in on what they had found.

Eyes wide, Kendra whispered, "Are we in danger?"

Gonzo's tense expression showed he was thinking the same thing.

"Our best guess is still that the killer's motives don't include us," Rob said, "that it's something about the relationships between the clients. That's why Tina and Paul are our top suspects, because Elsa was having an affair with Alex, and they were both with her when her harness was cut."

Kendra clutched Gonzo's arm. "But so were Les and Cool, and Gonzo's sharing a tent with Cool."

"It's possible that someone targeted Alex and Elsa for some reason other than the affair," Mandy said. *Or that they were chosen at random by a psychopath in the group.* "So we're not ruling out any of the clients or Cool. The only people we can trust are the four of us."

Gonzo drew Kendra in under his arm. "And Kendra's sleeping with three clients."

Rob nodded. "I think it's best if you two use the same excuse tonight as you did last night and put your sleeping bags together outside. We'll need to pull watch shifts again tonight anyway."

"And staying up two at a time is definitely safer," Mandy added.

A rustle in the willow thicket behind them made her turn and stare into the gloomy underbrush. She pulled her headlamp out of a pocket in her fleece jacket and shone the beam into the thicket. The light caught no eyes looking back at them or anything else unnatural. A glance back at camp, still lying in the dark shadow of the towering cliffs looming over them, showed all was quiet there, too.

She shrugged at the others. "Must have been a bird or chipmunk. Back to our problem. We'll all have to be on the lookout for anyone acting weird."

"Like what?" Kendra asked.

"Any behavior that's not typical for someone on a float trip, or anything that just doesn't feel right to you, even if you can't say why," Mandy said.

"What do we do if we see someone acting squirrelly?" Gonzo asked.

"Privately tell the rest of us, or as many as you can," Rob said. "Don't do anything on your own."

"And be super discreet and careful," Mandy added. "If we do find evidence of who the killer is, and he or she finds out we know, then we'll become targets, too."

Kendra sucked in a breath and clutched Gonzo, but before she could say anything, Cool emerged from his tent. He stood and stretched, then when he saw the four of them, he frowned in puzzlement and walked toward them.

"Why are you all up so early?" he whispered when he got near.

Mandy concocted a story about hearing a noise and looking for another camper then quickly directed everyone to start work on breakfast. She gave the excuse that if they got the clients up and moving on the trail to the Doll House early, the heat would be less likely to affect them. Also, they would be more likely to find campers, if there were any up there, before they broke camp.

Mandy had just finished slicing melons when Rob called, "Coffee!" She used the break in her activities to study the clients as they crawled out of their tents and lined up in front of the griddle. Manning the spatula, Cool was in fine form, flirting with the women and teasing the men as he flipped fried eggs and toast onto their plates. Of course, he was the only guide who had gotten a full night's sleep. Gonzo and Kendra ate standing up behind the prep table, as if afraid of getting near the clients and needing that barrier, flimsy as it was, between them and a hidden killer.

Rob moved among the clients, pouring coffee and asking how they slept. Mandy grabbed the juice pitcher and joined him. After all, if she was going to ferret out suspicious behavior, she had to start looking.

The five remaining Andersons ate quietly around one of the camp tables. Tina and Elsa sat next to each other at another table, so Mandy assumed Tina had made up with her mother. Paul, Betsy, Viv, and Mo gathered around the last table. Paul smiled good-naturedly while the three of them ribbed him about his snoring. No one was behaving like they had something to hide.

That raised a question in Mandy's mind. *How does a killer behave anyway, when not in the act?*

Cool broke her reverie by coming up to Rob with the radio in his hand. Mandy joined them.

"After I cleaned all the contacts with a cotton swab dipped in alcohol," Cool said, "I put the radio together this morning and tried it out, hoping I might be able to reach the repeater at the Confluence. It wouldn't even power on. Sorry."

Rob took the radio from him. "Bummer. Thanks for trying, though."

Cool left to help Kendra and Gonzo with the dishes, while Mandy studied the radio in Rob's hand. "You know," she said, "if Cool wanted to make sure we'd never be able to call out for help, he may have just achieved that."

"You think he disabled the radio deliberately? To me, he seemed genuinely interested in helping."

"Yeah, he did," Mandy said, peering at Rob. "But who's to say he didn't throw away some part after taking it apart, something vital?"

Rob stared at Cool. "Maybe I shouldn't have given it to him."

"It doesn't really matter," Mandy said. "You weren't able to fix it anyway. But, his generous offer seems a little suspicious to me. I'm keeping an eye on him." She moved over to a camp table and started folding it up. She glanced at Cool a moment later, but he was engrossed in talking to Gonzo, as if he had no concerns in the world.

After the breakfast cleanup was done, Rob organized the group for the Doll House hike, making sure everyone had water, sunscreen, cameras, and so on. All of the clients wanted to go, including Elsa. She insisted her ankle was better, and when Mandy checked it, she saw that the swelling had subsided.

"I'm not sure it's a good idea," Mandy said to Elsa. "You could make it worse by putting stress on it so soon after it was injured."

"No, it's fine." Elsa did a few turns around the camp to show she could walk on it without limping. Then she came up to Mandy and whispered in her ear. "And I'll be damned if I'll let anyone scare me out of going. I'm not giving up what's probably going to be my only chance to see the Doll House up close. Nobody would try anything in such a large group anyway."

"I hope not," Mandy said doubtfully. *Had Elsa forgotten how many people were around her when she had her accident?*

Rob joined them. Not having heard what Elsa whispered, he said, "We'll have enough guides along on the hike that if Elsa needs help, we can take turns giving her an assist. And Cool has a couple of retractable walking sticks, if she needs one."

From Elsa's determined chin, Mandy realized the woman would insist on going no matter what, so she nodded.

In a way, it was good that Elsa was adamant about going. Rob and Mandy had agreed that she would stay behind, with the pretense of guarding their stuff from animals and keeping an eye out for boats on the river. In reality, she planned to search all of the clients' gear for the grizzly bear claw and a hypodermic needle—if the killer had been stupid enough to keep either one. Unfortunately, a pocket camping knife—which was all that was needed to cut Elsa's harness—had been on the packing list, so everyone likely had one of those. Mandy also planned to look for journals, letters, or any other clues that might shed some light on what any of the clients were thinking.

After Rob had parceled out the first-aid kit, trail snacks, and other supplies among himself, Cool, Gonzo, and Kendra, the group was off. Mandy waved to them, then waited impatiently for at least ten minutes before starting her search. She and Rob had told the clients to leave their tents and gear where they were, so they could hike during the cool part of the morning and pack when it was hotter. That plan also made it easier for Mandy to search the gear.

She started with Cool O'Day's stuff in the tent he shared with Gonzo. She didn't find anything of interest, but she noted that he was even more slovenly than Gonzo. She was glad to get out of their funky smelling tent and move on to Paul Norton's solo tent. She didn't find a bear claw or hypodermic needle among his things, either, but he was keeping a trip journal, so she sat down to skim it. It was mostly dry notes about what he had done and seen each day. The entry for the evening when Tina had told him about Elsa's affair with Alex, however, included a paragraph about how upset his daughter was. He also wrote about how stupid his ex-wife was for doing such a thing. Mandy re-read the final paragraph over and over again.

I'm surprised I wasn't bothered more by Elsa's foolish affair. If we'd still been married, I would have been ready to kill her. But I feel nothing—other than worrying about the effect on Tina. Maybe that woman is really dead for me now—for good.

Mandy could interpret the passage two ways. Either Paul truly no longer cared what happened to his wife—or he wished her dead. And Tina had definitely been upset—but upset enough to threaten her errant mother's life? Mandy checked her watch. She was no closer to the truth, and time was wasting away. She moved on to Tina and Elsa's tent, but found nothing there. Neither woman kept a journal.

She decided to focus on the Anderson clan next. She searched Amy and Les's 2-man tent, but found nothing suspicious other than concealers in a variety of shades in Amy's cosmetic bag. To hide bruises from Les? Amy also had been recording every snippet of history that the guides had shared with the clients in a journal. From Amy's comments about where she needed to do follow-up research, Mandy wondered if the quiet woman planned to write a western history book someday. *What a surprise.*

Checking her watch, Mandy figured the group had probably reached the top of the canyon rim and were searching for hikers or campers and taking photos of the Doll House. Rob had planned on giving them about forty minutes to explore the formations and ancient granaries there, then they would head back down. And the return trip would take much less time than the steep uphill climb.

Mandy hurried to the tent that Diana, Hal, and Alice were sharing, along with Alex's gear. At first, she was going to leave Alex's gear alone, but then she realized there might be something in it that revealed his relationship with Elsa—or with others. She went through all of his stuff, but nothing shed any light on why someone would want to kill him.

Diana and Hal's things weren't enlightening either, but Diana's tear-stained notes about funeral arrangements for Alex made Mandy swallow hard and wipe away a tear of her own. Alice's dry bag turned up nothing but clothes, cosmetics, and a couple of paperback mystery novels. As Mandy was returning the items to the dry bag, she noticed that Alice had drawn in the margins of the novels.

She flipped through the pages to try to make sense of the doodles. Names of all of Alice's family members were embellished and turned into cartoon faces, animals and plants, but Les's name was the most frequent. The L often formed the bottom point of a heart. And some of the drawings made from Amy's and Alex's names had Xs scratched over them. Was Alice angry at her siblings or just not satisfied with the drawings?

A noise made her start and shove the books back in the dry bag. She stepped out of the tent and saw Alice Anderson running toward camp calling her name. *What the hell?*

Alice stopped in front of her. She leaned forward with hands on her knees and heaved a bit to catch her breath. "It's Dad. . . . He collapsed on the way down. . . . Rob said we need to make a stretcher to carry him. He said you would know where a tarp, some poles, and ropes are. Kendra and I volunteered to run down to get you and the supplies." She sucked in more deep breaths.

"Where's Kendra?"

"A few minutes behind me." Alice straightened and cocked her head at Mandy. "What were you doing in our tent?"

"Oh, I saw a chipmunk go in under the flap. They can do some damage chewing on fabric, so I chased it out." She leaned down to zip the entrance flap tight, which also hid her face from Alice's peering gaze. "Is your dad hurt? Is he conscious?"

"No, he's not hurt and he's awake. He's just too tired to walk any more."

"Okay, let's get those supplies."

While they headed for the rafts, Mandy wondered if this was another murder attempt. Could Hal have been poked with a hypodermic like Alex, or was what she had seen on the Lathrop ruins hike indicative of a health issue?

"Does your father have a health problem that we don't know about?" she asked Alice sharply.

Alice refused to meet Mandy's gaze. "He swore us to secrecy."

Mandy grabbed her arm. "We've got to know what's wrong so we can treat him. Is he diabetic? Does he have hypertension?"

Alice removed Mandy's hand. "No, nothing like that. Nothing you can treat. But you won't get it out of me. You'll have to ask him." She turned her head as Kendra appeared behind them. "And I suggest you ask in private. The damn man has his pride." She clamped her lips tight, indicating the conversation was over.

"Girl, you took off like a shot," Kendra said to Alice, while taking deep breaths. "I couldn't keep up."

"Well, I *am* a runner," Alice replied, then turned to Mandy. "So where's the tarp?"

Mandy clambered onto her raft and dug the tarp, poles, and rope out of the supply stash. She parceled out the items among Kendra, Alice, and herself and grabbed a water bottle. "Let's go."

They took off at a quick pace, but by the time they had scrabbled up the first gentle rise to the base of the switchback trail up the cliffside, Mandy could see the group slowly making their way down the last few hundred feet. Rob and Gonzo had Hal slung between them in a fireman's carry. They were picking their way sideways down the single-file trail while Cool preceded them and called out where to put their feet. The others followed silently.

Mandy put the poles she was carrying on the ground. "By the time we get this stretcher built, they'll be here."

She took the tarp from Kendra and used the grommet holes along the two sides to lash it around the poles. True to her prediction, by the time she and Kendra had finished tying the knots, the group had arrived. Rob and Gonzo eased Hal onto the makeshift stretcher and Diana fell down on her knees beside him. The others stood back, anxiety lining their faces.

Mandy studied Hal's face and didn't like what she saw. The man's skin was pale and clammy, and his breathing was shallow. *What's wrong with him?*

Before she could question Rob about what had happened, though, he said, "Let's get him to camp." He directed Gonzo, Cool, and Paul to each pick up an end of a pole while he took the fourth one.

Mandy helped Diana to her feet and led the way back to camp. She found a flat shady spot under a dying tamarisk a short distance from camp where they could lay the stretcher. She was determined to find out what was wrong with Hal, but was mindful of what Alice had said about asking him in private. So, as soon as the men lowered him to the ground, she addressed the group.

"Rob and I will stay with Hal, along with his wife. The rest of you need to break camp. Gonzo, Kendra, and Cool, you'll be in charge of lunch, too."

With a few last concerned looks at Hal, the others wandered off to do what they were told. Diana had lowered herself onto the ground next to her husband and was holding his hand. Hal's eyes were shut, but he had raised an arm to wipe sweat off his forehead, so Mandy knew he was awake—and being male, probably embarrassed about causing such a ruckus.

She knelt next to Diana by Hal's head. "Mister Anderson," she started, to show some respect, "do you need some water?"

He nodded, and she slipped a hand under his head to help ease it up so he could take a few swallows from a water bottle. After he lay back down, she caught his gaze and gave him a stern look.

"I understand your desire to keep your medical condition private, especially from the other clients." She swept a hand toward the bustling camp. "But Rob and I have to know what's wrong, so if you get in trouble on the trip, we can give you the right first aid. You were supposed to list any health issues on your confidential medical form, but since you didn't, you need to tell us now."

Hal shook his head, but Diana said, "We've got to tell them, Hal."

Rob sat down on the other side of Hal across from Mandy and Diana. "Yes, you need to tell us, but it will go no further than the two of us. We'll keep it private, whatever it is."

Hal sighed and nodded at Diana, then closed his eyes again.

She looked at Rob, then turned her head toward Mandy, exposing the bright tears pooled in her eyes. "He's got lung cancer. Terminal lung cancer. He's dying and there's nothing the doctors or you or anyone else can do to stop it." A tear splashed on Hal's hand that she held tightly in hers.

"Jesus," Rob whispered.

The horror of dealing with another death on the trip swirled through Mandy's head. Then she realized Hal's doctor probably wouldn't have allowed him to go on the trip if he was that close to dying—or had he told his doctor his plans?

She waited for Hal to open his eyes. "What did your doctor say about you taking this trip?"

Hal grimaced. "She wasn't happy about it."

"But she said he still had at least a few weeks before the cancer would incapacitate him," Diana added. "Once she realized how important this trip was to the family, she read your trip description and decided Hal should be able to handle it. But she told him not to try anything strenuous, that his remaining lung capacity wouldn't support it." She gave Hal a disapproving frown. "Then stubborn you insisted on going on that damn hike."

"I had to try it," Hal struggled to rise, and Rob helped him to a sitting position. "I'm sorry I caused all that trouble, but hell, this is my last chance to see views like that."

Mandy studied him to see if sitting up would make him dizzy, but his color seemed to be returning. "Did you get a chance to see the views before—"

"Before I wilted on the trail?" Hal finished for her. "Yes, it was on the way down that my legs gave out. I hadn't realized how shallowly I'd been breathing. My leg muscles just weren't getting enough oxygen to work right."

Diana nodded. "That's happened to him before."

Kendra called out, "Lunch is ready. Pasta salad!"

"I don't know about the rest of you, but I'm hungry." Hal rolled over onto his hands and knees. "I'm okay now. I think I can stand."

He pushed himself to his feet, but Rob stood close with a hand under Hal's elbow, just in case. Mandy stepped closer, ready to help support Hal on the other side. They waited for a moment while he took a few breaths.

He walked to Diana and took her arm, then turned and searched Mandy and Rob's faces. "Not a word to anyone, right?"

"Right," Rob said.

"But your family already knows, don't they?" Mandy asked. "When I asked Alice if you had a health problem, she seemed to know something. But she wouldn't tell me what it was, and said you swore the family to secrecy about it."

"Yes, they know," Diana said. "A couple of months ago, after we found out the chemo failed, Hal and I sat them down to tell them the news and talk about how the estate will be settled. Each of the three kids will get a fourth right away, with me getting the other fourth. We wanted them to know that they'll be comfortably well off and won't have to worry about anything after..." She bit her lip.

"After I'm gone." Hal patted her arm, and they turned and walked toward camp.

"Comfortably well off," Mandy said to Rob, after the couple was out of earshot. "There's a motive for you. A big inheritance. Either one of Alex's sisters could have killed him to make their share even larger."

A puzzled expression crept onto Rob's face. "That makes sense. But what about Elsa? Why go after her? And neither one of them was on the cliff with Elsa."

THIRTEEN

*The important thing to remember is that you're
dancing with the river—and you're not leading.*

—BOATMAN JOHN RUNNING

MANDY AND ROB GRABBED some pasta salad, then walked to where
the rafts bobbed in the water to eat a hurried lunch and to talk.
Mandy told Rob about her search. "Unfortunately, I didn't find either the bear paw or a hypodermic needle. And I never got to the
girlfriends' tent."

"They don't have a connection to either Alex or Elsa," Rob said,
"so maybe we can rule them out."

"That's why I left their tent for last," Mandy replied, "but I don't
think we can rule anyone out. Not yet."

Rob nodded solemnly. "True."

Mandy changed the subject. "I gather you didn't find anyone
up there."

"No, no hikers, and no evidence of campers, either. That couple we spotted yesterday must have just been passing through. They could be anywhere in the Maze now. I left Cool with the clients, and Gonzo, Kendra, and I split up and searched the whole Doll House area. We found nothing. I almost feel like I'm in one of those disaster movies, where the whole world's destroyed except for one small group of people."

Mandy shuddered. "More like the opposite. We're the disaster, and no one's around to help us."

"The only thing left to do is to keep moving down the river and make sure we rendezvous with our pick-up tomorrow morning." Rob ate his last bite of pasta salad and glanced at Mandy's watch. "I wanted to be on the river a half hour ago. Let's get moving. You ready the rafts and I'll ready the crew."

Mandy helped Kendra pack the kitchen gear. After they stowed it in the rafts, she checked the lashings on all of the other gear and on Alex's body bag in Rob's raft. Mandy wanted the ropes to be as tight as possible before hitting the rapids in Cataract Canyon.

"The last thing we need now is to lose Alex's body to the river after carrying it this far," she said to Kendra while tightening a knot. "His poor parents have been through enough."

When she got no response, she looked at Kendra and saw her fellow river guide was staring at the body bag. "You okay?"

"Why can't we smell him?" Kendra asked. "Shouldn't he be stinking by now?"

Mandy sat back on her haunches in Rob's raft. "Yeah, he is, plenty. But the bag's airtight, which keeps the odor from getting out." *Thank the river gods.*

They returned to the camp, where Rob was giving all of the clients a safety briefing and a review of paddling techniques. Cool and Gonzo circulated among the clients, checking their PFD straps and cinching them tight.

Les tugged on his PFD. "I can't breathe with this lifejacket so tight!"

"Our mantra is that if you can't breathe you can't drown," Cool said while rechecking Les's straps. He loosened the one over the middle of Les's chest a fraction of an inch. "We don't want the water ripping the PFD off you. How's that?"

"Not much better," Les grumbled.

After Cool's statement, though, no one else seemed inclined to complain. Mandy scanned their faces and recognized the familiar stink of nervous tension coming off the clients. As with all of her past whitewater rafting trip clients, eyes were bright, limbs couldn't keep still, and tongues were licking lips suddenly gone dry as they anticipated the excitement ahead. She hoped the only dangers they would face would be those posed by Mother Nature, not by their mysterious killer.

Rob finished his safety briefing with, "It may sound obvious, folks, but stay in the raft. If you have to, stop paddling to hold on. Okay, let's get this show on the river!" He turned and signaled for everyone to follow.

All of the clients had opted to try paddling the rapids, even Hal Anderson, so they piled into Kendra's and Gonzo's rafts. Cool joined Rob in his raft. Rob's raft was taking the lead position, and he needed Cool in the front. Since Cool had run the canyon multiple times, he and Rob would pick out the routes to run in each rapid.

Mandy took the sweep position in the rear since she would be running the canyon for the first time, having missed the scouting trip. She planned to watch the routes the other rafts took through the rapids before lining up her own. And, she was responsible for picking up any swimmers. She hoped there wouldn't be any.

When the flotilla rounded the sharp left turn the Colorado River made below Spanish Bottom, Mandy could hear the roar of the Brown Betty rapid. Her heart beat faster in anticipation, the adrenaline rush flushing her cheeks. She felt the familiar surge of joy, confidence, and pure power that kept bringing her back to whitewater for another fix.

Used to running the clear, blue-green waters of the Arkansas River, Mandy found the milk chocolate–colored waves of the Colorado disconcerting. But when she focused on the structures and features in the roiling water—the whitecaps glinting in the sunlight, the downstream and upstream Vs, the swirling holes—she began to feel at home. She watched Rob run Brown Betty cleanly and made a mental note of the turns and cross-river ferries he executed. Then she turned her attention to Kendra's and Gonzo's rafts.

Kendra's raft made a clean run, to the whoops and hollers of the passengers, then it was Gonzo's turn. Just as his raft reached the lip of the first drop, Paul let go of his paddle with one hand and grabbed the waterproof camera that hung on a lanyard around his neck.

Damn it, Mandy thought. *We told them more than once not to try to take photos while in the rapids.*

Paul compounded his error by raising himself to hold the camera above Tina's head in front of him.

Gonzo yelled, "Get down! Put your hand on your paddle!" at him to no avail.

The raft dove and smacked into the first standing wave of the rapid. As Mandy expected, the jolt pitched Paul out of the raft.

Gonzo had anticipated it, too. He shouted paddle instructions at the others in his raft and reached a hand out over the water. He tried to grab Paul as the raft bobbed past him.

But Paul was so disoriented he flailed away from the raft instead of toward it. He missed Gonzo's hand. After the raft passed him, Gonzo shouted at Paul to swim toward Mandy's raft.

Mandy gave up aiming for the rapid's ideal entry point. Hauling on her oars, she pointed her raft at Paul. She took a moment to cram the whistle tied to her PFD in her mouth and blow on it. She knew her voice wouldn't carry to Paul over the roar of the rapid, but she hoped he would hear the whistle.

Thankfully, he spun in the water as if searching for the origin of the whistle blast. When he saw her, he started dog paddling in her direction.

Good, Mandy thought, he's thinking clearly again.

When she got close enough, she yelled, "Grab the rope!"

Mandy angled her raft toward Paul so the side would graze him as they both bounced along one side of the rapid's train of standing waves. They had told the clients that if they fell in the river, they should immediately swim for the nearest raft and grab the rope running along the outside. They were to hang on for dear life and ride out the rapid that way until the raft guide or a passenger could haul them in.

When Mandy's raft hit him, Paul snatched frantically at the rope while waves crashed over his head, temporarily blinding him. He finally grabbed the rope with his left hand toward the back of the raft. Mandy pulled back on her oars, working against the current to slow the raft. She wanted to give Paul a chance to get his right hand on the rope before it was ripped out of the left.

She watched over her shoulder as Paul scrabbled for the rope. Finally, his right hand closed around it. Relieved, Mandy turned her attention to the rapid itself. The jagged edge of a mostly submerged massive boulder approached on Paul's side of the raft.

Shit!

Mandy hauled like a demon on the oars so they would skirt the rock with enough room for Paul to avoid getting hurt. Once they were past that, she saw that they had reached the short lull between Upper and Lower Brown Betty. She boated the oars and clambered back to where Paul was hanging on.

She knelt and grabbed the shoulders of his PFD. "On the count of three, kick hard and push up on your hands."

He did as he was told, and Mandy yanked as hard as she could. His upper body flopped over the pontoon. With Mandy pulling on his PFD, he managed to get a leg over and roll the rest of the way into the raft. He lay there panting.

"Stay there and hold on," Mandy yelled at him.

She leapt back into position between her oars.

Just in time, she plunged the blades back in the water while the raft dove over the lip of the next rapid. Water poured over the front and flooded the raft's floor. They rode that wave out, then Mandy spied the other rafts waiting for her in a quiet eddy on river right. She spun her raft in their direction and joined them. Rob grabbed the front rope of her raft. Safe at last, she rested her oars and took several deep breaths.

Looking sheepish, Paul climbed forward from the back of the raft. "Sorry about that."

"There's a good reason we told you not to take photos in the rapids," Rob said to him, his chin jutting out in anger. "As you found out, you not only put yourself in danger, you endangered others—the rest of the people in your raft as they tried to rescue you, and Mandy in the sweep raft."

With his face drooping as much as his wet clothing, Paul said with contrition, "I won't do it again."

"No, you won't," Rob said. "And if you do, I'll personally throw your camera in the river."

Mandy noticed Les tucking his waterproof camera under his PFD. He was smart enough to learn from Paul's example, at least. In fact, everyone looked a little shaken and apprehensive. There were no gleeful smiles like she normally saw after folks ran their first big rapid.

Rob had come down awfully hard on Paul. Why was that? Then it dawned on her. Rob had mentioned her name specifically. His macho protective instinct had reared its head, chewed up Paul, and spit him out. It was time to lighten the mood.

"Hey, no harm done," Mandy said. "Paul's wet but safe, and we all made it through our first big rapid. Let's hear a war whoop!"

She pumped her fist in the air and whooped. Gonzo and Kendra immediately joined her, with the others soon following. During the hollering, she caught Rob's eye and mouthed "lighten up" to him and drew a big smile on her face.

He got the message and grinned, but there was a hint of menace behind those pearly whites. No one messed with his gal.

Paul scrambled across the rafts back into his position in Gonzo's raft, then looked around him. His shoulders fell and he said, "Crap, I lost my paddle."

"No worries." Gonzo pulled a paddle out of bundle lashed inside his raft. "That's why we carry extras."

Paul accepted the paddle. "Again, I'm sorry."

Gonzo gave him a friendly clap on the shoulder. "Hey, someone has to make the first mistake. It just happened to be your unlucky day and you wound up with the short straw." He laughed good-naturedly and Paul visibly relaxed.

With everyone's mood now a little lighter, Mandy put her hands on her oars and said, "Well, I'm ready for some more roller coaster rides. How about the rest of you?"

Kendra and Gonzo grabbed their paddles and their passengers followed their leads. With a last exasperated eye roll at Mandy, Rob leaned on his oars and peeled out of the eddy to lead the way through Rapid Three.

The next four river miles flashed by with a steady stream of rapids—long jostling drops and rocking horse rides on haystacks made of water that periodically doused the rafters were interspersed with short recovery pools. All of the rafts managed to surf the rapids cleanly without swimmers or capsizes. While running them, Mandy had time to wonder whether she had just saved the life of the killer.

————

Later that afternoon, they came out of Rapid Ten into what Cool and his fellow local guides called Lake Cataract, a three-mile section of swift-moving but relatively flat water. It was punctuated by just two rapids, Eleven and Twelve, in the middle. It was the only long calm section of water in Cataract Canyon before they reached Lake Powell.

Everyone relaxed a little, and Mandy and her fellow guides were able to let down their guard some. Clients wrung out their wet hair and clothes and angled their faces to the sun. Paul and Les fished out their cameras and took photos of the striated canyon walls looming over them and of the people in the rafts.

After running Rapid Twelve, Rob beached his raft on a wide strip of sand on river left. Kendra, Gonzo, and Mandy beached their rafts a short distance downriver, and Rob and Cool walked over to meet them.

"We'll take a brief rest stop here," Rob announced. "Then everyone should prepare themselves for what's called Mile Long Rapid. It's really almost two miles of eight rapids, numbered Thirteen through Twenty. In high water, they run together to form one long monster rapid. We don't want any mistakes here because it could mean a really long, hard swim for anyone who ends up in the water."

Diana looked worriedly at the lowering sun. "How much longer before we stop for the night?"

"We plan to get all the way through Cataract Canyon today and camp at Waterhole Canyon," Mandy said. "That's about seven miles downriver, but as you can see, the river's moving fast here. We've already gone seven miles since Spanish Bottom."

Les whistled. "We're really chugging down the Colorado. So we're going to run the Big Drops today?"

Cool grinned. "You've heard about them, huh? The river's got some real attitude in those honkers."

Rob nodded. "We've got a lot of excitement ahead. But as long as we don't have any major spills, we should reach the campsite with enough light left to pitch tents and cook supper."

After a few more minutes, Rob whistled and waved for everyone to return to the rafts, and they were on their way. The river bent to the right and to the left, then the roar of churning whitewater greeted them again, echoing off the canyon walls. Mandy braced herself for the long run.

All of the rafts ran rapids Thirteen and Fourteen cleanly, but Rapid Fifteen held a special danger for rafters at low water levels. Capsize Rock jutted out of the seething river. As water collided with it, rooster tails fountained into the air. The rock had a reputation for seeming to reach out and grab rafts and wrap them around itself. Cool had told Mandy to steer clear of it, so when she saw Kendra's raft with the Anderson family aboard drift toward it, Mandy's mouth went dry.

Kendra yelled frantically for her crew to paddle. She ruddered as hard as she could on her rear paddle to turn the raft away, but to no avail. The powerful water smacked the raft against the rock. It flipped, spilling out bodies.

For a heart-stopping moment, the raft clung to the rock. Mandy wondered if it was pinned. She hoped no one was stuck underneath it, which would be life-threatening. Then the raft slowly slipped off. It spun upside-down in the frothy brown standing waves below the rock.

Heads bobbed in the water on either side of the raft. Mandy tried to count them, but she couldn't. She was particularly worried about Hal Anderson, whose health was already fragile.

Gonzo's raft, just ahead of Kendra's, moved toward one of the bobbing swimmers. Someone in his raft pulled the swimmer out of the water. Rob oared his raft toward a couple more swimmers on the other side.

Mandy pushed on her oars to propel herself into the maw of the hungry rapid. She aimed for swimmers while trying to steer clear of the treacherous rock. She managed to skirt it and catch up to Amy and Alice Anderson flailing in the water. She yelled at them to grab her ropes.

Alice snatched the rope right away, but Amy missed. She kept trying, while Mandy back-oared like mad to keep the raft abreast of her.

Mandy wondered why Amy was having so much trouble and why her sister didn't reach out and help her. Maybe Alice was too afraid to let go of the rope, even with one hand. Finally, Amy managed to grab on.

With both women holding on, Mandy snatched a peek at Rapid Sixteen coming up. "You'll have to ride it out through this," she yelled to the women, "then I'll haul you in."

Neither one replied as they gaped wide-eyed at the looming waves.

The answer from the river was a smack in Mandy's face with a wave of brown water. Mandy spit and blinked. Once she could see again, she hauled on her oars. Praying that the two women could hang on, she steered for calmer water to the side of the river.

She kept an eye out for pillows, water piled up on the upstream side of submerged boulders that might crash into her swimmers, and maneuvered the now sluggish raft to avoid a couple. She also scanned the water for more swimmers. She didn't see any and hoped everyone had been rescued.

When Mandy reached a momentary break in the rocking waves, she abandoned the oars. She moved first to Amy, the weaker of the two sisters. She grabbed the shoulders of Amy's PFD and quickly hauled her into the raft. Then she did the same for Alice, whose powerful kick helped propel her into the raft.

Mandy leapt back into her place between the oars, leaving it to the women to find seats and handholds on the raft. She steered them through Rapids Seventeen through Twenty, gaining a few more dousings in the process.

Then she aimed for river left, where she knew Big Drop Beach awaited. She saw that some of their clients had already been dropped off there.

Somehow Kendra's raft had been righted. She and Cool were in it, paddling toward shore. Rob and Gonzo plied the undulating water with their rafts, with Les and Viv hanging over the fronts. They were scouting for loose gear and snagging it as it floated by. That meant all of the people had been accounted for. Mandy silently thanked the river gods.

Mandy hit the beach and hauled her raft onto the sand. Alice and Amy spilled out of her raft and helped her pull it in, then all three of them collapsed on the beach.

After sucking air for a minute, Mandy scrambled back to her feet. She scanned the others flopped down in the sand and found Diana and Hal. "You okay? Anyone injured?"

"What a ride!" Hal panted, but that seemed to be all he could get out. At least his face wasn't white.

"We're okay," Diana answered. "We all made it out, but Les has a bloody scrape on his leg."

"Why's he back out in the raft, then?" Mandy asked.

"He's frantic about finding the dry bag with his expensive camera gear in it," Diana said.

Alice sucked in a breath between clenched teeth. "Oh shit. They'd better find it."

Mandy shielded her eyes from the sun and looked out at the river. Gonzo and Viv were paddling Gonzo's raft toward the beach. Rob was oaring his raft back in, while Les cradled a dry bag in his lap. "Maybe he's got it."

After the other two rafts landed and were pulled onto the beach, it was time to take stock. Kendra insisted on cleaning and bandaging Les's leg, since it was "her fault" he had been hurt. Mandy and Rob double-checked the others to make sure adrenaline wasn't masking the pain of any other injuries. Cool and Gonzo inventoried the gear they had salvaged and retied it into Kendra's raft.

While the clients sucked on water bottles, the guides held a conclave. "We lost Kendra's extra paddles," Gonzo said, "but we recovered all the dry bags that were in her raft. Not too bad." He put an arm around her shoulders.

Kendra looked crestfallen. "I messed up bad. Les's and Alice's paddles got tangled up, so that side of the raft wasn't helping at all. But still, I shouldn't have gone so close to Capsize Rock. I'm sorry. I remembered it from our scouting trip, but it's so much bigger in low water."

"Hey," Mandy said. "None of us are perfect. And the whole team worked together well to recover from it. Don't blame yourself."

"The river gods were just out to get you today," Rob said. "Tomorrow they'll be after someone else."

Hopefully not, Mandy thought. Hopefully tomorrow their motorized launch would meet them at Waterhole Canyon and extract them. They could contact civilization again and arrange for Alex's body to be taken care of. And they could get away from the silent killer in their midst and leave it to the police to figure out who it was.

But first, they had to make it through the worst part of the river.

"Should we just camp here for the night?" Cool asked. "A lot has happened today, and folks might need a rest."

"We need to make sure everyone can change out of their wet clothes before the sun sets and the temperature drops," Kendra added. "Already the river's mostly in shadow."

Rob's brow furrowed. "You're both making sense, but I'd feel a lot better pushing on to our rendezvous site. I wouldn't want the launch to miss us, particularly since we have no way to communicate with it."

"I agree," Mandy said. She checked her watch. "We still have a couple of hours of daylight left. But some of our clients may be too tuckered out to paddle well. Especially Hal. Let's offer them seats in our oar rafts."

"Good idea," Rob said. "We all agreed?"

Cool, Gonzo, and Kendra nodded.

Rob waved a hand toward the river. "Let's move on, then."

They broke up and gathered the clients around them. "We're about to head into the biggest water in Cataract Canyon," Rob said. "If anyone wants to get out of a paddle raft and sit this last section out in an oar raft, you're more than welcome to. We'll move gear if we have to."

Diana raised a hand. "Hal and I would like to move."

Mandy breathed a sigh of relief. She had been prepared to suggest it strongly to them.

Les stepped forward, holding onto his precious dry bag with one hand and to his half-drowned precious wife with the other. "Amy and I would like to move, too. We'll sit in your raft, Mandy."

Mandy was surprised Les didn't want to paddle the three Big Drop rapids, but she supposed that Amy's swim had frightened her and she had talked him into sitting it out with her. "Anyone else?"

No one else wanted to move.

Rob took Diana and Hal to his raft and Mandy took Les and Amy to hers. They were soon all launched and heading down the long V of accelerating current leading to Big Drop One.

"Hey diddle, diddle, right down the middle," Cool called out over the increasing roar of the squeezed funnel of water rushing over the horizon line.

Rob had coached Mandy to aim for the middle of the rapid to avoid the nasty pour overs and rock piles on both sides. That line also set the rafts up for an awesome ride atop the wave train at the end. She followed his lead, after Kendra's and Gonzo's rafts, and she heard whoops and hollers from the other rafts over the roar of the whitewater.

On her own raft, Les and Amy were silent, with Les clutching Amy tightly. Mandy concluded Amy must have been really traumatized by her swim. *Poor thing.*

Mandy eddied out to the left above Big Drop Two. Rob's raft cut right just below the large dome-shaped Marker Rock in the middle of the river. He aimed straight for Little Niagara, a massive falls to the right of Marker Rock. The goal was to ride the raft along the edge of its current, missing both the ledge hole below Marker Rock and "the Claw" on the left, a big hole with a huge wave curling over the top of it, ready to pounce on rafts.

It was a tricky maneuver, Rob had told her, and it would give their raft passengers a gut-clenching view of Little Niagara they would never forget. Mandy hoped Amy could stomach it.

With no place to pull out between Big Drop Two and Three, Rob continued on. Kendra's and Gonzo's rafts followed Rob's expert line and made it through cleanly, then bobbed down to Big Drop Three. Finally, it was Mandy's turn.

She took a deep breath and pulled on her oars to position the raft. The river grabbed hold of her raft and shoved it down the steep drop beside Marker Rock almost before Mandy could react. She quickly hauled on the oars, heading right for Little Niagara.

While the falls crashed and thundered in front of her, her belly tightened. She couldn't imagine how anyone could survive in the thrashing whitewater at the bottom. She felt the current grab the raft and send it in the right direction. She was about to line up to miss the ledge hole when the raft bounced hard.

What was that? She glanced at the front of the raft.

Amy was gone.

FOURTEEN

You drown not by falling into a river, but by staying submerged in it.
—PAULO COELHO

MANDY GLANCED AT THE base of Little Niagara. Amy bobbed face-up in the churning water, arms and legs dangling loosely as if she was unconscious. *Shit!*

Then the raft shot past, heading straight for the ledge hole. Mandy shoved on the oars, spinning the raft away from the hole. Her mind was spinning, too. How was she going to rescue Amy?

Les pointed at Amy and hollered. "Amy fell in!"

Mandy yelled back, "I'll head for her. You get ready to pull her in!"

Les nodded and got on his knees in the front of the raft.

Mandy spun the raft to face upstream. She oared against the current as hard as she could to slow the raft's downriver progress and ferry it across the river. The cross currents and boils made the raft buck like a rodeo bronco. She struggled to make corrections and keep the raft on course. She had to get in the right position to catch Amy once the boiling mess below Little Niagara spit her out.

After a few more muscle-straining hauls on the oars, Mandy saw Amy come out of the foam. She bobbed down the undulating river directly toward them.

"Grab her!" Mandy shouted at Les.

He reached out and snatched the shoulders of Amy's PFD, exactly as they had trained the clients to do. He dunked her in the water, a little deep, Mandy thought, but again, they had told them to do that. The swimmer's natural buoyancy would work together with the rescuer pulling from the raft to pop the swimmer out of the water.

Then Les fell backward into the raft. "Christ! I lost her!"

"We'll try again," Mandy shouted.

Les shook his head while he righted himself.

Thinking he was giving up hope, Mandy said, "Don't worry. We'll get her!"

Using his paddle as a third balance point, Les started climbing back in the bucking raft toward Mandy.

What was he doing? Mandy wondered if he had tried to say something to her and she missed it. He was probably worried to death about his wife.

Mandy yelled at him, "Sit down, Les! I'll go back for Amy!"

She glanced behind her, peering for Amy's body in the water.

When she turned back, Les was standing right in front of her. Before Mandy could register what he was doing there, he whacked her on the head with his paddle.

Reeling and confused, all Mandy could think was, *Why did he do that?*

As he lifted the paddle again, Mandy dropped the oars and instinctively raised her arms to protect herself.

He whacked her again on the shoulder, sending her flying into the river.

She smacked into the brown water and was instantly alert. Water filled her mouth, and the current pushed her underwater. Her body was churned and spun until she didn't know which end was up.

Mandy desperately searched for light and clawed her way toward it. Just as her lungs were about to burst, she popped out of the water. A standing wave smacked her in the face. Then another. Finally, she was able to spit out the gritty water in her mouth and suck in a breath of air.

She got oriented with her feet downstream, fended off a couple of boulders and rode out a few more head-crashing waves. When she could see something other than roiling brown water and whitecaps, she looked downstream. Les was at the oars of her raft, heading for Big Drop Three.

Not coming back for her or Amy!

Amy! She spun and searched the river. *There.* In the water behind her, Mandy spied a bright orange PFD.

Mandy turned and swam toward Amy's motionless form. She kicked and kicked and cycled her arms as hard as she could until inch-by-inch she made progress toward Amy's slackened body. Thankfully, the collar of the PFD had done its job, turning Amy's face up and out of the water so she floated on her back.

Mandy reached for Amy's leg first and grabbed hold of it to pull herself closer. She shook the woman's shoulder and shouted, "Amy!"

But Amy's eyes were closed, and she was unresponsive.

Mandy looped an arm through the shoulder strap of Amy's PFD so she wouldn't lose her, then glanced downstream. They were headed straight for Big Drop Three, home of the infamous Satan's Gut, a huge, deadly whirlpool.

Mandy frantically tried to remember what Rob had told her about running Big Drop Three. It was a river-wide boulder field. She sure didn't want Amy and herself pinging off rocks. Rob had said there was a narrow chute, the "Highway to Heaven." But where was it?

River left!

Mandy rolled onto her back. She pulled with one arm and kicked with her feet toward the left side of the river while dragging Amy with her other arm. Then she remembered that the chute was between a huge green rock named Big Mossy and Satan's Gut itself. She spied Big Mossy's green bulk jutting out of the water and aimed for it.

While she huffed and puffed and swam all out, Mandy wondered if she should have gone right instead and taken her chances with the boulder field. If she couldn't reach the chute before the two of them were swept over the drop, they would wind up churning in Satan's Gut.

Too late. She had committed to this course of action. She just *had* to make the chute.

Mandy swam until her muscles screamed in pain. *Hell, this is it. We'll both die in that whirlpool.*

Then a calm, masculine voice spoke in her head. "You can do it, Mandy."

She felt a renewed surge of strength and swam some more, gritting her teeth against the burning in her arms and legs. Big Mossy loomed closer and closer. Mandy prayed she would make it.

With a whoosh, the current swept them over the drop. They bounced and rolled. Mandy's arm looped in Amy's PFD felt like it was being ripped off, but she held on tight. Water splashed in her face. She couldn't see where they were.

Please, not in Satan's Gut.

Soon they were bouncing down a wave train at the bottom of the chute—the Highway to Heaven. Relieved, Mandy spit out a mouthful of water and sucked in a deep breath. They had made it! She remembered the voice, and silently thanked her late Uncle Bill for buoying her up once again when she was in trouble in a river.

She took a moment to gather her strength, then swam to the left again. She had to get Amy to shore before they were swept into rapids Twenty-Four and Twenty-Five, which roared downstream.

Finally, when Mandy feared she couldn't lift her arm one more time, she felt river bottom beneath her dragging feet. She pushed off, angling toward shore. When they reached still water less than knee-deep that was safe to stand in, Mandy stumbled to her feet. She grabbed Amy under the armpits and dragged her to shore.

Once they were out of the water, Mandy flopped down beside Amy, panting, and checked Amy's vitals. She was breathing but still out of it. Mandy shouted Amy's name and patted her arm until the woman's eyes fluttered.

"Wha?" Amy's eyes opened and searched unfocused around her. Then she moaned as if in pain and closed her eyes again.

Mandy gently shook her arm. "Amy! Amy, wake up. Where does it hurt?"

"L-leg," Amy mumbled.

Mandy scooted toward Amy's legs and ran her hands along each one. Then she felt it. A bump on Amy's calf signaled a bone break that hadn't broken through the skin. It was starting to bruise and swell, too, from internal bleeding.

Mandy looked around and spotted a pile of driftwood. Too tired to walk, she crawled over on hands and knees. She gathered a few strong straight branches that were at least a couple of feet long in one arm.

She crawled back to Amy and laid the smoothest two branches on either side of the break, then reached into her first-aid fanny pack. Mandy always kept some large rubber bands there. She looped the bands around the branches and Amy's calf to hold the splint in place.

By the time she finished, Amy's eyes were open again. Her gaze roamed the beach. "Where am I?"

"We're on a beach below the Big Drop rapids." Mandy searched downriver to see if anyone was coming back for them, but she saw no people or rafts.

Amy shifted slightly, eliciting a grimace and moan.

Mandy held her in place. "Don't move."

After a couple of breaths between gritted teeth, Amy asked, "What happened?"

"I pulled you out of the river after you went overboard in Big Drop Two. Do you remember how you fell in?"

Amy frowned as if thinking back, then her eyes grew wide. "Les!"

"What about Les?"

"I don't know why, but he stuck a needle in me just before we went over the first Big Drop." Her hand moved to touch her neck.

Mandy bent over Amy's neck. She saw a needle prick mark, with reddened skin around it, much like the one on Alex's neck.

A stark realization jelled in her mind. Les had killed Alex, making it look like an accident, and he had just tried to kill his wife the same way. And herself! When he realized that Mandy wouldn't give up trying to rescue Amy, Les must have decided he had to get rid of her, too. He probably hoped to stun her by whacking her in the head before he knocked her in the water. He wanted her to drown along with Amy.

Lucky thing I have a thick skull.

Mandy checked Amy's pupils. They seemed somewhat dilated, but they were at least the same size. "What happened after he stuck you?"

Amy wiped a hand across her forehead. "I got real sleepy." She yawned. "I'm still woozy. Head hurts, too. And my leg."

"I put a splint on your leg. You've got a break, probably from hitting a rock in the river. I bet your head hurts from whatever sedative Les used."

"Sedative?" Confusion wrinkled Amy's brow.

Mandy hoped the sedative wouldn't have any long-term effects. "Do you remember what happened next—after you got sleepy?"

"I don't know. I couldn't talk. I remember him holding me and the raft bouncing. Then wham, I was in the water and all wet, but I couldn't stay awake. I kept drifting off."

"Do you think Les pushed you in?"

Amy looked at Mandy in alarm. "No. He wouldn't. He couldn't have."

Taking a deep breath, Mandy decided it was time to be blunt with Amy. "He may have been trying to kill you."

"What?"

"I didn't see how you got in the water. But when I moved the raft over to you, so Les could pull you out, he dunked you under the water instead, then let go."

"Why would he do that?"

Mandy shrugged. "I'm confused about why, too. Rob and I figured Alex might have been murdered by someone in the family for your father's inheritance. But—"

"Murdered? I thought a bear mauled him!"

"No, Alex had a needle mark on his neck—just like you. The claw marks were suspicious, too. They were from a grizzly paw, and only black bears live here. And all the paw prints were from the same paw—the front left. We think the whole bear attack was staged, including sabotaging the radio, so we couldn't call out for help."

"Staged? I don't understand." Amy tried to prop herself up on her elbows, then fell back onto the sand. "Whoa, dizzy."

"Don't get up. But try to stay awake."

Amy frowned. "Wait, you're saying Les killed Alex and tried to kill me? That's crazy! I'm his wife. Les would never hurt me."

"Yes, it sounds crazy, but that needle mark in your neck says different. Les drugged you, pushed you overboard, and knocked me in the water. Then he took off in the raft and left us both to drown."

"Ohmigod!" Amy fingered her neck as what Mandy was telling her finally seemed to sink in. Her eyes reddened. "But why . . . ?"

With a nod, Mandy said, "That's what I don't understand. Why would Les try to kill you? Are you two having problems?"

"Yeah, some, but . . . murder?"

"What about money problems?"

"I don't know. Les handles our finances. But I don't think so. He hasn't told me to cut back on shopping."

"Does he have a big insurance policy on you?"

Amy shook her head.

Mandy chewed her lip while she tried to think. "Maybe he's after the share of the estate you'll get after your father dies. But wait, that doesn't make sense. If you die before your father, Les doesn't get any of the inheritance."

Amy blew out a breath. "God … maybe … but no." She shook her head then winced. "They wouldn't resort to killing."

"They? Who's they?"

Amy stared at Mandy for a long while, and Mandy could almost see the gears turning in her mind. Finally, Amy blurted out, "Alice and Les. Les is having an affair with Alice."

This new revelation sent Mandy reeling. She sat back on her heels. "What?"

Amy nodded. Tears welled up and ran down the sides of her face. "I saw them together last week, and, and …" She put a hand over her mouth to stifle a sob.

Mandy rubbed Amy's arm. "I'm sorry."

Sucking in a deep breath, Amy looked up at the strip of blue sky between the sheer canyon walls, obviously trying to pull herself together. She sniffed and continued. "They were having lunch together at a restaurant in the mall. I was supposed to be at a massage appointment, but my therapist was sick and had to cancel. So I went to the mall to look for these."

She raised her unsplinted leg to show off her water sandals. "I saw Les and Alice in the restaurant just as they stood to leave. I was going to go over and join them. Then they kissed. It wasn't a quick peck, like brother to sister, it was *passionate*! Tongues and everything." Amy made a face.

"Did they see you?" Mandy asked.

"Oh no." Amy shook her head furiously. "I didn't know what to do, so I ran off and hid behind a big planter. They walked right past me, and he said to her, 'I'll see you tomorrow at eight.'"

Amy grabbed Mandy's hand. "The next day was Wednesday, Les's poker night. He plays at eight—or he's supposed to be playing poker at eight. So, I didn't say anything to him, but I followed him the next night. He drove right past his poker buddy's house and went straight to Alice's."

"Did you confront him?"

"Nooo," Amy wailed. "I didn't know what to do. I can't live without Les. He takes care of me."

Yeah, in more ways than one, Mandy thought. "Amy, I noticed that Les seems to treat you pretty rough. That's where those bruises on your thighs came from, right?"

Amy bit her lip and nodded. "But he's not that bad. It's usually just when he's had too much to drink."

Which on this trip had been every night, in Mandy's opinion.

"I know he loves me!" Amy shouted. Desperation roughened her voice. "This thing with Alice is just a sordid fling. He'll get over it soon."

"If he's resorting to murder," Mandy said, "it's not just a fling."

The weight of that statement settled on them and quieted them both for a while.

Mandy did some thinking, then said, "Les didn't kill Alex because of a fling—or even a love affair. If his motive was love, he could have just asked you for a divorce. No, I think Les's plan was to get rid of both you and Alex on this trip, making both deaths look like accidents—in your case, a drowning, and in Alex's, a bear attack. That's why he sabotaged the radio when he killed Alex. He needed the trip to continue so he could kill you, too. Then he planned to marry Alice. She would inherit all of the money, and they'd live the high life."

Amy's brows knitted together. "So he did this for money, not love."

To Mandy, the statement sounded pathetically hopeful.

Then Amy gasped. "Maybe Alice is just using Les, pretending to love him, so he'd help her in this scheme. That would be like Alice. When we were kids, she always resented having to share with her little sister and brother."

"There's another possibility," Mandy said. "That Les is the one using Alice. We don't have any evidence that Alice is involved in the murders. Les could be acting all on his own. He may not even have any attraction for Alice at all."

Amy stared at Mandy. When her expression darkened, Mandy realized that Amy was reaching the conclusion that Mandy had already made—Les had been using her, too.

"No, no." Amy's tears started flowing again. She clamped her lips tight and hugged herself.

The action made Mandy realize that the air was getting chilly. The afternoon sun had slid behind the canyon wall across the river, and the long shadow had reached them. She glanced at her watch. She estimated over forty-five minutes had passed since she had dragged Amy to shore.

Where were the others? Why hadn't they come back to look for them yet? All of the guides were trained to go back upriver if they lost anyone, to find them and rescue them, no matter what story Les came up with. And if Les hadn't reached the group, they would come back searching for all three of them. Mandy decided some problem downriver must have held them up.

Then she had an awful thought. What if Les had beached the raft before reaching the others and was on his way back upstream to make sure she and Amy were dead? If he reached them before the others did, she and Amy would have to fight for their lives. She stood, straining her aching muscles, and carefully scanned the banks on both sides of the river. She saw no movement.

She realized that there was no way for Les to approach them unseen along the long, flat beach they were on, so if he came for them, they would have warning. She picked up a couple of strong lengths of driftwood and laid them at the ready nearby. That was the best she could do to prepare, other than continually scanning the banks downriver. In the meantime, with the temperature dropping, she and Amy were susceptible to hypothermia in their wet clothes.

"I'll get a fire going," Mandy said to Amy. "We've got to get dry and try to stay warm until rescue comes."

She made multiple trips up and down the beach until she had a large pile of driftwood and broken branches. Then she knelt near Amy to construct a small wood teepee around a waxy fire starter block that she took out of her fanny pack. Mandy lit the block with her fireproof matches. She kept feeding larger and larger pieces of wood onto the blaze until she had a good-sized fire going.

Then Mandy helped Amy to a sitting position. "Once your clothes are dry on the side facing the fire, I'll help you flip over so the other side gets dry."

Exhausted, she stood with her hands warming over the blaze and searched the shadows of the darkening canyon downriver. *Where the hell are the others?*

————

"I think I'm going to have to hike out," Mandy said to Amy two hours later.

They were sitting hunched over the fire, in the dark, cold, hungry, and thirsty. There had been no sign of the others coming upstream to look for them. Or, thank the river gods, of Les. Still, something was definitely wrong.

Amy winced as she shifted position to warm her other side. "Why hasn't anyone come for us?"

"I don't know. They should have." Mandy knew that all of the guides would have been driven to look for them. Rob, especially, would have come as soon as he could. He loved her! He would never abandon her. Unless…

"Something—or someone—has to be preventing them from coming." A looming dread crept into Mandy's thoughts. She peered at Amy. "What does Les have in that camera bag that he always keeps with him? Is he carrying a weapon?"

Amy stared at Mandy in disbelief. "You think Les is stopping them?"

Or has already killed them. But Mandy refused to believe that. The thought was too horrible to accept.

"Either that," she said to Amy, "or a landslide dammed the river. Which we should have heard. And since the water level hasn't changed, it couldn't have happened." Mandy held out her hands palms-up. "What else could be the reason?"

"Maybe the guides decided to keep moving, to go on to Lake Powell and send someone else back for us."

Mandy shook her head. "That's not our training. We rescue first, make sure someone who's hurt, like you are, is stable, before we go for help. They have no idea whether we're alive or dead or hurt. They'd find out first. So, back to my question. What does Les have in that camera bag?"

"I don't know," Amy wailed. "He kept it with him all the time. Said he didn't want me messing with it because his expensive camera gear was in it."

"That makes me even more suspicious." Mandy hugged her knees close to her chest. "Les probably kept the bear claw and hypos in there, and whatever sedative he used on you and Alex. He was hoping to make your and your brother's deaths look like accidents—and I got in the way."

Then an idea formed in her head. "Or he overheard Rob and me talking, or me talking to Betsy, and learned that I suspected Alex's death wasn't an accident. So he decided to get rid of me, too."

"I still can't believe he'd do something like that," Amy whispered.

Mandy remembered Les's grim, determined expression when he struck her with his paddle. "I can."

And if Les overheard her talking to Rob about Alex, he would go after Rob, too. If it came to hand-to-hand combat, Rob could probably defend himself against Les, but not if Les was able to inject him

215

with the sedative first—or if he had a gun. She turned to Amy. "Does Les own a gun?"

Amy nodded. "Yeah, he has a couple of handguns and some hunting rifles."

"If I was Les, I'd be carrying a handgun with me, in that camera bag, in case the plan went wrong or someone found out." Mandy could no longer tamp down her fear for Rob. She leapt to her feet. "I've got to go. I have to stop him from hurting Rob or anyone else."

If he hasn't already. But Mandy had to have hope to cling to. *Stop it!*

"I don't want to be left here alone." Renewed tears dribbled down Amy's cheeks. "It's not safe."

"You're safer than the others, who have a killer among them. And if I don't go and warn them and get help for all of us, the two of us might never be found here." Mandy dug in her fanny pack, took out a thin folded space blanket and an energy bar and handed them to Amy. "I'll leave these with you. Bundle up in the space blanket and keep the fire fed, so you'll stay warm tonight. If you get hungry nibble on this. Don't eat it all at once."

"I'll go with you." Amy pushed on her hands, struggling to rise.

Mandy put a restraining hand on Amy's shoulder. "You can't travel with that broken leg. It's safest for you if you stay. If you try to walk on it, you could hurt yourself more, or tear an artery in your leg and bleed to death."

"I'm scared."

"So am I." *For us, yes, but especially for Rob.*

Mandy reached down and hugged Amy. "I'm sorry, but this is our only option. I can't stay, and you can't go. I promise that I'll come back for you or send someone for you as soon as I can." She stared into Amy's wide, pleading eyes. "I promise."

Then she turned and headed downriver, into the dark unknown.

FIFTEEN

The man who is swimming against
the stream knows the strength of it.
—WOODROW T. WILSON

MANDY TRIPPED OVER A boulder in the dark and fell down once again with an "oof." She lay there cursing her clumsiness until a stone under her stomach made itself known. She wiggled on the sand until at least that part of her wasn't resting on rocks. Her body felt like it had spent time in a washing machine full of cement blocks on fast-spin cycle. The beatings came from her swim in Big Drop Three, clambering over rock piles and through willow thickets, and her frequent falls in the dark while hiking.

One side of her brain pleaded for rest, begged to lie there just for a few minutes. But the other side knew that would be a fatal mistake. With a groan, she sat up.

She pressed the light button on her waterproof watch and saw that she had been stumbling downriver for over an hour. The moon wasn't yet visible in the thin wedge of star-studded black sky that sliced through the towering canyon walls, so she had had to rely on starlight to pick her way. She had estimated that the distance between the beach where she left Amy and Waterhole Canyon, where the group had planned to camp, was about three miles. If she had been walking on a flat trail in daylight, she would have been there in less than an hour. But from what she remembered of the river map, she had gone only half that distance.

Damn.

Of course, Mandy had no idea if the others actually were at Waterhole Canyon. She tried to put herself in Les's mind, figure out what he would do. What was his exit strategy? She could only hope that he still planned to rendezvous the next morning with their pick-up motor launch.

At least Mandy had a pretty good idea where she was. She had passed two dry, rock-strewn ditches in the sand, indicating small side canyons that sometimes dumped water into the Colorado River after rains. And she had been listening to and observing the river beside her. She had passed the roar of three long rapids, and she was still alongside the third one. So, she figured she was at Rapid Twenty-Six.

But she had yet to cross a large ditch that would indicate she had reached Imperial Canyon, a mile upstream from Waterhole Canyon. Just past that was where she planned to make a swim across the swift-flowing Colorado River, which she'd been dreading.

Mandy rubbed her chilled arms. If she was cold now, she would be freezing after the swim. But Waterhole Canyon was on the other side of the river. If she wanted to sneak into camp, she had to make the river crossing a fair distance upstream.

And that's what she planned to do. Sneak into the camp—if they were there. Try to find Rob's tent and hopefully him in it, figure out what was going on and what to do next. She refused to listen to the fearful small voice in her head that whispered Les may have already killed Rob—and possibly the other guides. And if the man was really that crazed or desperate, the other clients, too. No, she had to believe that Rob and the others were still alive.

She licked her dry lips and pushed herself to her feet. *Onward*, she told her sore legs. She took one step, then another and started moving again.

Finally, Mandy approached a large ditch with a trickle of mud at the bottom. She searched the canyon wall to her left and thought she saw a break in the outline of its looming, dark expanse against the starry sky. She gingerly picked her way across the ditch, scrambled up the other side, then stopped and scanned the canyon rim again, hugging herself against the bitter cold. Yes, there was a large divot in the jagged edge, indicating a sizable side canyon.

She walked a little farther, and the river to her right quieted again. "Okay," she told herself, "that means I've gone past Imperial Canyon and Rapid Twenty-Six. Next is Rapid Twenty-seven, then I swim." She remembered Rob saying that the gap between Rapids Twenty-Seven and Twenty-Eight was fairly long, so that was her best option for a safe swim.

She shuddered at the prospect, but pushed on. When she passed a cottonwood tree, a loud hooting overhead startled her. Looking up she saw two glowing yellow eyes focused on her. A great horned owl. Normally she would be excited to see one, but at that moment she hoped it wasn't an ominous sign. Many Native American tribes in the west believed that the owls carried the souls of the dead to the underworld.

Mandy hoped this one wasn't waiting for her soul.

Soon thereafter, she heard the roar of Rapid Twenty-Seven. She hiked along its length, fell once and skinned her knee, then reached a point where the river quieted. She walked to the water and stood there looking across the Colorado. It flowed by, powerful and almost silent, with just a few undulations breaking its smooth shiny black surface. She couldn't see the river bank on the other side.

She stepped into the water and felt the cool current slide across her toes. It was actually warmer than the air, but she dreaded the swim. There was the danger of soaking herself and coming out wet into the cold air on the other side, inviting hypothermia. And, there was the risk of hitting something in the river in the dark and injuring herself or knocking herself out. Or, the risk of not making it to the other side before she was swept into Rapid Twenty-Eight. Or…

Stop it!

Mandy had no choice. She took a deep breath and waded in. When the water came over her knees, she sank down and launched herself out into the current on her stomach. She gasped as the icy water soaked her nylon swim trunks and shirt.

Her PFD kept Mandy buoyant and atop the surface of the water, but the water's force spun her legs downstream. She started swimming at an angle somewhere between directly upstream and across to the opposite shore. Hopefully keeping her body at that angle would help the current ferry her to the other side before she was swept into Rapid Twenty-Eight and past the camp.

Soon, she was far enough out into the river that she couldn't see the river bank on either side. All she could do was keep on swimming and hope she was making progress. As long as she felt the push of the current against her right side, she knew she was still headed in the correct direction.

Mandy swam and swam until her arm and leg muscles screamed in agony, but she knew that if she stopped, the current could shove her back into midstream. Just when she felt her leaden arms and legs couldn't make another stroke or kick, a flush of warmth infused her.

Hypothermia or Uncle Bill?

Whichever one it was, it gave her a renewed sense of strength. She forged ahead again. She started a counting cadence to stroke to. Finally, she saw a glimmer of shoreline on the other side. That gave her a burst of energy, and she kicked faster and harder.

When her foot hit bottom, she breathed out a sigh of relief. But she couldn't stop. Not yet. She kept swimming until her knee banged on a rock and she realized she was in quiet water again where she could safely stand.

Mandy went into a crawl on her hands and knees until she was out of the water and lay panting on the beach. A breeze made her shiver—a signal to get moving. She pushed herself to her feet and started picking her way downstream. With her teeth rattling in her head from violent shivers, she hugged herself and rubbed her arms, willing the goose bumps to fade. She hoped the breeze would dry her off eventually, but in the meantime, it was damn cold.

After about a half hour, she ran out of sand and had to start scrambling over large boulders, with sharp driftwood sticks piled between them. That slowed her progress, because she didn't want to crash into a stick pile or send any rocks tumbling, either of which would announce her presence, and could hurt like the dickens. And she couldn't afford to get injured. She had no idea how wide the rock fall was and how far she would have to scramble before she reached the sandy beach in front of Waterhole Canyon on the other side.

At least the effort of picking her way through the rocks kept her from feeling the cold too much. And, when she dropped down between large boulders, their mass cut the breeze. But her jaws hurt from clenching her teeth to keep them from chattering.

The climb over and through the rock fall added to her numerous scrapes and bruises until Mandy thought there couldn't be a single spot of skin on her that wasn't damaged, except where her PFD protected her chest. Finally, she spied beach ahead and tents—familiar tents.

Thank the river gods!

Mandy stopped to rest behind a large boulder and checked her watch. Ten thirty. By that time on past nights in the canyon, everyone had gone to sleep in their tents. She couldn't be sure of that tonight, though.

She hunkered down and slowly pushed sticks aside until she had cleared a flat space on the sand to sit. She hugged herself to try to generate some warmth and scanned the camp. All was quiet, except for the dissonant sound of Paul's snores coming from the far side of the beach and the lapping of the river against the shore, from waves coming off of Rapid Twenty-Eight. The sound was much like what Mandy had heard when she camped out on an ocean beach on the California coast a few years ago. If she hadn't been shivering so violently, the waves could have almost lulled her to sleep. She was exhausted and her body craved rest.

But she couldn't rest. Not yet. She had to find out what was going on. She scanned the campsite for movement. If Les had overpowered the guides somehow, it would make sense for him to stay awake and guard against any of them escaping. If he killed them, though, he wouldn't need to do that—unless the other clients rebelled. At least Mandy knew he hadn't killed the whole group, because she could hear Paul.

The fact that all of the tents were pitched gave her hope, too. Les wouldn't pitch tents for dead people.

Then she realized that Rob's and her tent was at the end of the beach closest to her. What luck. She would only have to skirt the girlfriends' tent to get to it. She checked her watch again. A half hour had passed with no movement or sounds other than Paul's snores, the waves against the shore, and her own teeth chattering in her head.

Mandy slowly unfurled her cramped body, flexed her stiff fingers and toes, and crept out of the rock pile. The tents all lay along the low-water beach that spread out below a head-high sand shelf above which lay the entrance to the canyon. She stayed on hands and knees as she inched along the beach so she could feel for rocks and driftwood in the sand and avoid them. Slowly and anxiously, she crawled around the back of the girlfriends' tent and came to the door of Rob's tent.

She gingerly unzipped the flap. The slow rip of the zipper sounded like a thunderclap to her ears. She paused to listen for anyone stirring.

Nothing.

Mandy unzipped it some more, then slithered inside. She inched toward the back of the tent, searching for Rob's face in the lump of sleeping bag beside her with her heart in her throat. When she reached his head, she realized his eyes were open.

In a choked whisper, he said, "*Mi querida.* You're alive."

She kissed him, her heart soaring with relief. She breathed a whisper into his mouth, "Thank goodness, so are you."

She hugged him to her and placed her cheek, damp with tears, next to his. His cheek was wet, too. Both their bodies shook as they wept silently together.

Finally, Mandy pulled back and wiped her face. She realized he hadn't returned his hug. "Are you tied up?" she whispered.

"Yes."

She reached into his sleeping bag and ran her hands down his back until she found his wrists bound together with rope. Before she could undo any knots, a violent shiver shook her frame.

"You're freezing. Change into dry clothes first," Rob whispered. "They're in the bag by my head."

Mandy realized her frozen fingers wouldn't make much progress on the knots anyway. They were having a hard enough time unbuckling her PFD. With clumsy fingers, she pulled off the wet lifejacket and clothes and pulled on dry sweatpants and a sweatshirt as quickly and quietly as she could. Finally she slid into Rob's sleeping bag, feeling so, so grateful for the heat of his body.

Rob turned his back to her so she could reach his hands. She pulled her pocket knife out of her first aid fanny pack and used that to saw away at the rope around Rob's wrists rather than try to untie the knots.

When his hands were finally free, he rolled over. "You're so cold. Let me warm you." He enveloped her in a tight hug.

Mandy couldn't stop the "ouch" that came out.

Rob loosened his grip. "Did I hurt you?"

"Every inch of my body hurts. But don't stop hugging. I need it."

"Babe, I'm so sorry for what you must have had to go through." He pulled the top of the sleeping bag over their heads and kissed her gently. "This will muffle our voices. Les is sleeping at the other end of camp, but we can't be too careful. How did you get here? Where's Amy?"

She whispered a quick summary of how Les had dumped both of them out of the raft, of Amy's injury and status, and of her nighttime journey down the river to get there.

Rob caressed her back and kissed her. "My dear *querida*. You suffered so much. I wish I could have helped you."

Mandy smiled. "Me, too." Her stomach growled. "And I missed the end-of-the-trip steak dinner. Did you fix that?"

"Ye-es, between other stuff going on. Sorry there's no food in the tent for you."

"We've got bigger problems than my noisy stomach to deal with." Then she asked, "What happened here?"

"After Big Drop Three, we eddied out below Rapid Twenty-Four to regroup. When I saw Les at the oars of your raft, I almost died." Rob clutched her tighter then continued. "He sped right past us, yelling that he couldn't control the raft. I got Diana and Hal out of my raft and had Gonzo and Cool get in. I told everyone to stay with Kendra while we went after Les. With Cool and Gonzo paddling and me oaring, we caught up with Les just past Rapid Twenty-Five.

Gonzo leapt into your raft and took over the oars. We got the two rafts to shore, then Les told his story."

"And I bet it was some tale," Mandy said.

Rob nodded. "He said Amy fell in the river in Big Drop Two and you fell in trying to rescue her." Rob kissed Mandy and she could tell he was smiling. "Les painted you out to be quite the heroine, sacrificing yourself to save Amy."

Mandy's body indeed felt like it had been sacrificed to the river gods.

"But the details were suspicious," Rob said. "Les had you doing things that go against our training. When I said we'd hike back up the river and look for you two, he said no, it was hopeless, that he was sure you were both dead. He even made a credible act of holding back tears for his wife. His voice broke."

"He's been acting the whole trip," Mandy said.

"Yep. Anyway, the four of us argued back and forth, with Les saying we should continue downstream and get help rather than go back. Cool backed him, but I insisted on going upriver and Gonzo backed me. Finally, Les gave Cool a strange look and unzipped his dry bag. He pulled out a gun and held it on me, then he tossed the bag to Cool and said, 'They aren't buying it. We've got no choice.' Cool pulled another gun out of the pack and pointed it at Gonzo."

Mandy could barely believe what she heard. "Cool's in on it?"

Rob nodded. "I couldn't believe it either. I asked Cool how he got mixed up in a murder scheme. He said he agreed to help Les for a share of the inheritance. The total of the three kids' shares that Alice would get is almost ten million. Les promised him a tenth of it."

"Cool's probably dreaming of spending all of his time climbing and rafting while he lives off that." Mandy thought for a moment. "When did Les recruit him?"

"Not until this morning. Apparently, Les eavesdropped on our meeting this morning and learned that we knew Alex's death and Elsa's fall weren't accidents, that we knew a killer was in the group. With his secret plan unraveling, he figured he needed a guide on his side and chose Cool."

"And we unwittingly helped him choose Cool when we didn't include him in our talk this morning. It showed we didn't trust him. But why did Les cut Elsa's harness? What did she have to do with anything?"

"I don't know. There're still some parts of all this that I don't understand."

"Me, too," Mandy said. "So, what's his plan now? To kill the rest of the group and have Cool get him out of the canyon? I can't believe Les would go that far. And I can't believe Cool would agree to help him kill everyone!"

"No, Cool told Les he wasn't doing any killing. And Les is smart enough to realize they'd have no hope of getting away if they left so many dead bodies. Instead, he said he'd take one guide hostage and make that person return to Nebraska with him. As long as the rest of us guides kept quiet and didn't tell anyone, including the other clients and the police, about how Alex, Amy, and you really died, Les said he would put the hostage back on a plane to Colorado once he had the inheritance and could leave the country."

"That scheme sounds lame. And it could take weeks, especially if Hal takes a long time to die from the cancer."

"Les plans to use some of the sedative to help that along, figuring if Hal dies in his sleep sometime in the next few days, no one would question it since he's terminal anyway."

"Man, he's one cold-hearted bastard, to plan to kill his wife, his brother-in-law, and me, and to woo his sister-in-law into marrying him to get his hands on her millions. Does Alice have any idea what's going on?"

Rob shook his head. "As far as I know, no. Neither do any of the other clients."

"And Cool believed Les would do what he said and not just kill the hostage guide?"

"Either he did, or he didn't care," Rob said with a shrug. "All he had to do was help Les get the hostage and get out of the canyon and keep it all a secret."

"So you're the hostage?"

"No. Kendra is."

"Kendra! Why'd he pick her?"

"Les decided that Gonzo and I would be more cooperative if he chose Kendra, because she's both Gonzo's girlfriend and my employee."

"You agreed? I can't believe either of you thought that Les wouldn't kill Kendra when he was done with her."

Rob cracked open the sleeping bag to let in some fresh air, then covered them again to mute their voices. "No, I didn't believe him, and Gonzo didn't either, but we agreed to keep quiet to buy some time. I was hoping we could figure out something before the trip ended and Les left with Kendra."

"Where's Kendra now?"

229

"She and Gonzo are both tied up in Gonzo's tent. After Gonzo and I agreed to the plan, Gonzo and Les hiked upriver to the rest of the group. Les hid his gun under his PFD then but kept his hand on the trigger. The two of them pulled Kendra away from the others and filled her in on Les's plan."

"I bet she was shocked."

"She was ready to fight," Rob replied, "but when Les drew his gun, Gonzo convinced her to cooperate. In the meantime, Cool held his gun on me until the others made their way downriver. Believe me, I tried to talk him out of helping Les, but the asshole wouldn't listen."

Rob fisted his hands, then he let out a breath and eased them open. "After we regrouped, Diana had a meltdown about Amy, insisting we go back for her. She pleaded with me, too, asking how I could leave you, knowing you might be hurt."

Mandy squeezed him. "That must have been hard for you."

"Damn right. I had to pretend that wasn't our way, that the best strategy was to go downriver and meet our extraction boat, then radio for help. Les and Cool chimed in, and Les made a convincing show of saying he was worried about his wife, too, but he realized that getting to civilization and sending help for you two was best."

"Which we'll need to do for Amy," Mandy said, "if we get out of this alive. I left her with a space blanket and a fire, but I'm still worried about her. What happened next?"

"After that," Rob continued, "we made our way downriver with no incidents. Les sat in my raft, holding a gun hidden in his PFD on me, and Cool oared your raft. Then we made camp and fixed dinner with Les watching us like hawks the whole time. After the rest of the clients went to sleep in their tents, Cool tied up Kendra, Gonzo, and me while Les kept his gun on us so we wouldn't try anything."

"I don't see how Les thinks he can pull this off." Mandy worried her lip. "What is he going to tell Hal, Diana, and Alice? I mean, about Kendra coming with them?"

"I asked that question, too. Now that his careful plan has been shot out of the water, he seems to be making it up as he goes along. And he's getting more and more desperate. He said he'd tell them a story about Kendra needing to visit a dying relative in Omaha and offering her a place to stay."

Mandy flashed to a mental image of Alex and Amy's bodies in coffins and shivered, which made Rob rub her back and arms.

"I'm not cold," she said, "just creeped out. Okay, now that I'm caught up, we've got to figure out how to stop Les and Cool. And we've got to do it before the launch meets us tomorrow morning to take us to the Hite Marina. Once Les is off the river with Kendra, we lose our chance and seal Kendra's death sentence."

"I agree." Rob shifted. "They have the two guns, most likely in their hands or next to their heads, but we have the element of surprise. They think I'm tied up and you're dead. If we can sneak over to Kendra and Gonzo's tent and untie them without waking anyone, then we outnumber Les and Cool. We can creep up on them, overpower them, and grab the guns."

"There're a couple of big ifs in that plan," Mandy whispered grimly. "First it's going to be tough to untie Gonzo and Kendra without making any noise. Then, if whoever we attack first gets a chance to shout, whoever has the other gun can come out shooting."

"One thing in our favor is that they're sharing a 2-man tent. But it's also risky since we'll have to attack them both at the same time. On the other hand, what choice do we have?"

"None." Desperation roughed Mandy's voice, and her heart revved up as she realized how slim their chance of success was. "We're risking getting shot, but if we do nothing, we know Kendra's going to die, and Amy might, too, from hypothermia. This whole situation sucks."

Gripping her arm, Rob said, "All we can do is try our best."

Mandy put her palms on his cheeks and kissed him, hard. He responded in kind. If their plan failed, one or both of them could wind up dead.

"I love you," Mandy whispered hoarsely.

"I love you, too, *mi querida.*"

Mandy squeezed his hand. "Let's do this."

SIXTEEN

*Nature cannot be tricked or cheated. She will give up to you
the object of your struggles only after you have paid her price.*
—NAPOLEON HILL

MANDY CRAWLED OUT OF the sleeping bag and slipped her cold
wet river sandals onto her feet. Rob put his on, too. Then she peeked
out of the tent and observed the camp for a while. The half moon
finally had risen over the canyon wall, so she could make out the
shapes of the other tents and of the rafts tied to sand anchors on
the shore. Waves from the rapids upstream lapped at the shore,
but otherwise the camp was quiet and still.

She slithered out of the tent and Rob followed. Slowly and carefully, they picked their way around the backs of other tents. They
crawled on hands and knees in the dark, trying to avoid sticks that
might crack or rocks that might tumble.

When they reached Gonzo and Kendra's tent, Mandy led the way
to the front. She slowly unzipped the door flap while Rob cupped

his hands around the zipper to muffle the sound as much as possible. Thankfully, Kendra and Gonzo were sleeping with their heads toward the flap, so Mandy placed a hand over Kendra's mouth and Rob did the same with Gonzo. That startled both of them awake, their eyes wide with surprise and fear.

Mandy put a finger to her lips and waited for the pair to recognize them and nod before she removed her hand from Kendra's mouth. She and Rob cut Kendra's and Gonzo's ropes with their pocket knives. Once they were freed, Kendra gave Mandy a spontaneous hug and whispered in her ear how glad she was to see her. Mandy whispered back to get dressed and follow them. Rob signaled the same to Gonzo.

Kendra and Gonzo slipped on shoes and fleece jackets. Then the four of them made their way quietly to the other side of Paul's tent. The farthest tent downriver, it lay well past Les and Cool's tent. Mandy hoped Paul's sonorous snores would mask their conversation, and being the sound sleeper he was—how else could he sleep through his own noise machine?—their conversation shouldn't wake him either.

Rob took off his jacket and put it over their heads to further mute their whispers. He quickly told Kendra and Gonzo their plan, which wasn't much of one—basically, to surprise and overpower Les and Cool before they could get their hands on the guns.

"You all shouldn't be risking your lives for me," Kendra whispered. "I'll just go quietly with Les and he'll let me go."

Gonzo took Kendra's hands. "You know that's not what's going to happen, given what Les has already done. Once he gets what he wants, he'll just kill you, too, because you're a witness. Then he'll hightail it out of the country before we figure out you're dead and spill the beans."

Mandy nodded. "We aren't going to let that happen—or let him get away with killing Alex."

Kendra shook her head. "But—"

"No buts," Rob said. "We're doing this and we're doing it together."

They sealed the pact with a fierce clench of each others' hands. Then Rob slid his jacket back on, and the four of them crept slowly toward Les and Cool's tent.

Mandy thanked the river gods for Paul's loud snores—and for the waves from the rapids lapping against the shore. Both helped mask the sounds of their progress. But when Gonzo put a foot down on a twig, snapping it, they all froze.

In front, Mandy peered at Les and Cool's tent and counted to sixty while her heart hammered in her chest. When she detected no sound or movement, she gave a forward wave to the others. They continued their slow creep.

Once they reached the tent, Mandy and Kendra stood on either side of the tent door as they agreed earlier, while Rob and Gonzo bent down in front. Kendra grabbed the zipper pull. With her heart hammering against her rib cage, Mandy held up a hand and ticked down three fingers.

Three-two-one. Go!

Kendra yanked down the door zipper and pulled the flap aside.

Les and Cool lay with their feet nearest the door. Rob and Gonzo each grabbed a sleeping bag and yanked hard, hauling the bags and their startled occupants out of the tent. Mandy and Kendra fell on top of the bags, pinning Cool and Les under them.

The two men yelled and flailed, trying to escape from their bags.

Mandy groped through Cool's sleeping bag, hunting for the hard metal of a gun. Kendra did the same with Les's.

Gonzo and Rob pummeled the sleeping bags while the two men inside squirmed and clawed to get out. Then Les rolled, pitching Kendra off him.

Rob yanked the sleeping bag off Les and leapt on his chest. He pinned one of Les's arms under a knee. While Kendra scrabbled into the tent to look for the guns, Rob punched Les in the face. Les flailed back with his free arm, but Rob managed to block his punch.

Holding onto the foot of Cool's sleeping bag, Gonzo yelled, "Clear."

Mandy rolled off Cool.

Gonzo jerked Cool's sleeping bag off and fell on top of him. He landed a couple of punches in Cool's sides before Cool kneed him in the gut. With an "oof," Gonzo buckled over, holding his stomach, but he fell on Cool's chest, trapping him.

Since Kendra hadn't found a gun yet, Mandy desperately searched the two empty sleeping bags for one. They had to find the weapons before Les or Cool grabbed them.

"Gun!" Kendra yelled from where Les's and Cool's heads had been inside the tent. She backed out of the tent and stood up, aiming it at Les. "Stop now!"

Les threw a couple more punches at Rob until Kendra shoved the gun in front of his face. "Stop, I said!"

Finally getting the message, Les stilled. Rob started tying him up with the ropes they brought with them that had been used to tie up Gonzo, Kendra, and him.

Mandy still hadn't found the second gun in the sleeping bags. She helped Gonzo pin down Cool and frantically felt all around Cool. When she came up empty-handed, she said to Gonzo. "Hold him while I search their gear for the other gun."

She went to the tent, pulled out the men's gear bags and started pawing her way through them.

Suddenly Gonzo yelled, "No!"

Mandy whirled in time to see Cool buck Gonzo off of him and leap up. He ran downriver.

"Stop," Kendra yelled and shot at him, but she missed.

Mandy realized two things in rapid succession. Kendra had never fired a gun before, so she couldn't be counted on to hit Cool. And, the sand shelf behind the tents dipped down toward the beach downriver, giving Cool easy access to an escape route back into Waterhole Canyon.

"Help me get him, Gonzo!" she yelled. She took off running after Cool along with Gonzo.

"Don't shoot, Kendra," Rob yelled behind them. "You might hit Mandy or Gonzo!"

Mandy and Gonzo were fast, but so was Cool. He sprinted to the other end of the beach, but since he wore no shoes, the rocks there slowed his progress. He winced and clawed his way through them.

Mandy and Gonzo reached him just as he clambered up on to the sand shelf, which was only a couple of feet high at that end of the beach. Gonzo grabbed Cool's leg and pulled, but Cool kicked free, knocking Gonzo on his rear.

Mandy jumped onto the shelf and grabbed Cool. They rolled into the brush away from the lip. Mandy grimaced as the low-lying prickly bushes raked her skin, adding to the scratches and scrapes all over her body.

Gonzo scrambled up, leapt onto the sand shelf and ran after them. He aimed some quick kicks into Cool's side, barely missing Mandy, who was stuck under Cool.

When Cool rolled off Mandy and stood to face Gonzo, she snatched him around the knees and yanked. He flopped down on his chest in the sand, and Gonzo leapt on his back. Gonzo pulled Cool's hands behind him and held them while Mandy grabbed his legs. Finally, the two of them had Cool pinned to the ground.

Mandy only had one concern at this point. "Where's the other gun?"

Cool just looked back at her and grinned.

Uh-oh.

"Gonzo, let Cool go," Rob yelled. "They've got guns on us."

"They? Who's they?" Gonzo asked.

The question was answered when Alice hollered from the dark camp, "Get back in your tents and stay there!" Presumably the ruckus had awakened the other clients. "Fucking idiots," she yelled at Les. "The whole plan is shot to hell now. Everyone else knows what's going on."

"Alice," Mandy hissed to Cool. "She was in on this all along, wasn't she?" She couldn't see the camp, but she realized Alice must have snuck up on Kendra with the other gun and made Kendra drop hers.

Cool snorted. "She's the one in charge, came up with the whole plan in the first place. And she has the other gun." He bucked against Gonzo's weight. "Now get off me."

"Call your boyfriend, Kendra," Les yelled, "or you and Rob here get it."

"Come back now, Gonzo," Kendra shouted. "Or Alice and Les will shoot us for sure."

That was the second time they had called for Gonzo and not Mandy. She glanced at the sky and saw a cloud was blocking the moonlight. The whole beach was plunged in the cloud's dark shadow.

"They aren't using my name," Mandy whispered to Gonzo, "so maybe Les didn't see me in camp. And they can't see us now, just like we can't see them. Les and Alice may not know I'm here, and Rob and Kendra are trying to tell us that."

Cool sucked in a large breath and opened his mouth.

Mandy lunged forward. She clamped a hand on his mouth and put his whole head in a lock hold with her other arm, muffling his yell. "Tell them you're coming," she said to Gonzo.

"Don't shoot! I'm coming!" Gonzo yelled toward camp, then turned to Mandy. "Now what?"

"We've got to knock Cool out," Mandy said, "so he doesn't tell them. There's still a chance if I can sneak away."

Cool's eyes widened. He struggled harder to get out of Gonzo's grasp and get Mandy's hand off his mouth.

Gonzo scanned the ground around them, found a hefty piece of driftwood and walloped Cool in the head with it.

Cool went slack and blinked. His eyes stayed open, but they seemed unfocused.

Mandy released her lock hold but kept her other hand on his mouth. "Again, but don't kill him, just knock him out."

Gonzo whacked Cool again. Finally, Cool's eyelids fluttered closed.

"What's taking so long?" Les yelled. "Cool?"

Mandy nodded at Gonzo.

"I knocked Cool out when we were fighting," Gonzo yelled back. "I have to drag him back."

"God damn it," Alice shouted at Les. "What a cluster fuck this is. How do we get out of this?"

"Don't panic, damn it," Les replied. "We'll tie up the guides and think."

"Go," Mandy whispered. She helped Gonzo push Cool down off the sand shelf.

"Back in the tent," Alice shouted again, and Mandy guessed one of the clients had poked a head out.

Gonzo slid his hands under Cool's armpits and clasped them across his chest, then started dragging him back to camp.

"What's going on, Alice?" Diana yelled from her tent.

"Shut up, Mother," was the terse reply, followed by, "Shit, shit, shit."

Mandy crept along behind Cool's legs, keeping Gonzo's bulk between her and camp so she wouldn't be seen in case the moon came out from behind the cloud. When they reached Paul's tent, she slipped behind it. Gonzo went on alone.

A minute later, she heard Alice say, "About time, asshole. Dump him there and come over here."

Mandy peeked out from around Paul's tent. The moon was out again, its light flooding the camp. Alice held both guns, one in each hand. One was trained on Gonzo and the other on Kendra, who had her hands raised in the air. Les was working behind Rob's back, holding some lengths of rope. Mandy realized he was tying Rob's hands.

Gonzo moved next to Kendra, so Alice had to turn and face away from Mandy to keep her guns trained on the two of them.

Smart thinking, Gonzo.

"After you finish with Rob, tie up Gonzo," Alice said to Les. To Gonzo she said, "Stop there and hold your hands up, just like your dumb-ass girlfriend."

Gonzo stiffened but wisely kept his mouth shut. He raised his hands over his head.

"What the hell are you doing, Alice?" Hal shouted.

"Get back in your tent and stay there," Alice yelled back, "or so help me God, I'll shoot someone."

"No!" Diana shrieked between wracking sobs.

"Who's there?" Paul whispered from inside his tent.

Surprised, Mandy jerked back behind the tent.

"Shhh. Keep quiet. It's me, Mandy," she replied in a whisper through the tent wall.

"Thank God. What's going on?"

"Alice, Les, and Cool plotted to kill Alex and Amy so Alice can inherit her father's estate. We guides found out and tried to overpower them, but Alice has two guns on the others now. She doesn't know I'm here, though."

She heard shuffling in the tent. "I'm getting dressed," Paul whispered. "How can I help?"

Mandy did some quick thinking. If they were going to act, they had to act fast, before Rob, Gonzo, and Kendra were all tied up and Les got one of the guns from Alice.

Or before Alice decided to start shooting.

"I swear it'd be easier to just shoot them," Alice said, presumably to Les, confirming Mandy's thought.

"No, wait," Les said, "We'll figure something out."

"Hurry the fuck up, then!"

"Alice is losing it." Mandy blew out an anxious breath, trying to calm her roiling stomach. "This is a long shot," she whispered to Paul, "but maybe we can get the jump on her before Les finishes tying up the others—or before she decides to start killing more people. It's risky, and she might shoot us before we can get to her."

"We have to take that chance," Paul said.

Mandy shook her head. "No, I have to do this solo. You're not involved in this. I can't ask you to risk your life."

"If she's not stopped," Paul said quietly, "she might kill everyone—me, Tina, and Elsa included. I *am* involved, and I *am* helping you." He started to slowly unzip the tent door.

"Hands behind your back," Les said.

"He's tying up Gonzo," Mandy whispered to Paul. "We've got to move now."

She said it as much to galvanize herself as Paul. Her breath came in short gasps, and her palms were slick with nervous sweat. While Paul slid quietly out of his tent, she wiped her hands on her pants. "You go for the gun in her left hand, and I'll grab the one in her right."

"Let me see where everyone is." Paul crouched next to her behind the tent and peeked around the edge. He gave a nod, then glanced back at Mandy, his eyes black in the moonlight. "Ready?"

He held up a fist, and Mandy bumped it with her own. "Ready."

To die?

Paul leapt up and Mandy followed. They charged straight for Alice. To Mandy, their footsteps sounded like elephant stomps.

This isn't going to work, she thought, as Alice jerked and turned toward them.

Paul sprang toward Alice, reaching for her left arm.

A surprise burst of speed in Mandy's legs powered her forward. She flew at Alice just as the woman's face appeared, grim and twisted with raw anger. Mandy zeroed in on the gun in Alice's right hand.

Get that!

Paul hit Alice first. They both grunted and Alice stumbled back.

Mandy slammed into Alice's right arm. While the three of them fell, she groped for the gun and yanked it out of Alice's hand. She rolled away and came up on her knees, gun in her grasp.

Bang!

Shrieks came from the tents.

At first, Mandy thought the gun in her hand had fired, but no, it hadn't. She hadn't felt anything.

Then Kendra leapt on Alice's chest, pinning her right arm under a knee. She started fighting with the maddened and kicking woman along with Paul.

Had Paul been shot?

"Paul! Are you okay?" Mandy looked for Alice's left arm. It was under Paul. Both of his hands were under him, too. He seemed to be struggling with Alice for the gun.

"I'm fine," he said between clenched teeth.

Mandy crawled over to Alice's head and shoved the gun in her face. "Stop! Now!"

Alice's eyes were unfocused, hazed with anger. She continued to fight and roll against Kendra and Paul.

Mandy didn't want to risk shooting Kendra or Paul, so she turned the gun in her hand and whacked Alice in the head with it. Finally Alice stilled.

Diana screamed again, and Mandy realized she must have come out of her tent and seen her whack Alice. She prayed that Alice's parents would stay out of this fight.

Grunts and yells told Mandy that Gonzo and Rob were fighting with Les behind her. She turned to see if she needed to help them, thinking both of them had their hands tied. Gonzo's hadn't been yet, however, so he was beating on Les's prone body with his fists, while Rob stood beside Les and rammed kicks into his side.

"Stop," Les said, his voice muffled by the sand. "I give."

Mandy turned back to Alice.

"Got it!" Paul rolled off Alice's arm and held up the other hand-gun triumphantly.

Then Mandy saw the bloom of dark blood on his shirt.

SEVENTEEN

*The highest good is like water. Water gives life to ten thousand
things and does not strive. It flows in places that men reject.*
—THE TAO TE CHING

MANDY LEANED BACK ON her haunches and surveyed her bandaging handiwork on Paul Norton's side by the light of her headlamp. He had only been grazed when the gun in Alice's hand went off while they were struggling. That didn't stop Tina from crying hysterically, though, when she emerged from her tent and her flashlight illuminated the blood on her father's torso.

Elsa had comforted both her daughter and ex-husband while Mandy ran for the first-aid kit and patched up Paul's wound. When the frightened women friends piled out of their tent, full of curious questions, Mandy directed them to Rob so she could focus on taking care of Paul. Diana and Hal were with Rob, too. Diana sobbed while Hal held her and demanded answers from Rob, who tried to answer them while tying up the captives.

While Mandy worked, she explained to the Nortons what had happened. With horrified expressions on their faces, they listened to her story of how Les had tried to kill both Amy and her in Big Drop Two and her harrowing journey in the dark to camp.

"The outer layer of gauze is still white, so I think the bleeding has stopped," Mandy said to Paul after she finished her story. "You should lie still for a while longer, though."

He lifted his head to peer at the bandage. "Thanks. But I'm cold. I need to get out of this wind." A shiver coursed through him.

"Of course," Mandy said. The night breeze lifted her hair, and she tucked it behind her ears. Now that the adrenaline was wearing off, she, too, was feeling chilled. She chafed her arms to warm them inside her fleece jacket.

"Tina, go get his sleeping bag," Elsa directed. After Tina took off running, she removed her fleece jacket and draped it over Paul. "Can't have our hero catching cold."

Paul smiled up at her. "Thanks."

With a smile of her own, Mandy turned away to pack up the first-aid kit.

"Don't be getting any romantic ideas, now," Elsa said. "The divorce is still final."

"I'm not," he replied. "It's just that I've never heard you call me a hero before."

"You took a huge risk to save all of our lives. I didn't know you had it in you." Mandy glanced back at them in time to see Elsa grin and give his shoulder a pat. "I'll be looking at you with different eyes now."

"So maybe we can be friends instead of enemies?" Paul's voice held a hopeful note.

Elsa nodded.

Tina returned at a trot with her father's sleeping bag. Elsa and Mandy helped her unzip it and lay it next to Paul, so he could roll into it. Then Elsa zipped it closed and bent down to kiss Paul on the cheek. "Thank you, friend."

Tina clapped her hands with glee. "So you two have finally made up?"

Paul gave her a chiding stare. "We've agreed to be friends, Tina, nothing more."

Tina looked from her father to her mother, then heaved a sigh. "That's a lot better than the sniping I've had to put up with until now. I guess I'll take what I can get."

Paul lifted a hand out of his sleeping bag to take her hand, and Elsa put an arm around Tina's shoulders. "You're still our daughter, honey," Paul said. "We both love you."

"And that will never change," Elsa added.

Mandy picked up the first-aid kit and stood, stifling a groan as various aching body parts made themselves known. "Well, since Paul's in such good hands, I'll check on the others. Take a look at his bandage in about ten or fifteen minutes. If he hasn't bled through, you can help him move—slowly—into a tent." She glanced at her watch, pressing the button to make its face glow. "It's one thirty in the morning. You may want to try to get some sleep."

Viv, Betsy, and Mo approached and each gave Mandy a hug and words of thanks and praise. Though they had obviously heard the story from Rob, they still buzzed with questions for Mandy. She answered a couple, then said she needed to check everyone who had been in the fight for injuries. With a promise to answer any more questions they had in the morning, Mandy suggested the three girlfriends return to their tent.

"If you think we're going to go back to sleep, you're sadly mistaken," Viv said, "but we'll get out of your way." She pulled Betsy and Mo with her toward their tent.

Mandy walked over to where Rob and Gonzo were standing guard. They aimed their headlamps and the two handguns at Les and Alice, who sat on the sand with arms bound behind their backs and duct tape wrapped around their ankles. Cool lay on his back beside them, being similarly trussed up by Kendra, but with his hands tied in front.

Kendra cut the duct tape wrapped around his ankles from the roll and stood. She flipped the roll into the air and caught it. "We ran out of rope, so I used this," she said. "As they say, 'One only needs two tools in life: WD-40 to make things go, and duct tape to make them stop.' I'd say these three are well-stopped."

"Ha ha," Alice said with a sneer. "Gloat all you want, but don't expect anyone to laugh at your lame jokes."

Mandy knelt beside Cool and shone her headlamp on his face. His gaze tracked her movements, which was a good sign. He probably had a concussion from being knocked out, but it seemed to be a minor one—both eyes were dilated the same amount. "How's your head?"

"Got a mother of a headache," he answered.

"Dizzy?"

"Only when I sit up."

Mandy nodded and stood. "We'll keep checking on you through the night, and I'll let the cops know you've got a head wound."

"Fuck," Cool whispered and closed his eyes. Mandy could imagine that he was picturing his dream of spending his days free climbing and living off his cool million flushing down the drain.

"Anyone bleeding?" Mandy asked the others.

Rob and Gonzo shook their heads, and Gonzo said, "Battered, bruised, and scratched, but not bloodied."

"I checked Les and Alice when I tied them up," Kendra said. "No blood on them."

"What's that, then?" Mandy pointed at a maroon stain on Kendra's hand.

Kendra gazed at her hand in surprise and turned it over, then looked at her other hand. "Well, I'll be damned, there's a cut here. Never felt it."

Mandy cleaned the cut with an alcohol wipe, making Kendra wince, then bandaged it.

"How about you, *mi querida*?" Rob looked her over, concern wrinkling his brow.

"Gonzo summed it up about right. I'm okay." *Not really.* She was dog-tired, almost dizzy on her feet with fatigue, and she didn't think there was a single place on her that wasn't bruised or scratched. But she wasn't going to reveal any of that to their prisoners.

She felt a hand on her arm and turned. Bundled up in a fleece jacket and sweatpants, Diana Anderson looked at her with sorrowful, pleading eyes, dried tears staining her cheeks. "Where's Amy?" she asked tentatively, as if afraid to hear the answer.

Mandy put a comforting hand on top of Diana's. "She's on a beach upriver and has a space blanket and a fire to keep her warm."

Diana's shoulders drooped with relief. She leaned back against Hal, who was standing behind her. "Thank God."

"Amy's injured, though," Mandy added. "She's got a broken leg, which I put in a splint. She's in pain, but otherwise she's okay."

Hal embraced his wife from behind with shaking hands. He nodded at Mandy. "Thanks for taking such good care of her. Can someone go back up the canyon to rescue her now?"

"It's too dangerous in the dark," Mandy said. "I barely made it here alive. And we've got our hands full guarding these three. As soon as the launch comes to collect us, and I can get my hands on a working radio, I'll make sure a powerboat gets sent to pick her up."

"Damn it!" Alice kicked Les with her bound feet. "You can't do anything right, can you?"

"Hell," he grumbled. "You screwed it up the first time."

That caught Mandy's attention. "First time?"

Les sneered at Alice. "It wasn't Kendra's fault that her raft tipped. Alice and I maneuvered that quite well. But then she didn't finish the job."

Kendra gasped while Mandy's mind whirled back to her rescue of Alice and Amy in Rapid Fifteen. Alice hadn't helped her sister grab onto the raft when Amy seemed to be having extra difficulty grabbing on. Mandy couldn't see what was going on under the murky water. Maybe Alice had actually been kicking Amy away from the raft.

"I was having enough trouble keeping my own head above water," Alice spat back to Les, "to make sure hers was below. I'd like to see you try to do that in the middle of a Class IV rapid."

Mandy glanced at Rob, who along with her was listening intently to the two bickering murderers. Were Alice and Les really that stupid, or were they just so mad at each other—and the fact that their whole scheme had failed—that they didn't realize they were digging their own graves? She wasn't about to say anything that would make them stop and think. She still had questions, though. Which one of them had killed Alex, and why had they gone after Elsa?

"Rob explained some of what happened to us," Hal said to Mandy, interrupting her thoughts. "But Diana and I are still trying to understand." He and Diana turned to look at Alice, disbelief and shock in their gaze.

Alice and Les's words had degenerated into flinging insults at each other, so Mandy decided it was okay to stop paying attention to them. "I'll tell you what I know," she said to Diana and Hal, "but it may take a while, so we'd better sit down."

She pulled the older Andersons over to some camp chairs a few feet away and righted two that had been knocked down. After they had all taken seats, she explained what she had managed to put together. Alice and Les were having an affair and wanted the whole inheritance from Hal's death to themselves. When Alex had suggested the remote trip through Cataract Canyon, Alice and Les saw their chance. They hatched a plan to work together to kill her brother and sister and make their deaths look like accidents.

Diana shook her head. "I can't believe this. Alice wouldn't kill her own flesh and blood. What proof do you have?"

Mandy waved Kendra over. "Go get Les's camera bag and bring it here."

Kendra trotted over to Les and Cool's mangled tent and searched through the contents by the light of her headlamp until she found a small dry bag. She brought it back and gave it to Mandy. "This one has his name on it."

Mandy opened it and inverted it to dump the contents in the sand. She shone her headlamp on the scattered contents.

"Hey," Les shouted. "Don't get sand all over my camera gear."

Alice kicked him again. "You fool. You've got a lot more to worry about than your stupid camera and lenses."

"Stop kicking me!" Les returned her kick. "That equipment cost thousands of dollars."

"And what do you think criminal lawyers cost?"

That was the first indication that either one of them knew how much trouble they were in. While Diana gasped, Mandy peered at Alice's face, which bore an expression of worry now, instead of the pure bile that had distorted her features earlier. Maybe Alice's temper had finally cooled enough that her situation had sunk in. Mandy doubted that they would hear much more from the woman, unfortunately.

Mandy turned back to the small pile of Les's gear and pushed around the contents with a stick. She pointed the stick to a preserved bear claw. "There's the bear claw that scratched Alex."

Diana put a hand to her mouth.

"Good God almighty." Hal reached out for the claw.

Mandy stopped him with a hand on his arm. "Don't touch it. The police will need to test it."

After Hal dropped his arm back into his lap, she poked at a small box labeled "disposable hypodermic needles" and a plastic disposable syringe. "Here're the needles and syringe that were used to sedate both Alex and Amy. And this must be the sedative he used."

A small medicine bottle lay in the sand. Mandy rolled it over with the stick to read the label, which contained the words "animal tranquilizer" along with a bunch of words she had never heard of.

"How'd Les get those?" Hal asked woodenly.

Mandy glanced at him, worried that the shock might have been too much for him and that he might pass out. But when Diana grabbed his hand, and a look of horror passed between them, she realized they were both still struggling to absorb the bombshell that their daughter and son-in-law were killers.

She bent down to focus her headlamp on the labels on the box and the bottle so she could read the small print. "Looks like a veterinary supply company. Les probably just ordered them over the Internet."

"You're too stupid to live, you know that?" Alice yelled at Les, her face reddening. "Why didn't you throw that stuff in the river?"

"Because I thought we might need it again," Les yelled back.

Nope, Mandy was wrong. She suppressed a grin. Alice was at it again.

"Yeah, I need 'em again," Alice mumbled, "to use on you." She tugged against her bonds, as if anxious to free her hands and get them on the animal tranquilizer. After a few tries, she blew out a breath, then glared at Les. "At least I don't have to pretend to love you anymore, you fucking asshole."

Les rocked back and gaped at her. "Pretend? You mean—?"

An evil grin split Alice's face. "You thought I was going to share that money with you? As soon as I inherited, I was going to drop you like a hot potato. Hot? Ha! More like a cold flabby couch potato."

"Hey, I work out!"

Alice sputtered. "Oh, you're a piece of work, all right. Your ego is five times the size of your pea brain. A little stroking, and I could get you to do anything."

Les's face fell. "You don't love me?"

"Oh, please!" Alice turned away from him.

Diana had watched the scene with her mouth agape. While tears filled her eyes, she clutched Hal's arm. "What in the world happened? I can't believe this is our little Alice."

"She's turned into a scheming, manipulative bitch," Hal whispered. He stood and walked unsteadily over to his daughter. "How could you stand by while Les killed your brother?"

"Stand by?" Les snorted. "That's a laugh. I had nothing to do with Alex's death. That was all her doing."

"Shut up!" Alice yelled.

Les just gave her a venomous smile and said, "She stuck him with the needle, waited for him to conk out so he couldn't fight her, then she—"

Alice rolled toward him, kicking and yelling, "Shut up, shut up, shut up!"

Rob gave Gonzo his gun and ran over to pull Alice off of Les.

"She clawed him with the bear claw," Les went on, "then sat there and watched him bleed out. She actually enjoyed it." Les glared at Hal. "He'd always been your pet, got most of your love and support and the best gifts. Alice actually gloated to me later that the favored son was gone now."

Diana had come over and now stood by Hal, trembling and clutching his arm. She looked from Les to Alice in wide-eyed shock, until the dawning realization twisted her features into an anguished grimace. She started sobbing again.

Mandy bit her lip. She didn't know what she could do to help them. The terrible realization that one of their children had killed another must be almost too agonizing to bear.

"You killed your own brother—." Hal choked up. He and Diana held each other and wept for their dead son while they stared at their daughter—a monster.

———

The next morning, Mandy raised her face to the welcome sunlight breasting the east canyon rim across the river. Shards of white light danced on the water's surface, blinding her eyes and forcing her to squint. She hoped that the sun's warmth and the hot cup of coffee she brought to her lips would rouse her tired, aching body into some kind of action. She was almost too exhausted to chew, but she bit into a bagel slathered with peanut butter anyway. She needed the energy the calories would give her.

The camp was stirring behind her, at least an hour later than their usual morning wake-up call. Rob had forgone the coffee call to let those who had been able to go back to sleep in their tents get some added rest. Mandy hadn't been one of them. She had tried, thinking she would take a later guard shift. But after lying awake in her sleeping bag for over an hour, she got up and relieved Gonzo as a guard over Alice, Les, and Cool.

They had wrapped sleeping bags around the three captives but left them outside, so if they said anything to each other, the guards would hear it. Mandy had sat watch with Kendra, periodically waking Cool to check for signs of concussion, until Rob relieved Kendra at six in the morning. He had asked Mandy then if she wanted to grab some sleep, but she shook her head. She wouldn't be able to rest until she knew Amy had been rescued. Instead, she and Kendra took Alice to the portable toilet under guard, then Kendra woke Gonzo so he and Rob could do the same with Cool, followed by Les.

Mandy took another sip of coffee while watching the sun's rays illuminate the canyon walls until they came alive again, glowing in layered shades of pink, white, beige, gray, and red. She took a moment to feel grateful that, although battered, she was alive, and to thank the river gods for bringing them safely to the end of their journey. Then she glanced at Rob's raft, tied some distance downstream, with Alex's body bag in the water next to it.

All safe, but one. And hopefully not two. She glanced upstream and prayed that Amy was also warming herself in the sun while awaiting rescue.

Then Mandy remembered the odd conversation she'd had with Les and Alice after the toilet break and all three captives were tied up and sitting on the sand again. One unanswered question had been nagging her throughout the night. She had hoped to get the answer out of them before the three were handed over to law enforcement. She had decided to be blunt and hopefully surprise Les into a straight answer.

"You were the one who cut Elsa's harness, weren't you?" she said to him.

"You obviously think so," he answered cryptically.

"Alice had already rappelled down," Mandy said, "so it wasn't her, and you two hadn't recruited Cool to help you yet, so I don't think it was him, either."

"No way, José," Cool said vehemently. "You're damn straight it wasn't me. And you'd better not try to pin that rap on me!"

Les just shrugged.

"Why did you do it?" Mandy studied him with hands on her hips. "What did you have against Elsa? Was it because you knew about her affair with Alex?"

Alice's brows went up, and Les chuckled. "Well, what a surprise. Alex was banging his professor."

So that wasn't it, Mandy thought. Then a dawning realization hit her. "You didn't have any reason to hurt Elsa. That was the whole point. You or Alice must have overheard my conversation with Betsy about the grizzly paw. That rustling I heard in the brush was one of you. You realized your attempt to make it look like a bear had gone after our food on the raft and killed Alex had failed. So, you decided to sabotage Elsa to throw us off track, make us think someone else was trying to kill people for some other reason."

Les said nothing.

Alice kicked him, then peered at Mandy. "I had nothing to do with Elsa's accident. It was all his idea."

"Like hell," Les yelled. "You agreed. And it almost worked, didn't it?" Les said to Mandy with a gloating smile. "After that, Paul and Tina were your number one suspects."

"As I said," Alice said smugly. "It was all your idea."

"Fuck you!" His face mottled red, Les scooted away from Alice. He clamped his lips tight, and Mandy knew she would get no more out of him.

She had gone to work laying out a cold bagel and fruit breakfast. After that was done, Mandy had walked to the water's edge to look and listen for their pickup launch, which was due soon.

She couldn't wait to turn over their captives to the authorities and to end her responsibility for the other clients, too. Her whole body craved relief from the tension that was the only thing keeping her on her feet now. She wanted nothing more than to climb into a warm bed and to fall into a worry-free deep sleep.

Not yet, though, not yet. We aren't out of the canyon.

The three women friends came up to stand with her and watch the sun rise over the rim. They silently picked grapes off a cluster that Mo had brought with her and chewed on their bagels. Then Viv put an arm around Mandy's shoulders, glanced at Betsy and Mo, and cleared her throat.

"We all just wanted to let you know how much we admire you, Rob, Kendra, and Gonzo, and how grateful we are that you kept us safe. You risked your lives for us."

Mandy blushed. "Thanks. Paul helped, too, though, and I feel bad that he got injured."

Mo stepped forward. "We'll thank him, too. I'm sure Les, Alice, and Cool would have killed us all if they'd gotten the chance. We were all witnesses, and they had the weapons to do it."

"Especially me," Betsy added. "I've been thinking. I'm sure that one of them must have heard me tell you about the grizzly prints when we went to fetch the toilet that day. Remember the noise in the willows that we thought was a squirrel? I bet it was Les or Alice."

Mandy nodded. "It was. That's when Les and Alice realized their ploy to make Alex's death look like an accident wasn't going to work. And that's why Les cut Elsa's harness."

All three women stared at Mandy.

"That wasn't an accident either?" Mo asked.

"No," Mandy said, "but we didn't tell anyone her harness had been cut, because we didn't want everyone to panic."

"Then Les tried to kill you." Betsy's eyes went wide and she wagged a finger at Mandy. "Because you knew about the fake paw—and the harness being cut. I'm sure I would have been next."

Mandy couldn't disagree with that, but before she could say anything, Betsy gave her a fierce hug. "Thank you. For everything."

The distant roar of an outboard motor echoed off the canyon walls.

Mo looked eager. "Is that what I think it is?"

Mandy shielded her eyes from the sun's glare and peered down-river. A motor launch appeared from around the bend, dwarfed by the towering striated cliffs hemming in the river. The boat headed toward them, and Mandy waved at it.

"Yes, that's our pickup," she said. "Hopefully he's got a radio."

And hopefully Amy had survived the night.

EIGHTEEN

And this, our life, exempt from public haunt,
finds tongues in trees, books in the running brooks,
sermons in stones, and good in everything.

—WILLIAM SHAKESPEARE

WITH HOPE AND RELIEF lifting her spirits, Mandy sent Betsy, Mo, and Viv to alert the others that the motor launch had arrived. The tanned, wiry boatman nudged the bow to shore. While exchanging howdies, Mandy took the anchor he handed to her and seated it firmly in the sand. Then she climbed aboard and said, "I need your radio."

With a question in his gaze, he handed it to her. She contacted the Canyonlands Park Service dispatcher, reported that an injured client needed rescue, and gave directions on where to find Amy. "Please radio back as soon as you find her," Mandy said. "I'm worried about her."

"Why didn't you take her with you?" the boatman asked.

"That's a long story," Mandy replied. "A very long story." Then she told the dispatcher that they had a body in a body bag and three captives to turn over who had committed murder and attempted murder.

"What?" both the boatman and radio dispatcher exclaimed.

Mandy summarized the events quickly for the dispatcher while the boatman looked on, gape-mouthed and periodically shaking his head in disbelief.

The dispatcher said, "Hold on." After a few moments, she came back on and said, "We're sending a helicopter down the canyon. They'll locate your injured client and relay the GPS coordinates back to us so we can send a boat to rescue her. Then they'll drop a ranger at your campsite to arrest your captives and secure them. He'll take over custody."

"Good," Mandy said. "I'm more than ready to get them off my hands."

"They'll have to ride to Hite Marina with you, though," the dispatcher said. "We don't have room in the helicopter for all four of them. State police will meet you there."

The boatman took the radio and spoke into it. "I'm more than a little wigged out about having killers on board."

"That's why we're sending an armed ranger," the dispatcher said, then added with admiration in her voice, "Plus it sounds like Miss Tanner and her crew have things under control and can lend a hand if the ranger needs it."

After signing off, the boatman turned to Mandy. "Damn! You've had more excitement on this trip than a spring run at flood stage."

"I'd much rather have that kind of excitement," Mandy replied. "Fighting for our lives against the river gods would've been a lot less scary than battling armed human killers."

The boatman nodded somberly. As the clients arrived with armloads of gear to be stowed in the rafts, he said, "Let's get this flotilla roped up. Hopefully the chopper will arrive by the time we're done, and I can get you back to the marina as fast as possible. I'll have the willies until those crooks are off my boat."

It took about an hour to fill the rafts with gear and link them in a chain behind the motor launch. By mid-morning, they were ready to go. The helicopter landed at about the same time, and a National Park Service ranger hopped off with a bag of gear.

Mandy hurried over. "Did you spot the injured woman?"

"Yes," he replied, "though she didn't make any movements when we flew over."

Mandy's knees went wobbly. "Uh-oh. I can't believe she didn't hear the helicopter. I hope that doesn't mean she's too weak to move or unconscious." *Or dead from exposure and her injury.*

The ranger's expression was sympathetic. "We were pretty high. If she was sleeping, she may not have heard us."

"How long will it take to get a boat to her?"

"One of our rangers came down the Green River in a motor launch yesterday and spent the night at the Confluence. Dispatch is sending him to pick up your client, so it shouldn't take too long. Now, where are your captives? I've got handcuffs and ankle cuffs in here." He hefted his gear bag. "I'll feel much better once I get them properly restrained."

"Me, too," Mandy said. She motioned the ranger to follow her as she started walking toward the campsite. "And I'll feel much better when you take charge of them."

She took him to where Rob and Gonzo stood over the captives, who sat in the sand and glowered in the sun, since there was no shade on the beach. Mandy pointed to each one. "Alice Anderson, Les Williams, and Tom O'Day, who likes to be called Cool."

Cool winced. Obviously, he wasn't feeling very cool that day.

The ranger read the three of them their rights. Then he had Mandy and Gonzo replace their rope and duct tape constraints with the ones he brought while he and Rob stood guard.

Mandy breathed a sigh of relief when the ranger confiscated Les's two handguns from Rob and put them in an evidence bag. Though she had some law enforcement training as a seasonal river ranger, weapons training hadn't been included. This guy was an armed career officer, and his no-nonsense approach showed he knew how to manage the situation.

The ranger watched over them with his gun raised while the guides lifted Alice, Les, and Cool to their feet, helped them duck-walk in their ankle restraints to the water line, then assisted them into the motor launch. Then Mandy got into the first raft in the chain behind the launch, which held Diana and Hal. She gave them the news about Amy.

"She didn't move? Oh my God," Diana cried, her anxiety evident in the way she tightly clutched Hal's hand.

"She could have just been sleeping," Mandy said. "It doesn't mean anything bad." Mandy mentally crossed her fingers. "We'll know how she is as soon as the ranger gets to her."

"I'm sure she's fine," Hal said to Diana. "Our little girl is stronger than you think." But his worried glance to Mandy belied what he was saying to his wife.

The boatman fired up the launch engine and pulled slowly away from the shore.

"Better hold onto the raft," Mandy said to Diana and Hal. "There will be a jerk once he gets underway."

The three captives rode in the motor launch under the watchful eyes—and gun—of the ranger, while the rest of the clients and guides were scattered among the rafts for the two-hour trip to the marina. The Nortons and the three girlfriends had readily agreed to skip the last planned hike into Dark Canyon so they could get to the Hite Marina as soon as possible. Plus, Diana and Hal were obviously anxious to be reunited with Amy.

Mandy spent the whole ride back fretting about Amy—her leg injury and possible dehydration and hypothermia—while trying to seem unconcerned in front of her parents. Finally, as they crossed under the high arch of the Route 95 bridge across northern Lake Powell, their first sign of civilization in days, the boatman got a call from the National Park Service dispatcher on his radio. He cut the engine so Mandy could hear him while he relayed what the dispatcher had to say.

The park ranger who had spent the night at the Confluence had just called in that he had found Amy and examined her. She was awake and in some pain. But she was glad to see him and asked for water. He was going to load her on the launch and bring her to the marina. Mandy whooped and shouted the good news to the others in the rafts behind hers.

Diana and Hal beamed and hugged each other while everyone else clapped and hollered with joy. Everyone, that is, except Alice, Les, and Cool. Alice's face was twisted in an angry scowl and Les's eyes were shooting fire. Cool's pale forehead, though, was lined with fear. Mandy was sure he was regretting throwing his lot in with the two conspirators.

Then the flotilla rounded a bend, and the Hite Marina boat ramp and white support buildings came into view. Another cheer went up from the rafters.

Mandy spotted their vehicles, the fifteen-passenger van and the pickup truck and raft trailer, sitting in the parking lot. On the road between the parking lot and the boat ramp sat a coroner's van and three Utah State Police cruisers with their lights flashing. The officers from those cruisers stood on the dock with arms crossed and sunlight flashing off their dark shades.

———

A couple of hours later, Mandy and Kendra packed up the remains of the last meal they had served the clients in the parking lot of the marina—a smorgasbord lunch of sandwiches and whatever leftover food would get thrown out if it wasn't eaten. Mandy glanced at Rob and Gonzo securing the rafts on the trailer. They had already loaded all of the gear onto their vehicles other than the trash the women were bagging.

"Looks like we'll be able to leave soon," she said to Kendra.

"I can't wait to jump in a hot shower," Kendra replied and rolled her shoulders.

"Me, too." Mandy smiled at the thought of her aching muscles melting in the hot steam. "But we've got the long drive back to Moab first."

Kendra nodded. "Makes me wish I could hop on the sightseeing plane with the clients."

"I don't think I want to ever see Cataract Canyon again, even from the air," Mandy replied.

The Nortons and the three girlfriends had opted to take the forty-minute flight back to Moab in a small plane over the Canyonlands. They had already said their goodbyes to Rob, Mandy, Kendra, and Gonzo, and pressed generous tips into their hands. They would see and be able to take photos of the route they took on the river from above. And, they would be snug and clean in their motel rooms by the time the guides arrived three hours later with the vehicles and gear.

It would be dark by the time they pulled in, but the delay hadn't been up to them. After sending two cruisers with Alice, Les, and Cool in the back seat to the jail in Monticello, Utah, the remaining two Utah State Police investigators had insisted on interviewing everyone in turn before they left.

Mandy's session with one of the investigators had taken almost an hour, the longest of everyone's by far. He took her camera and promised to mail it back to her after he had made a copy of the photos she took of Alex's death scene. When he wrote down her contact information, he assured her there would be more questions later and she would be called to testify if the three captives didn't plead out and the case went to trial. Though she wouldn't be on the Colorado River again anytime soon, Mandy figured she would be seeing a lot more of Utah.

She slung a trash bag over her shoulder and gazed down at the boat ramp, where an ambulance sat waiting for Amy. Hal and Diana stood nearby, shielding their eyes and scanning the entrance to the long, skinny finger of Lake Powell that stretched into Cataract Canyon. After making plans to meet later with the coroner, they let the van with Alex's body in it leave without them. Instead, they both planned to ride with Amy in the ambulance to the hospital.

The ranger who had picked up Amy had radioed the marina that he was close. Mandy could see from the tense set of the older Andersons' shoulders that they were anxious to see their youngest daughter.

She was, too.

A faint hum sounded in the distance. Mandy scanned the water and spotted a launch approaching the marina. She dropped the trash bag she was carrying on the ground.

"Can you finish here?" she asked Kendra. "I've got to see Amy,"

Kendra gave an understanding nod. "No problem."

Mandy trotted down to the boat ramp, arriving in time to help the ranger tie up at the dock. Diana and Hal hovered close by, peering into the boat. Amy lay pale and still atop a bench seat on the launch, her eyes closed.

"Can we get on the boat?" Hal asked.

"Oh, sure." Mandy tore her gaze from Amy and turned to help Diana climb aboard. Then she gave Hal a hand up.

Diana leaned over her daughter. She reached a hand out to gently swipe a lock of hair off her brow, then bent down to kiss Amy's forehead.

"Amy? How are you, honey?"

Amy's eyes fluttered open. She squinted at her mother. "Not great. I'm a little seasick, and every time the boat bounced, I felt it in my leg."

Hal caressed Amy's shoulder. "We'll get you fixed up soon. We've got an ambulance to take you to the hospital in Monticello."

"Not Moab?" Amy asked plaintively.

"Monticello's an hour closer, and I talked to the emergency room physician," Hal said. "He assured me that they can take good care of your leg."

"But what about our car and stuff?"

All of that was in Moab, except for what they had taken on the river trip. Having climbed aboard, too, Mandy felt relief washing over her that Amy was feeling well enough to complain.

She stepped up next to Hal. "Don't worry. We've arranged to get everything to you."

Rob and Hal had been busy making calls from the marina office while Mandy was being interviewed by the police. They changed the Andersons' motel reservation, and Rob had found someone to drive their car from Moab to Monticello.

Mandy patted Amy's arm. "You just focus on healing."

Amy grasped Mandy's hand in hers. She squeezed it hard and stared at Mandy. "I'm so happy to see you. I spent the night worrying about you—having to swim across the river in the dark and cold, then fighting it out with Alice and Les."

Mandy smiled. "And I spent the night worrying about you! I'm glad to see you here safe and sound."

"Only because you left me all your survival gear. While I lay there wrapped up in the space blanket and nibbling on the granola bar, I thought of you, wet and cold and hungry, with nothing."

Mandy felt her face flushing while Hal and Diana stared at her. Anxious to get the spotlight off herself, she straightened and stepped away from the boat. "I could walk, though, and you couldn't. Speaking of which, let's get you on this thing." She waved over the EMTs, who had wheeled a stretcher down the dock.

While the two EMTs worked to get Amy moved and strapped on the stretcher, Hal pulled Mandy aside. "Will you be in Moab tomorrow, or are you heading straight back to Salida?"

Mandy thought about all they had to do and said, "I doubt we'll leave before noon."

Hal nodded. "Good. I want to talk to you and Rob before you leave."

Before Mandy could ask him what he wanted to talk about, he said, "Gotta go."

The EMTs were wheeling Amy up the dock and Diana was walking alongside her daughter with a hand on Amy's arm. Hal strode after them.

Mandy watched them go. At least part of the story had ended happily.

NINETEEN

*He who postpones the hour of living rightly is like the rustic
who waits for the river to run out before he crosses.*

—HORACE

"AND THAT'S WHY COOL'S in jail," Mandy said. She had just finished telling the long story about their trip to the outfitter whose building they had borrowed, and who employed Tom O'Day.

The man's coffee had grown cold while he listened in awed silence, perched on a stool across his check-in counter from Mandy. When he realized she had stopped talking, he scratched his day-old salt-and-pepper beard. "I still can't believe O'Day would do such a thing. How stupid can a guy get? What the hell was he thinking?"

Mandy looked at the dregs in the bottom of her coffee cup— her third that morning. The four guides had shared a room after returning to Moab past midnight the night before. After taking hot showers and gulping down aspirin, they had all collapsed into bed and conked out. It had taken a lot of caffeine to get them moving again. Especially Mandy, who woke up feeling like an arthritic old woman with all her bumps and bruises.

"I have no idea," she said, then peered at the outfitter. "You going to bail him out?"

The man made a face and waved a dismissive hand. "He'd just skip town and leave me in debt to the bondsman. Nah, I think that asshole needs to sit and stew in his own juices."

He tapped the inventory sheet that Mandy had prepared, showing what gear they had borrowed and returned. "As for you and Rob, you two have been total professionals. Anytime you want to use my building again for a similar trip off-season, I'll be happy to rent it to you. And hopefully you'll trust me to loan you another climbing guide." He shook his head. "Though I would have sworn Cool was reliable. He was one of our best. I'm real sorry about that."

Mandy smiled. "Not your fault, not at all. He fooled everyone. But I think we'll bring our own climbing guide next time." She nodded at Gonzo, who was walking past them with an armload of rinsed-off PFDs. "Gonzo should be fully trained and experienced by next fall."

Gonzo smiled and gave a bow. "Just call me a Renaissance guide —a man of many talents."

Mandy snorted. "Modesty not being one of them."

With a hearty laugh, Gonzo went outside.

Rob came in the door soon after, rubbing his hands together. "We're about ready to leave. Paperwork all set?"

The outfitter slid off his stool and held out a hand to Rob. "All set. Pleasure doing business with you." After they shook hands he did the same with Mandy. "Now you two better skedaddle before the reporters come looking for you."

Mandy rolled her eyes. "Too late. One cornered us as we were checking out of the hotel. He wanted an exclusive, said he'd be willing to pay us for it."

While she had been talking, the door opened and Betsy, Viv, and Mo walked in.

Betsy held up a hand, palm out. "Whoa, hold it right there. I hope you didn't make a deal with him."

Mandy shook her head and glanced at Rob. "Not yet. This is all new to Rob and me. We need to figure out what we want to do."

"I hope you'll consider an offer from me, first," Betsy said. "I write for an adventure magazine myself." She gave the name, and Mandy recognized it.

"I contacted the editor-in-chief last night," Betsy said, "and told him what happened. He wants me to write an article for the magazine, and he authorized me to pay you for an exclusive. I hope we can match the other guy's offer."

The outfitter winked at Mandy and Rob. "Looks like you two stand to make quite a profit from this trip."

Rob looked at Mandy. "What do you think?"

"I'd rather talk to Betsy, no matter what her offer is. After spending so much time on the river with her, I feel like I can trust her."

With a nod, Rob said, "I agree."

Betsy smiled and clapped her hands. "Great! I'll get a contract to you in a day or two. And we'll throw in free ad space for your business. I'm sure the article will provide lots of exposure for RM Outdoor Adventures."

"Exposure of the right kind, I hope," Mandy said. "I don't want anyone thinking that people die all the time on our trips."

Viv came up and put an arm around Mandy's shoulders. "More people would have died, if not for the bravery you guides showed. If Betsy doesn't make that damn clear, she'll hear from Mo and me."

Mo mimed punching her hand into her palm, and Betsy laughed. "Don't worry, Mandy! I'll make sure our readers know how safety-conscious you and Rob are."

The three women gave out hugs all around, said their goodbyes and left. On their way out, they said hello to someone just outside. It was soon obvious who it was when Diana, Hal, and Amy walked in. Amy was leaning on crutches, her lower leg in a cast.

Mandy ran over to hug Amy, then pulled out a chair and helped Amy ease into it. "How are you?"

"Pretty good, considering," Amy said. "The doctor said the bone should heal pretty quickly, and there wasn't much muscle damage. He said you did a great job on the splint. Said that if you hadn't splinted it and I had tried to move it, the damage could have been a lot worse." She squeezed Mandy's hand. "I owe you so much. I don't know how to thank you!"

Mandy blushed. "Any guide who was with you would have done the same thing."

"Well, I know how to thank you." Hal moved forward and placed a check in Mandy's hand.

She looked at it and gasped. "We can't accept this!"

Rob came up and looked over her shoulder at the check. He let out a low whistle. "I agree. That's way too much for a tip."

Hal put up his hands, palms out. "It's not just a tip. It's a lot more. Think of it as an investment in a business that we believe in and a thank you for saving our daughter's life."

Mandy glanced at Diana and wished that she had been able to save their son's life, too.

Diana gave her a nod, as if she knew what Mandy was thinking. "Yes, and it's also a wedding gift from us to a beautiful, strong, and dependable couple we've come to admire and love."

That brought a tear to Mandy's eye, and she gave Diana a hug. When she could trust her voice, she pulled back and said, "Thank you. Very much."

She hugged Amy and Hal, and Rob joined in the hug fest.

Finally Hal cleared his throat. "We also thought you should know something else. We've made a decision about what to do with my estate after this cancer has its way with me."

An involuntary moan escaped Diana's lips, and Amy reached out to take her mother's hand.

Hal glanced at his wife. "Diana and I talked it over with Amy, and she agrees with the decision. I'll be cutting Alice out of my will, obviously." He pursed his lips in a thin, hard line then continued. "Diana and Amy will split half of the estate. The other half will go to a river preservation nonprofit that has pledged to fight to save the Colorado River."

He named the organization, and Mandy smiled. She sent a small donation to the organization each year herself.

"After traveling a hundred miles down the river on this trip with you," Hal continued, "we all fell in love with its beauty and power, just like Alex thought we would." He paused for a moment, while

Amy and Diana bowed their heads with him in a brief silent remembrance of their departed son and brother.

"We want to take an active part in protecting the Colorado River," Hal continued. "The nonprofit will open a special account to receive the money from the estate, and Amy and Diana will share the responsibility of administering it."

The outfitter gave out a cheer and started clapping. Rob and Mandy joined in.

"That's wonderful news," Mandy said.

Gonzo and Kendra came in hand-in-hand and looked around. "What's the celebration about?" Gonzo asked.

In an excited jumble of voices, everyone jumped in to explain. Soon the two of them were thanking and congratulating the Andersons, too.

Mandy held up their check. "And you two are getting a big piece of this, too."

"Oh, no," Hal said, shaking his head.

Momentarily confused, Mandy opened her mouth to speak, to say that Kendra and Gonzo deserved a tip, too. Then she saw Diana draw two more checks out of her purse.

With a smile, she handed them to Kendra and Gonzo. "You get your own checks."

When they saw the amounts, Kendra's and Gonzo's eyes grew wide. "Ohmigod," she said, while he whispered, "Jesus, this is way too much."

Hal grinned and rocked back on his heels. "I think there's an echo in here."

Mandy laughed and explained. "We said the same thing when he gave us our check." And she knew that Hal appreciated their appreciation. His chest was swelled with the accomplishment and pride of doing something meaningful before he passed away. She wasn't about to take any of that thunder away from him. "Just take it and say thanks."

Gonzo and Kendra didn't disappoint her. They were effusive in their hugs and expressions of gratitude.

After a time, the Andersons left, a momentary lightness in their steps that temporarily lifted the pall of grief Mandy was sure they were all feeling for Alex. Arm-in-arm with Rob, she watched them go and gave out a little sigh. When he crooked a quizzical eyebrow at her, she said, "I'm all right. I'm just thinking of the grieving that they'll have to go through."

Rob nodded. "Yes, you would know about that."

Mandy leaned against his chest and closed her eyes for a moment to send a silent message to her Uncle Bill. *Please welcome Alex, wherever you both are.*

Within a half hour, Mandy was ensconced in the front passenger seat of the pickup truck next to Rob as he drove north out of Moab pulling the equipment trailer. Kendra and Gonzo followed in the passenger van behind them.

"In less than six hours we'll be home," Rob said.

"I can't wait to fall asleep in my own bed," Mandy replied. She reached into her jeans pocket and pulled out her cell phone—that had been turned off since the night before the trip. "Let's see if anyone missed us."

After the phone powered up, a message appeared announcing new voice messages. "I don't believe it," Mandy said, as she paged through the list. "There's a whopping twenty-seven messages here," she said to Rob, "and all but two of them are from your mother." She threw her head back against the seat and groaned.

Rob's brow crinkled in worry. "I'll talk to her after we get back, tell her to back off on the wedding plans."

Mandy looked out the windshield at the highway winding toward the horizon in front of them, a fitting metaphor for their life to come. Given the life-and-death experience they had just gone through, an overeager mother-in-law no longer seemed like such a big deal.

She put a hand on Rob's knee. "No, don't. I love your mother, Rob, I really do, and I can do this for her."

Rob covered her hand with his. "You sure?"

"I'm sure." As sure as she was about spending the rest of her life with the man next to her.

THE END

ACKNOWLEDGMENTS

I had a lot of help researching the Colorado River in Utah and its Meander and Cataract Canyons for this book, particularly from the staff of Tag-A-Long Expeditions (http://www.tagalong.com/), the outfitter that organized the scouting trip my husband and I took down the Colorado River from Moab to Lake Powell. Jennifer, Sarah, and the other office staff at Tag-A-Long were very helpful. Our boatman, Dave Pitzer, and river guide, Justin King, provided a wealth of information and colorful stories and lingo while taking excellent care of us on the trip. Dave Pitzer was kind enough to stop at all the beaches where a 5-day trip would stop, even though we were on a 3-day trip, so I could take notes and soak in the atmosphere of each while my husband took photos. And I owe another huge debt of gratitude to Dave, who later provided me with expert and detailed descriptions of the paths for running various rapids, because all I remembered was fun roller coaster rides and water splashing in my face!

Thank you to my husband, Neil, for the wonderful photos and videos you took of that trip, so I could reconstruct locations and experiences months later. I read many reference books and articles about the area, but the most useful book that I referred to often was *Belknap's Waterproof Canyonlands River Guide*, and I recommend it to anyone planning a trip on the Colorado River. The state and national park rangers at Dead Horse Point State Park and Canyonlands National Park were helpful in answering questions and providing brochures on the geology, flora, fauna, and history of the parks.

Thanks to my critique group, Jeff Campbell, Vic Cruikshank, Maria Faulconer, Barbara Nickless, MB Partlow, and Robert Spiller, for making it abundantly clear when my writing wasn't up to snuff and I had more work to do. Their high standards made me work that much harder to turn out a quality story. I don't know what I'd do without my literary agent, Sandra Bond, who works tirelessly on my behalf and keeps me out of contract trouble. Thanks, Sandra! Terri Bischoff, Acquisition Editor at Midnight Ink, and Connie Hill, Senior Editor, made sure the book's prose was the best it could be. Thanks to Donna Burch for the book design and to Lisa Novak for the gorgeous cover art that was exactly what I asked for and more. Thanks also to all of the staff at Midnight Ink who toil behind the scenes to produce and market the books in my RM Outdoor Adventures series.

And lastly, I would like to thank the avid readers of the RM Outdoor Adventures who take the time to write me and tell me what they like—and don't like—about the books. I write them for you!

ABOUT THE AUTHOR

Beth Groundwater was an avid "river rat" in the 1980s, running whitewater rivers in the eastern United States in an open-boat canoe. She has enjoyed reacquainting herself with that subculture and its updated boating equipment while researching the RM Outdoor Adventures mystery series. Beth lives in Colorado and enjoys its many outdoor activities, including skiing and whitewater rafting. She loves to speak to book clubs about her books. To find out more, please visit Beth's website at bethgroundwater.com and her blog at bethgroundwater.blogspot.com.